BY AVON RIVER

UNIVERSITY PRESS OF FLORIDA

Florida A&M University, Tallahassee
Florida Atlantic University, Boca Raton
Florida Gulf Coast University, Ft. Myers
Florida International University, Miami
Florida State University, Tallahassee
New College of Florida, Sarasota
University of Central Florida, Orlando
University of Florida, Gainesville
University of North Florida, Jacksonville
University of South Florida, Tampa
University of West Florida, Pensacola

UNIVERSITY PRESS OF FLORIDA

Gainesville · Tallahassee · Tampa · Boca Raton
Pensacola · Orlando · Miami · Jacksonville · Ft. Myers · Sarasota

BY AVON RIVER

H.D.

Edited by Lara Vetter

28 27 26 25   6 5 4 3 2

First cloth printing, 2014
First paperback printing, 2016

Library of Congress Control Number: 2014937642
ISBN 978-0-8130-4997-7 (cloth)
ISBN 978-0-8130-6237-2 (pbk.)

The University Press of Florida is the scholarly publishing agency
for the State University System of Florida, comprising Florida
A&M University, Florida Atlantic University, Florida Gulf
Coast University, Florida International University, Florida State
University, New College of Florida, University of Central Florida,
University of Florida, University of North Florida, University of
South Florida, and University of West Florida.

University Press of Florida
2046 NE Waldo Road
Suite 2100
Gainesville, FL 32609
http://upress.ufl.edu

Contents

Acknowledgments

Working with H.D.'s writings is a labor of love for me, but I am not the only one who has worked to bring this project to fruition. First and foremost, I would like to express my gratitude to Cynthia Hogue and Jane Augustine. I benefitted greatly from their incisive reading of the manuscript and their useful suggestions. My friend and colleague Annette Debo, who is likewise incredibly generous, continues to serve as an expert sounding board within a broader community of H.D. scholars. As always, I must also thank Randy Malamud for introducing me to H.D. all those years ago. The organizers of "Rereading Poets Reading" at the University of Maryland, College Park, invited me to share my earliest work on *By Avon River*, and the response from the symposium's participants—including Rachel Blau DuPlessis, Alicia Ostriker, Martha Nell Smith, and Christina Walter—persuaded me that there was genuine interest in seeing this book come back into print. The University Press of Florida is to be commended for taking on the task of publishing so much of H.D.'s late prose, and I am especially grateful for my editor, Shannon McCarthy, who has been enthusiastic in her support of the project. Elizabeth Detwiler copyedited the manuscript. Nevil Parker and Louise OFarrell shepherded it into print. My graduate assistant, Arthur Basler, helped me proof and index the final text.

Profuse thanks go to Nancy Kuhl, curator of poetry in the Yale Collection of American Literature, and to the ever-efficient and knowledgeable staff of librarians at the Beinecke Rare Book and Manuscript Library. A fellowship awarded by the Beinecke Library Visiting Scholars program and a faculty research grant from the University of North Carolina at Charlotte (UNCC) afforded me two invaluable research trips to read the H.D. Papers. I would also like to acknowledge the generosity and hospitality of H.D.'s grandson, Val Schaffner, who granted me access to the Bryher Library at his home. A small grant from the College of Liberal Arts and Sciences, UNCC, helped to facilitate that trip. The patient and resourceful librarians at the Berg Collection at the New York Public Library helped me navigate the May Sarton Papers. Another grant from UNCC's Department of English permitted me to obtain materials I needed to complete this project.

Declan Spring and the Schaffner family have been very supportive of this edition, and they kindly granted me permission to quote from published and unpublished writings by H.D. and Bryher (copyright © 2014 by The Schaffner Family Foundation, used by permission of The Schaffner Family Foundation and New Directions Publishing Corporation, agents). I am thankful, too, for permission to quote from letters by H.D. and Bryher held by the Henry W. and Albert A. Berg Collection of English and American Literature, New York Public Library, Astor, Lenox, and Tilden Foundations.

Finally, I must thank my family and friends. I am especially appreciative of the unwavering support of my father, Fred Vetter, for whatever endeavor I undertake. My greatest debt of gratitude is reserved for Kirk Melnikoff, whose love sustains and inspires me. His expertise in the English Renaissance has been an indispensable resource in completing this particular project, and it was his delight in discovering that H.D. wrote a book about his field that initially piqued my own interest in this forgotten volume.

Introduction

The modernist poet known as H.D. (Hilda Doolittle) declined offers of refuge and remained in London during World War II, enduring the relentless bombings of the Blitz that overtook London from the fall of 1940 to the spring of 1941, the food rationings that left her ill and malnourished, and a second wave of doodlebug and V2 bombings near the close of the war.[1] She stayed in her South Kensington flat, and she wrote, penning her well-known epic *Trilogy* and several other works, even as she lived under unremitting anxiety and strain. Near the end of the war, when peace seemed imminent, she made a pilgrimage to Shakespeare's birthplace, Stratford-upon-Avon, visiting the grounds of his lavish home New Place and his tomb in Holy Trinity Church. Out of this experience came *By Avon River*, a hybrid volume of poetry about Shakespeare's late play *The Tempest* and prose about him and his contemporaries. H.D. had a particular affection for this, her first postwar book, reportedly carrying it with her "for re-reading and memorizing": "I am almost 63 & have been writing for 40 years but *Avon* is the first book that really made me happy," she gushed to her friend George Plank after its publication in 1949.[2]

H.D. had been known as the Imagist par excellence, an innovative transatlantic poet composing in a genre that tends toward stasis—a glimpse, a snapshot, a moment in time. But for H.D., *By Avon River* and her other writings of the 1940s signify a shift she was more than ready to embrace: upset over a negative review of the first book of *Trilogy*, H.D. complained, "Why one must write at 60 (or near 60) what one wrote at 16, must remain a mystery!"[3] With this volume, Horace Gregory argues in his contemporaneous review of *By Avon River*, we can see clearly that "H.D.'s writings have outgrown their early associations."[4] With her fictionalized story of her childhood, *The Gift*, and her long poem *Trilogy*, *By Avon River* launches her into a late career guided by a more expansive, dynamic vision. From this point, she is to compose epic poems such as *Helen in Egypt*, memoirs of various stages of her life, and the long historical fictions she pens in the late 1940s. As H.D. reflects in a letter to her literary executor, Norman Holmes Pearson, with *By Avon River* "I had crossed literally my Rubicon, albeit AVON y-clept!"[5] This book represents, then, a singular turning point for a major modernist poet, who will evolve away from the short Imagist lyric and toward the path of late modernism in verse and prose reflections on issues of nationality and on the vexed intersection of the personal and the political.

The first part of *By Avon River*, "Good Frend," is verse. Titled after a phrase from Shakespeare's epitaph, the three-poem sequence revives Claribel from *The Tempest*, the unfortunate daughter of Alonso whose arranged marriage to the King of Tunis is the catalyst for the action of the play. The shipwreck survivors are traveling home from her wedding when they are waylaid by the rage of Prospero's storm. Though Claribel never appears on stage—never speaks a word of dialogue—H.D. creates for her a plot and a quest. In the first poem, "The Tempest," the speaker meditates on Shakespeare's "poaching": his sources for *The Tempest* and his theft as a Stratford youth of Sir Lucy's deer. She identifies Claribel as a forgotten character and reflects on her arranged marriage to the King of Tunis, subtly aligning those nuptials with the 1613 arranged union that was thought to be the occasion for the play, that of the daughter of James I of England, Elizabeth, to Frederick of Bohemia, the Elector Palatine. The more lyrical second poem, "Rosemary," picks up this thread, overlaying Shakespeare with Prospero, and Claribel with the present-day speaker who, like H.D., makes a pilgrimage to Stratford. The final poem of the sequence, entitled "Claribel's Way to God," liberates Claribel from Shakespeare's play, transporting her home to medieval Italy where she aids the Order of the St. Clares and attends a fallen soldier.

The three poems that make up the first half of this hybrid book are more regularly iambic than is typical of her oeuvre, obviously at play with Elizabethan verse forms. The first poem of the sequence, "The Tempest," is closest to her more familiar vers libre while generally employing a fair amount of rhyme and slant rhyme at line endings, particularly in its opening and closing cantos. Written in couplets, mostly rhymed, the opening canto of the poem references Shakespeare returning to Stratford after he has finished *The Tempest*—beginning, in effect, with an ending. The poem then shifts to freer verse, taking on a conversational tone as the speaker emulates the cant of Elizabethan gossip. At the end of "The Tempest," as our present-day speaker emerges to stand solemnly at Shakespeare's gravesite, the rhythm of the verse becomes more regular, the internal and end rhyme more pronounced. The effect is funereal and ceremonial.

"Rosemary," the second poem, begins at Shakespeare's tomb in a variable iambic meter. This second poem as a whole ultimately pushes the repetition of sound to an extreme degree, but in this first canto, it is excessive, and we see this, for instance, in the final couplet: "*Blest be ȳ man*—that one who knows / His heart glows in the growing rose."[6] This is not bad writing. Rather, the effect borders on parody rather than tribute in a poem that critiques Shakespeare more than it lauds him; after all, in "The Guest" she will quote considerably darker verse from Sir Walter Raleigh that recalls these very lines: "Say to the Court, it glows / And shines like rotten wood."[7] The shift, then, from this tightly structured and repetitive initial canto to the lyricism of the remainder of the poem is striking. H.D. uses the repetition of sound to push Shakespearean verse to its breaking point in the first canto, forcing a breach through which Claribel can emerge. The lyric voice that then overtakes much of the remainder of "Rosemary" mimics the sound of bells, summoning the shadowy figure of Claribel. As Kate Chedgzoy notes perceptively, the "tightly woven pattern of assonance," and the very rhythm of the verse, serve as an incantation, designed to call forth her presence.[8]

Once brought to life, Claribel is the speaker of the third poem, "Claribel's Way to God," and she renders her experience in a ballad verse form. Shakespeare has been lodged in iambs, while Claribel is freed by the lyric to investigate the roots of Elizabethan poetry. As Claribel travels back in time—from her bare existence in Shakespeare's *The Tempest* to medieval Italy during the time of the Crusades—the verse form, then, shifts from Elizabethan to the aubades of the troubadours H.D. cites as Elizabethan forebears near the end of "The Guest," the prose half of the volume. It is this form that is radical and heretical, a challenge to Crusaders who meant to drive underground worship of a female deity, she explains in "The Guest." It is this form that at once conceals and reveals the subversive devotion to the Lady, a figure who is (as in *Trilogy*) at once the Virgin Mary and the goddess of any number of ancient religions.

The second part of the book, "The Guest," intermingles fiction and nonfiction prose: critical commentary on Shakespeare's contemporaries, fictionalized episodes imagining Shakespeare in Stratford toward the end of his career, and a literary history of England from the time of Richard the Lionheart through the seventeenth century. If Shakespeare is a "Good Frend," "The Guest" constructs a complex portrait of his cohorts in the English Renaissance, tracing an intricate web of influence, collaboration, and friendship between nearly sixty lyric poets of the period. The titles of the two sections are suspended in an almost eerie tension between earthbound permanence and ethereal impermanency—between coming together and coming apart—for the phrase "The Guest" is taken from a poem attributed to an indignant Sir Walter Raleigh, who pleads his desire to cast aside the earthly body—the vessel in which the soul has merely been "guest"—welcoming a death that will prove "the World the lie!"[9] This delicate network of poets is ever under threat by a corrupt state, always on the brink of unraveling.

Opening "Remembering Shakespeare always, but remembering him differently," much of the essay, in fact, scarcely mentions Shakespeare, treating instead nearly five dozen Elizabethan lyricists, quoting her favorites among their poems and contextualizing each biographically and historically.[10] Her choices are telling, for she stresses at once poets' bonds with one another and their desire to be freed from the chains that bind them to corporeal existence, at times manipulating their birth and death dates to emphasize those connections ultimately and inevitably dissolved at the end of their lives. The final third of "The Guest" relies heavily on Denis de Rougemont's *Love in the Western World*[11] to broaden her meditation on the Elizabethan era into a contemplation of the origins of English poetry, which she locates in the songs of the troubadours of Provençe and the French tradition of courtly love. H.D. traces what she sees as the thread that runs through the troubadours' ballads and aubades, the early modern sonnets and songs, the religious lyric, metaphysical verse, and Cavalier poetry of the seventeenth century. Interwoven throughout "The Guest" are fictionalized episodes of an aging Shakespeare at home, as, nearing the grave, he tries to remember his past.

The speaker for much of the second half of the book is a literary critic, as H.D. addresses the life and verse of Shakespeare's many contemporaries and traces a genealogy of English poetry from the medieval period to the Jacobean. Periodically, though, the fictionalized thoughts of an older Shakespeare—rendered in stream of consciousness—erupt into the text, distracting the critic and the reader from the topic at hand. Utterly disintegrating, the forgetful mind of an elderly Shakespeare intrudes upon, usurps perhaps, textual space devoted to other poets with musings on his estate, his garden, his standing, and his legacy. In the final pages, Shakespeare finally does claim the book, as his thoughts interrupt H.D.'s outline of literary history, but he claims that space only to die.

H.D. made three trips to Stratford-upon-Avon at the close of the war, between April and August of 1945.[12] The first trip was taken at the urging of her lifelong companion Bryher "as a sort of premature peace-celebration."[13] Bryher, H.D., and their close friend Robert Herring braved overcrowded trains to make a trek to Stratford for Shakespeare Day, April 23, 1945, where they took part in the festivities, marching in the processional to Holy Trinity Church and laying flowers on his tomb ensconced at its altar. They listened approvingly to a "sermon" that stressed "that poets were the most important thing" in times of strife.[14] Bryher's memoir of the early 1940s, *Days of Mars*, recounts how meaningful the ceremony was to a broad spectrum of survivors of a war-torn nation: "It was an experience that none of us can have again because that year it was truly a festival of the people.... We came from cities, camps and the adjoining villages for love of Shakespeare and with him, on this particular occasion, England."[15] What is most striking to Bryher, perhaps, is the deeply communal nature of this swath of people from all walks of life, a sense of "a unity of joy" she had never before felt: "We walked slowly along the main street and I was thinking, I am sure, the same thoughts as my neighbors."[16] She characterizes it solemnly as "a religious experience, one of the most profound

I have ever known."[17] H.D.'s dedication of "Good Frend," to both Bryher and Herring, pays homage to this visit.[18]

Even as her compatriots were periodically escaping to the English countryside in the early 1940s, H.D. had been stubbornly resistant to leaving London, even during the worst days of the war. Following this initial journey to Shakespeare's birthplace, however, H.D. becomes ecstatic about staying in Stratford for the summer,[19] scheduling two return trips on her own, a week in June and then a longer stay from mid-July to mid-August, interrupted with a brief side trip to Chipping Campden in the Cotswolds.[20] These jaunts were Bryher's gift to H.D., commemorating the anniversary of their first meeting (July 17, 1918), offered with the hope that a change of scenery would promote recovery from the trauma of the war.[21] While in Stratford, H.D. wrote regularly in a favorite tea shop, attended several Shakespeare performances numerous times,[22] and spent much of her time in the gardens of New Place. The descriptions of flowers in "The Guest" reflect her time spent studying the flora of the region, and her depictions of the town in "Good Frend" are taken from her own experiences there.[23] By the end of the summer, H.D. speaks to both Bryher and Plank about her intention to relocate to Stratford more permanently, to secure a house of her own there. "I am *at home* here," she pronounces in July.[24]

Before the war, as early as 1938, H.D. was reading about the Renaissance, amassing literature about Henry VIII, Hampton Court, Elizabeth I, and Mary, Queen of Scots, after seeing Alexander Korda's *The Private Life of Henry VIII* (1933).[25] In 1940 she sees Bette Davis and Errol Flynn in *The Private Lives of Elizabeth and Essex* and Errol Flynn again in *Sea Hawk*, about the 1588 Spanish Armada.[26] By the end of the war, in 1945 and 1946, H.D.'s reading about the Elizabethan era had intensified. Her copy of *The Tempest* is thoroughly marked in her hand, as is her edition of G. Wilson Knight's blatantly patriotic 1944 study of Shakespeare's history plays, *The Olive and the Sword*, which she was delighted to find in a Stratford bookstore in the summer of 1945.[27] She probably read, too, George Garrett's 1937 bold indictment of Prospero when it was printed in *Life and Letters Today*.[28] Most important, the book from which all of the biographies and verse of other Elizabethan poets mentioned in "The Guest" derive is an 800-page anthology of Elizabethan poetry, *The Book of Elizabethan Verse*, compiled by African American literature professor William Braithwaite in 1908, a work she referred to as her "out-dated demodé, beloved Elizabethan Anthology."[29]

Letters between Bryher and H.D. document that Bryher was also sending her many books on loan from the London Library and her personal library, including one on the flora and fauna of Stratford and another on Edward Dyer, and recommending others, for which H.D. diligently searched in the Shakespeare Press bookshop in Stratford.[30] Bryher sent as well Edith Sitwell's *Fanfare for Elizabeth*, which H.D. read avidly to learn more about Henry VIII, and when H.D. was proofreading "The Guest," Bryher put Shakespeare's complete works in the post to her. Having a life-long interest in the period, Bryher herself was a fount of knowledge about Elizabethan writing and culture and was probably one of H.D.'s most significant sources of information.[31] "People say I have an Elizabethan ear," Bryher notes in *Days of Mars*, and during the war she, too, turned with renewed interest to that period of literature, especially to three writers who feature in *By Avon River*, Sir Walter Raleigh, Christopher Marlowe, and Francis Beaumont.[32]

In fact, the Shakespeare Day trip in 1945 was not Bryher's first wartime pilgrimage. In 1943, Bryher set out to find Shakespeare's one-time lodgings on Silver Street. She then traveled to St. Mary's in Aldermanbury, London, the parish church of John Heminge and Henry Condell, the actors who compiled the First Folio.[33] When she stumbles upon a memorial to Shakespeare, Heminge, and Condell in the gardens of St. Mary's, she is deeply moved: "The moment was one of the closest affiliations with the Elizabethan age that I have ever felt."[34] She returned to Aldermanbury, in 1945, one last time before moving back to Switzerland: "It seemed to me that the heart of London . . . was in the parish where Shakespeare and his fellowship of the Globe had lived, written, and worked."[35] In the 1940s, Bryher and H.D. were both studying the Renaissance and undoubtedly found this shared interest the foundation for a generative exchange.

The three poems that comprise "Good Frend" were probably composed in London at some point between H.D.'s trips to Stratford and the acute illness in the spring of 1946 that precipitated her move in May from England to a medical facility, Klinik Brunner, in Switzerland on Lake

Zurich.[36] She does not share the poems until September of 1946, when she offers them to Bryher, bestowing her with the dedication to the sequence. Given the magnitude of her own experience that Shakespeare's Day, it is not surprising that Bryher responds effusively that she is "enchanted with Claribel." She compares the sequence to H.D.'s first volume of poetry, *Sea Garden*, and insists she send the poems to Herring to appear in *Life and Letters Today*: "How much your poems bring back Venice and Greece and the lands no longer to be wandered—so very beautiful."[37] As editor, Herring readily agreed to publish the poems, and the entire sequence was typeset by the journal and proofed by H.D. In the end, though, only parts of the first poem, "The Tempest," and all of the second poem, "Rosemary," appeared in that periodical.[38]

"The Guest," originally entitled "The Body's Guest," was composed later, at the Klinik Brunner in the final months of her recovery, September and October of 1946. She is inspired to begin the essay after reading her notes taken a year previous for an invited series of lectures at her alma mater, Bryn Mawr.[39] Contacted in November 1945 by the College to teach a spring semester seminar on poetry, H.D. began making plans to travel to Pennsylvania, writing comrades for lists of their favorite lyric poems to guide her preparation and corresponding with her friend Molly Hughes, an educator, about teaching tips. Her sudden illness in the spring prevented that engagement, but as she recovered, her notes, her Elizabethan anthology, and her memory of Shakespeare's plays lead her on a foray into the genre of literary criticism.[40]

Bryher's letters that autumn are encouraging, and H.D. broaches the subject of publishing both "Good Frend" and "The Guest" in late October with her friend Norman Holmes Pearson, who had begun to play a central role as her American literary agent and who, in his capacity as professor at Yale University, was arranging space in the Beinecke Library for her papers. Though the draft is finished by this point, however, H.D. continues to revise the manuscript and check dates and references for another year, finally mailing to Pearson the manuscript of both pieces in late September 1947. H.D. suggests to Pearson that "the two really do go together," and he readily agrees that she publish the poetry and prose as one volume, proposing the title *By Avon River*.[41] By July of 1948, Pearson's efforts—along with classicist Horace Gregory's strong advocacy of the book—are rewarded with an acceptance by Macmillan for publication in 1949.

Blurbs from William Rose Benét, Horace Gregory, and Marianne Moore adorned the book jacket of *By Avon River*, praising its lyricism—its "haunting music," its "overtones of sound and meaning"—and its perceptiveness—its "acute intelligences" and its "uninsisted upon implications."[42] The description inside the book jacket stressed its celebratory and elegiac qualities. It was reviewed widely—and overwhelmingly positively—in a range of newspapers across the United States. It is, in fact, one of H.D.'s only volumes to enjoy this kind of mainstream appeal, a phenomenon she predicted when she wrote her former husband, British writer Richard Aldington, that the book would be "useful" to Macmillan and when she commented to Bryher that the book was "fool-proof" in terms of popular interest.[43] For the most part, reviewers happily accepted the book as advertised—as Bardolatry, a tribute to a great man. Though one reviewer did note his delight at the portrait of Shakespeare as "a man very like all of us,"[44] most reviews characterized the volume as "the perfect greeting from one poet to another,"[45] "a tribute and emotional response to Shakespeare's genius,"[46] inscribed with the "felicity and love only a poet of H.D.'s stature can invoke and evoke."[47]

The largely positive reviews stressed the melodic quality of the verse and the deft use of imagery to bring the Elizabethan era to life for a modern audience. A particularly incisive review at the *Chicago Tribune* is appreciative that her poetry is "allusive and delicately lyric rather than the pompous and official thing a Shakespeare day poem is so likely to be." The reviewer rightly observes that H.D. strives for an Elizabethan rhythm with a decidedly modernist edge: "The rhythms themselves, tho varied, are more regular than those for which H.D., a pioneer imagist and free-versist, is best known. Yet they do not have the deadly da-dum da-dum monotony found always in the minor sonneteers and never in real poets."[48] While Floyd Logan of the *Fort Wayne News-Sentinel* most enjoyed "The Guest," he lavishes praise on the lyricism of "Good Frend" as well: "[I]t has the old-fashioned poetic virtues of being pleasant to the ear as well as an instrument for the fashioning of mental images; it is a graving tool for the craftsman's wax." Kenneth Rockwell, for the *Dallas Daily Times Herald*, stresses the "literary perfection" of her poetic lines, linking this verse to her Imagist beginnings. The reviewer at the *New York Herald Tribune*, however, notes that H.D.'s sense of tonal qualities and sound has only intensified over time: "The present volume is less striking than such early imagist work, but its beauty of cadence—and H.D. has always been famous for haunting music—is even greater."[49]

As for the prose, a reviewer in the *New Haven Register* wisely observes that it is best viewed as "a marvelous impressionistic painting rather than a detailed character portrait."[50] The observation of a *New York Mirror* reviewer—"The writer's feeling for the Elizabethan era is so vividly alive"— is a constant refrain.[51] "[S]he brilliantly achieves her expressed intention," enthuses one reviewer, "'to recall echoes of a great period by way of its minor satellites.'"[52] It is, for David Daiches of the *New York Herald Tribune*, the "provocative power of H.D.'s prose" that lets "new men live and their songs have new meaning." A reviewer for the *Richmond Times Dispatch* particularly values the skill with which H.D. embeds the figure of Shakespeare within his milieu: "At the end Shakespeare himself is brought before us through an elaborate and very beautiful stream-of-consciousness—the consciousness of the great dramatist when he is old enough to be pushed aside by younger, more fashionable men. He remembers his life—trivial detail mixed with heartbreaking moments—and sees how it colored his work. This is an extraordinary thing to attempt: perhaps only H.D. could have achieved success."

Several reviewers use the volume to champion the cause of modernist poetry. Indeed, this is the thrust of a lengthy review essay by Horace Gregory in *Poetry*, the periodical that had first published H.D.'s Imagist poems in 1913. Gregory first asserts the significance of earlier forms of verse to contemporary poetry: "H.D.'s lyricism . . . arrives at a moment that seems to anticipate a revival of traditional melodies in modern verse."[53] He pushes his argument further, then, to claim that *By Avon River* is "proof of the hardiness of lyric poetry in what has so often been regarded as an age of prose."[54] H.D., he contends ultimately, stands apart from her contemporaries whose talents have been devastated by World War II: "*By Avon River* . . . is also proof that the imagination and sensibility of a highly gifted poet have survived a tempest in which whole groups of fashionable writers have lost their bearings."[55] Kenneth Rockwell puts forth vigorously a case for the superiority of H.D.'s verse over that of younger poets when he sneers that the youth of the era will not like her poems because "[t]hey are not obscure; they have something to say, and that something is said in lines that sing." Her verse, full of "charm and delicacy," lacks the "tougher ironies of our modern poets and critics," according to the *New York Herald Tribune*. "It is good in these times," writes Martha Bacon pointedly in the *Saturday Review of Literature*, "when there seems to be some uncertainty concerning the purpose and the validity of poetry, to be reminded of our betters."[56]

If the *San Francisco Chronicle* reviewer commends H.D.'s "skillfully wrought intimacy with the Elizabethan poets" and her "serious scholarship,"[57] however, several reviews note factual errors committed in the book. "It seems ungracious to point out chronological inconsistencies in an imaginative survey by a poet," a reviewer from the *Philadelphia Inquirer* notes wryly, "but a poet as addicted to dates as H.D. . . . and as perceptive in her interpretation of the meaning of dates in the tides of cultural movements, must allow her stream of consciousness to be checked by the stream of history. . . . A little history combined with an active imagination is a dangerous thing."[58] Kenneth Rockwell, in fact, seems to anticipate this inevitable criticism when he chides his readers, "We have the plays. Let the scholars play their research crossword puzzles. They all finish with different answers to their problem. H.D. is not convinced by their games."

New York Times reviewer Herbert Barrows takes issue with the verse, praising that which was modeled on the Elizabethan lyric in "Rosemary," but condemning the first poem, "The Tempest," for its vers libre. Barrows and others in the mainstream press found the prose section difficult to follow at times: "H.D.'s occasionally valuable points of perception are lost in a confusion," he grumbles.[59] The review in *The Nation* likewise observes that "more than a tendency to wander makes the essay difficult to read with concentration; the sentences are gracious and lovely, the quotations generous, the information relevant, and the conclusions modest, but a kind of distrait air makes the total a bit distracting."[60] An otherwise glowing review in the *New Haven Register* tactfully questions her feminization of Shakespeare: "if there is one fault with 'By Avon River' it is that

Shakespeare comes out of it solely a delicate lyricist, which he partly was, and not the lusty creator of people like Falstaff."[61]

A Macmillan publication, the book was mostly reviewed in the United States; however, a brief notice did appear in the *Times Literary Supplement*, judging the poem "sensitively written" and the essay "imaginative and critical."[62] A review in the *Canadian Forum* was mostly positive, though exhibiting preference for the poetry over the prose.[63] The Canadian reviewer applauded its "combination of fragile remoteness and ecstatic warmth, which, at best, H.D. is able to touch." This shrewd reader also noted the "cumulative" effect of her verse, her "steady maintenance of control." The first part of the essay is praised as well for its "delightful" selections from the various poets, but the pieces of the prose that fictionalize a dying Shakespeare were seen as less affecting.

Several years later, in 1955, a German-language translation of *By Avon River* appeared with Suhrkamp Verlag.[64] While Macmillan had marketed the text to a mainstream audience, Suhrkamp Verlag used it to launch a highly specialized series of poetry books with limited print-runs.[65] Bryher had arranged for the translation to be done by Johannes Urzidil, a Prague writer who became a refugee when Nazi Germany occupied Czechoslovakia in 1939. Bryher had rescued Urzidil and his family from Italy, where they were hiding from the Gestapo, and with her financial help, he had made a home first in Britain and then, permanently, in the United States, where he acquired citizenship in 1946. His translation of *By Avon River* was undoubtedly one way to express his gratitude to his benefactor. The German-language edition presents "Good Frend" in a side-by-side format, with English and German renditions of the poems on facing pages; "The Guest," however, appears only in German (including the quotations from the various Elizabethan poets discussed).

Urzidil wrote an afterword to the text, which argues for privileging a poet's interpretation of another poet over the meticulous research of scholars, though he does take care to praise H.D.'s knowledge of Shakespeare and his contemporaries, and her carefully drawn representation of the Elizabethan age. Much of the essay expounds upon the difficulty—the impossibility even—of translating Shakespearean verse and poetry more broadly, citing the tremendous gap between Shakespeare's language and German translations of his language, a chasm that remains even after centuries of attempts to fill it. He warns, too, that German and English appear to be much closer than they are. Urzidil reminds his readers that most of Shakespeare's contemporaries have been ignored by German scholars, a neglect that serves to heighten his burden as translator for an audience with little knowledge of the Elizabethan lyricists. For Urzidil, German scholars have so idealized Shakespeare that Shakespeare has practically become German himself. He notes as well his own past research into seventeenth-century literature, and he concludes with the assertion that language springs from the ethos of a people, and thus translation is always a fraught enterprise.[66] Urzidil also prepared five pages of annotations to the text, but these notes were not printed in the edition, perhaps because his relationship with Suhrkamp Verlag had become strained during the proofing stages.[67]

Despite the limited print run, the German-language *By Avon River*—entitled *Avon, von H.D.*—was reviewed by several German periodicals, and it was featured on a Voice of America German-language radio program on September 26, 1955.[68] For H.D., Urzidil prepared a German-language transcript of the broadcast and meticulously translated the reviews and notices of *Avon* in German periodicals. In the broadcast, H.D. is characterized, with Marianne Moore, as an American poet residing behind the scenes of modernist poetry who had nonetheless wielded great power and influence. Interestingly, the description of *Avon* by the radio announcer emphasizes first the link between the source texts for *The Tempest*—accounts of new world exploration and shipwrecks—and the Elizabethan age, when English imperialist efforts began, before shifting to a brief mention of Claribel. For this radio audience, issues of nation and imperialism took precedence.

A preeminent writer H.D. much admired, Hermann Hesse, praised the German edition as a "very very strange and complex, wonderful work of poetry" and its "verses of a sweet and wild peculiarity and dream-power." Perhaps not surprisingly, then, the reviews that followed were quite positive, echoing the American reviewers of the Macmillan edition. In a lengthy review, Emil Belzner for the *Rhein-Neckar Zeitung* expresses his utmost admiration for the book, citing the poetic nature of the prose, its lively representation of Shakespeare's milieu, and its intuitive grasp of Shakespeare's genius. Alfred Günther reviewed the book for both the *Deutsche Zeitung* and the *Stuttgarter Zeitung*, dubbing it "the most unique and touching homage to Shakespeare which one could think of," particularly in light of the clumsy efforts of her predecessors who, in their "flood of poetic homage," have always been found lacking. The difference, Günther contends, is that "[f]or her Shakespeare is not only the occasion for her own poetry, his words and their characters are not only material for poetic reflection: she invents her poet." So pleased with Günther's insight into her work, H.D. read one of his books on Shakespeare and sent him a personal copy of the English-language *By Avon River*.[69]

As with the 1949 version of the text, there were few negative chords struck in these German reviews. One reviewer for the *Rheinische Post*, Richard Gerber, writes a laudatory review but wonders why Shakespeare has to appear as a drunken, senile, old man in the text. Gerber also vents his frustration at his confusion over the avalanche of lyricists she mentions with whom non-English readers were unfamiliar. The one truly dismissive review was authored by Czechoslovakian Willy Haas, who Urzidil warned H.D. "harbour[ed] an old prejudice" against him.[70] An exasperated Haas cites her "amateurishly arbitrary use of language": "Heaven knows what may have attracted Hesse to it."

The following year, in 1956, the musician Eric Walter White corresponded with H.D. about the possibility of setting "Good Frend" to music. They had long been friends, and he suggested treating the three poems individually and using two voices for "Rosemary." Her reply was enthusiastic: "What an exciting idea! It fills me with a wild fantasy of myself coming to Stratford," she responded from Switzerland.[71] If White did make such an attempt, however, it was never published.

Clearly, one key historical context for reading *By Avon River* is World War II. *The Tempest*'s storm evoked in the opening lines of the poem—"I came home / Driven by *The Tempest*"—is, on one level, the war, for H.D. had chosen to remain in London for her second world war, having faced World War I as the wife of a poet-soldier, Richard Aldington. As Susan Stanford Friedman astutely observes, "To H.D., Shakespeare was inseparable from war."[72] Bryher, too, draws a parallel between the early modern and modern periods when she writes, "We had stuck it somehow as England had stuck it at the time of the Armada." Indeed, to Bryher's mind, the Renaissance is firmly tied to war. Her passion for the period came and went with each war: "My knowledge of Elizabethan came to me during two wars and seemed to vanish 'into thin air' when they were over."[73]

In the poem, the present is the past. "We stand with our flowers.... Today? Yesterday?" the poet asks, conflating the two historical periods as she stands at Shakespeare's tomb in 1945.[74] The idea for the parallel between the two periods may have come to H.D. early on, when the Blitz began. In 1940, she writes excitedly to Bryher that England is a ship, caught in a terrible storm: "A radio commentator said something I have felt and said to myself for a long time. We are on a SHIP. That is what it is. The island IS a ship—and things going on, on 'land' as it were (America) are simply out of another element—especially when ship is in storm."[75] With this observation, H.D. invokes the threat of shipwreck as well as the Americas. She thus references Shakespeare's sources for an account of the sinking of the *Sea Venture* off the coast of Bermuda, a story she marked in the preface to her copy of *The Tempest* and inserted into her poem:

> Some say the *Sea-Adventure* set out,
> (In May, 1609, to be exact)
> For the new colony, Virginia;
> Some say the *Sea-Adventure* ran aground
> On the Bermudas....
>
> ....
> It is all written in an old pamphlet....
>
> ....
> The flagship, the *Sea-Adventure*
> Was one of nine ships; it bore
> Sir Thomas Gates and Sir George Somers;
> So the poet read.... [76]

But there probably isn't one single source for the connection drawn between the two periods. As Neil Corcoran has argued broadly, "Shakespeare as a cultural category becomes one of the focal points for modernism because he contains all the positive and negative, conflicting possibilities of modernity."[77] Modernists write about Shakespeare, simply put, to make Shakespeare their own. But, in a time of strife, the sense of urgency is heightened. As Kathleen Crown explains, Shakespeare during World War II becomes a symbol of national pride:

> Literary London . . . turned in wartime to Shakespeare as a symbol of nationalism and patriotism. H.D. was not the first to note that the situation presented in *The Tempest*—an island beset with rough magic, strange aerial visitations, and a father mourning the loss of his son and heir—was much like that of England during the First and Second World Wars. Nor was she the first to use the upheavals of the English Renaissance as a screen for discussing the disruptions of the twentieth century.[78]

Indeed, Laurence Olivier's award-winning film *Henry V* was intended as propaganda, partly underwritten by the British government, to boost morale in 1944 when the Nazis began a second major strike of bombing. The story of Henry V's heroic win over a French army at Agincourt that vastly outnumbered his own forces resonated with London audiences who were beginning to grow weary that the war would never end, and H.D. viewed the film positively.[79] The battle at Agincourt features, too, in "The Guest," when H.D. quotes from Michael Drayton's "stirring ballad" about the battle and defends its importance: it "stands by itself, with or without Shakespeare's *Henry V*":

> O when shall English men
> With such acts fill a pen?
> Or England breed again
> Such a King Harry?[80]

As Susan Stanford Friedman and Diana Collecott note, the overtly patriotic 1944 *The Olive and the Sword* by G. Wilson Knight, which H.D. read closely and annotated, articulates strongly the parallels between Shakespeare's day and her own. H.D. penciled in a mark next to Knight's comment about *Henry V*: "The King is to lead a united nation to war. Shakespeare's mood is therefore ripe for some fine comments on national harmony."[81] Knight's introduction in particular vigorously makes the connection between eras, calling on a war-torn England to turn to

Shakespeare, "a national prophet if ever there was one." For Knight, England's war with Germany is spiritually mandated, and Knight's study of the history plays shows that "Shakespeare's life-work might be characterised as expanding, through a series of great plays, the one central legend of Saint George and the Dragon." King George VI, in Knight's imaginary, becomes St. George, the patron saint of England, and Germany is the dragon to be slain, a land of "dark presences" straight off the pages of *Macbeth*. Knight insists that England must return to its "Shakespearian heritage" as a way of "re-awakening the national imagination." H.D.'s dedication to "Good Frend"—commemorating both Shakespeare Day and St. George's Day—mirrors the parallel drawn in Knight between national and literary history: "It would be well to face and accept our destiny," he opines, "in the names both of Shakespeare and of Saint George, the patron saint of our literature and nation."[82]

The consistently grim focus in "The Guest" on poems evoking the death of the body and the flight of the soul no doubt reflects H.D.'s postwar despair. H.D. had been married to a poet-soldier in World War I, and she continues to be preoccupied with that figure at the close of World War II. A number of wars and warriors are cited throughout the prose part of the book. Military service is almost invariably mentioned in her brief biographies of the various playwrights and poets. On the very first page of "The Guest," in fact, H.D. tells us not of the great literary achievements of Philip Sidney and Christopher Marlowe, but rather that they went into battle with the French Huguenots, as did Raleigh. She highlights Sidney's participation in the Massacre of Saint Bartholomew; his death in yet another war completes the paragraph.[83] Two stanzas from Michael Drayton's *The Ballad of Agincourt* appear in the essay, recalling one of the shining moments of England's military history. She dwells on Robert Herrick's "To Anthea," lines of which serve as a refrain for several pages. Sir John Suckling fights against the Scotch and the Royalists. Most notably evoked, though, are the medieval Crusades, which appear as well in "Claribel's Way to God" when Claribel encounters an injured soldier. The last third of "The Guest" is devoted to a discussion of how the Crusades' violent suppression of heterodox forms of spirituality led to the birth of English lyric poetry. For poets who were not soldiers, H.D. emphasizes other tragedies in their lives. Many, such as John Webster and Thomas Nashe, were affected by the plague, another dark metaphor, like the tempest, for war. The plague swept through London like the Blitz, leaving a trail of corpses in its wake.

If London is the site of storms, wars, and shipwrecks, Stratford, for H.D., becomes a place of sanctuary, a refuge from the memories of the war. "In the presence of a storm such as World War II," Horace Gregory wrote in his review of *By Avon River*, "individual sensibility turns to its islands, returns to its earliest faiths, its Crete, its Utopia, its imagined place of rescue from the storm."[84] H.D.'s pilgrimage with Bryher and Herring in April 1945 was just such a return. Herring in fact claims that, at some spiritual level, that trip ended the war: "it was when we started moving—to Stratford in April—that the war began to end." "[I]t's been a kind of spring-board," he writes, "it was *our* V-Day."[85] Bryher eagerly encouraged H.D.'s other trips to Stratford that summer because "it is so much more of a change if you get right away from the London district and its bombing memories and great fun that you are in the Elizabethan vibration."[86] The journey and the book that resulted from it were healing for H.D. as she struggled to recover from the trauma of living through a second world war. The book itself comes to represent that recovery. When she hears of Macmillan's acceptance of the book, she writes to Bryher that "it is a great deal to the UNK [unconscious] to feel they have just snatched AVON RIVER."[87]

There are other significant critical and historical contexts that may illuminate *By Avon River*. In her memoir *Days of Mars*, Bryher muses that H.D. may have identified with Claribel, "married to the King of Tunis and left in a foreign land": "Had Hilda not been born in Pennsylvania, married to an Englishman in 1913 but treated throughout the First War almost as if she were an alien, and now in the second one 'come home' through sharing it and offering her tribute, on that just-past April day, to Shakespeare?"[88] One approach to reading *By Avon River* is found in most of the sparse scholarly attention to date. H.D.'s focus on Claribel, a forgotten female character of *The Tempest*, and her critique of Shakespeare for denying Claribel a voice constitute an important feminist subtext to the volume. As many have argued, H.D.'s recovery of Shakespeare's neglected character Claribel can be seen as a strategy by which she rewrites literary history and England's most significant literary forebear in an effort to authorize herself as woman writer.[89] Friedman argues that "Shakespeare's reinterpreted greatness authenticates the female poet: her existence, her quest, her woman-centered vision."[90] And Chedgzoy agrees, "In *By Avon River* and *Tribute to Freud* she confidently rewrites a powerful male precursor as an enabling source of intertextual material and revisionary methodology, in order to create a self-authorising female voice which acknowledges its relation to cultural tradition while asserting a difference from it."[91] For Friedman, too, "H.D. repeatedly personified her confrontation as a woman with male culture in a series of dialogues with men."[92] Like *Tribute to Freud*, *By Avon River* examines H.D.'s ambivalent relationship with one of the most powerful male figures of Western culture.[93] This focus on Claribel and female authorship is not unwarranted; indeed, her recovery of Claribel is absolutely crucial to the text's project.[94]

The first poem in the sequence, "The Tempest," introduces Claribel through Shakespeare's language, which is rendered in italics:

> *'Twas a sweet marriage,* we are told;
> And she *a paragon ... who is now queen,*
> *And the rarest that e'er came there;*
>
> We know little of *the king's fair daughter*
> *Claribel. . . .*
> . . . .
> And we read later, *in one voyage*
> *Did Claribel her husband find at Tunis. . . .* [95]

Here Claribel is the object exchanged in a political alliance. She has no presence, no voice: "She is not there at all."[96] In "Rosemary," the chiming bells at once call to Claribel and recall her name. Near the end of "Rosemary," Claribel—who has no lines in *The Tempest*—becomes the speaker of H.D.'s poem,

> I only threw a shadow
> On his page,
> Yet I was his,
> He spoke my name. . . . [97]

Granted life, Claribel is freed from the bounds of Shakespeare's page and goes on a quest in the final poem of the sequence, "Claribel's Way to God."

She returns home to Italy a queen, only to find a victim of war, a fallen crusader, to whom she offers rosemary, memory. As Chedgzoy remarks, it is the third part of the sequence that represents the fulfillment of H.D.'s feminist vision: "Here [Claribel] ceases to be Shakespeare's creation and acquires an autonomous existence as she moves beyond the boundaries marked out for her in *The Tempest*, undertaking her own pilgrimage to the source of the female-centred esoteric tradition manifested in courtly love poetry and the worship of Sophia, the female incarnation of 'Wisdom, the Supernal Light.'"[98]

In the poem, H.D. asks, "why did I choose / The invisible, voiceless Claribel,"[99] and in our own era Friedman responds with a biographical reading, attributing H.D.'s decision to write about one of Shakespeare's weaker female characters to her fragile mental state in the mid-1940s. But it is also possible that by choosing *The Tempest* over her favorite play from her girlhood, *As You Like It*—a play that likewise haunts "The Guest"—H.D. may not be embracing a weak character but rather showing that Shakespeare has. The text underscores, in fact, a troubling trend in Shakespeare's career. Shakespeare's early plays present strong, powerful female presences, while the late plays offer characters such as Miranda and Claribel—mere "marriage token[s]," H.D. dubs them[100]—who are no match for the intelligent, defiant Rosalind, the character a young H.D. was inspired to perform at home, reveling in the cross-dressing scenes.[101]

Moreover, H.D.'s feminist aims, I would argue, are not limited to her own concerns with female authorship or to the recovery of forgotten female figures. Embedded in *By Avon River* is a critique of marriage and how it functions in courtly society, for both Claribel and Miranda serve as objects of exchange. Arranged marriages in Europe have been essential to imperialist aims, consolidating power and amassing territory and wealth. As Stephen Orgel's introduction to the Oxford edition of *The Tempest* notes, speculation about Queen Elizabeth's potential marital alliances, and the relentless matchmaking of James I for his progeny, form a powerful backdrop to the poetry of the period.[102] Arranged marriages are foundational to the politics of nation, H.D. suggests in *By Avon River*, and thus women's bodies are part of an intricate exchange of power.

Arranged marriage is a topic raised on the opening pages of "Good Frend." H.D. had undoubtedly read George Garrett's irreverent commentary in *Life and Letters Today*[103] on Prospero's self-serving plot to "stag[e] a come-back" by uniting Miranda with the king's son: "We can imagine the old schemer saying to himself: 'Be patient, girl. Daddy has a big surprise for you. A real live prince? For you're a princess, my dear.'"[104] Miranda's marriage to Ferdinand is mirrored in Claribel's to the king of Tunis, and H.D. parallels these arranged unions with yet another associated with the play when she references a "wedding-feast" on the first page of the poem. Citing the popular belief that *The Tempest* was written in honor of the arranged marriage of Elizabeth, daughter of James I of England, to Frederick V of Bohemia, H.D. thus alludes to a marriage contrived to foster deeper connections between King James and the coalition of Protestant princes of the German states. In her own copy of *The Tempest*, H.D. marked the section on Elizabeth of Bohemia that lamented the "sorrowful adventures" that awaited the young queen and her eventual return to England decades later to die.[105]

Later, in "The Guest," H.D. will explain to her readers that "*The Tempest* was written to celebrate the marriage of James' daughter, Elizabeth, later known as Elizabeth of Bohemia or the Winter Queen" and quote generously from Sir Henry Wotton's poem in tribute to her.[106] But in the poem, H.D. pointedly forefronts the impersonal and public function of the union between Elizabeth and the German prince:

> Elizabeth, our princess, is to wed
> The Elector Palatine—who's that?
> Frederick, I think. And where's the place—
> Bohemia? I don't think so,
> But anyhow it doesn't matter,
> A foreign fellow is to wed our princess,
> The grand-daughter of Scotland's Mary;
> Occasion—compliment—another play![107]

The subject of London gossip, Elizabeth is *our* princess; she belongs to England. And it "doesn't matter" whom she marries—just that she weds a "foreign fellow."

This alliance is referenced again, albeit less directly, in "Good Frend" with a bit of misdirection. About Claribel's marriage, H.D. creates a refrain from lines that appear to be from the Old Testament Song of Songs, but also echo the refrain in a poem by Francis Quarles, cupbearer for Elizabeth of Bohemia, who will figure in "The Guest." On the surface, what seems to be a celebration of Claribel's love match is clouded by the reference to the unhappy Elizabeth Stuart lying beneath it.[108] "So they say, *my beloved is mine / And I am his*," H.D. writes of what *"they"* say, but then immediately revises it, "Our belovèd is ours, / Our belovèd is ours," changing singular to plural pronouns and adding (as Quarles does) an Elizabethan accent over the second "e" of beloved.[109] In this way, she responds to the final stanza of Quarles' poem, which critiques "those glittering Monarchs," who "tender in exchange their shares of land": "The world's but theirs," he writes, "but my Belovèd's mine." Emphasizing the public nature of the union, she makes clear that these marriages belong not to a *me* but an *us*, the nation, the then emerging English nation under the reign of Queen Elizabeth I.

Another telling instance of revision comes when H.D. rewrites Shakespeare's *"in one voyage did Claribel her husband find at Tunis"* to read instead: "The king's fair daughter / Marries Tunis."[110] Shakespeare's line grants her a name and a husband, but H.D.'s rewriting points out what Shakespeare elides, that Claribel loses her name, her identity, in the marriage; that she is defined entirely in terms of her relationship to her father, the king; and that she weds not a man but a geopolitical entity, Tunis, long a pirate stronghold. In Shakespeare's period, this alliance would have strengthened ties to the Turks, invaluable for Venice, a major trading port, in consolidating power against Spain. The opening of "The Guest" reasserts this theme when H.D. recalls that Sir Philip Sidney witnessed the Massacre of St. Bartholomew, a bit of biographical data that directs the reader to contemplate the bloodshed that can stem from arranged marriages. When Catherine de Medici orchestrated a marriage between her unwilling Catholic daughter and a Protestant, the bride was physically and violently compelled to consent, and days later thousands were dead in the massacre. It is not lost on H.D., in "Rosemary," that it is Shakespeare himself who arranges the marriage of Claribel to the African monarch. Shakespeare, like Prospero, takes the stage for a world and marries off the daughters of the play.

A feminist theme carries through to "The Guest" in H.D.'s references to Judith, Shakespeare's daughter, and in her extended discussion of the culture of courtly love, which, she argues, gives birth to the English lyric.

It is Judith to whom Shakespeare returns in his old age when he retires to Stratford: "He had come home," H.D. finishes the essay, "because he loved Judith."[111] Sifting through memories of his late mother, remembering the death of his son, Hamnet, Shakespeare must look for his legacy in his daughter and her children: as Crown notes, "At the book's close, the scholar-narrator imagines William Shakespeare thinking back through his mother, Mary, and forward through his daughter, Judith."[112] His relationship to Judith, for Friedman, suggests "his own androgyny," and "[t]he presence of woman within Shakespeare counters the absence of women in the Elizabethan anthology."[113] As one dismayed contemporaneous reviewer observed, H.D. feminizes Shakespeare.[114]

As in *Trilogy*, the Lady is a goddess resurrected near the end of her essay, "The Guest." Drawing on one of her favorite books—Denis de Rougemont's *Love in the Western World*—H.D. argues that it is the religious suppression of the Lady, by Simon de Montford in the Albigensian Crusades that sought to quash worship of the Virgin Mary, that spawned the courtly love motif. Forced to secularize their songs, troubadours wrote subversive aubades, or ballads, for and to an unattainable ideal, as Dante did to Beatrice. The mother of Richard the Lionheart, Eleanor of Aquitaine, brings this tradition from Provence to England. H.D. alleges, "This worship [of the Lady], forced to renounce the official language of the Church, disguised itself in terms of earthly passion. But this passion was never requited. In other words, the love of the troubadour was love of the Spiritual. This love could not be satisfied on earth." If, as she argues, "[t]he Inquisition had destroyed the cult of Our Lady," then "the Lady banished from the churches of Provence, found refuge elsewhere."[115] According to the code of courtly love, the medieval knight was caught between his allegiance to the lady and his allegiance to the king; this Lady, for H.D., is to be interpreted spiritually, so that the choice is really between heavenly and material desires. Here the verse and the prose of *By Avon River* are brought into dialogue. The very Crusader who had fought to suppress the worship of Mary—"Wisdom, the Supernal Light"—(mis)identifies Claribel as just this spiritual entity when she gives him rosemary for remembrance. The Goddess will not be forgotten. Claribel's quest in "Good Frend" is fulfilled in "The Guest."

Robert Herring asks H.D. in 1945, "Do you think, H.D., there has *ever* been anyone who has left such an absolutely *unadulterated* aura around him as Shakespeare?"[116] Recent studies of modernism and Shakespeare—such as those by Cary DiPietro[117] and Neil Corcoran—demonstrate a wide range of responses, by a number of modernist writers (from Yeats to Auden), to this phenomenon. H.D.'s own response to Herring's question, in *By Avon River*, does not serve to fortify and insulate that *"unadulterated aura"* but rather to trouble it. Ever ambivalent, she celebrates while she denigrates. H.D.'s reconstruction of Shakespeare is not of the playwright as genius, at his prime. Rather, Shakespeare in "Good Frend" is a plagiarist and arguably a misogynist, and in "The Guest" appears elderly and frail, plagued by the memory loss that comes inevitably with old age, at home in Stratford because "[h]e couldn't compete with the new wits."[118]

Though critical assessment of the text—from its publication to the present day—univocally locates Shakespeare at the center, he is, in fact, barely mentioned until the final pages, his presence sensed only at the margins; we are not, after all, *at* Avon River but *by* Avon River. But the specter of Shakespeare drifts in and out of the poem of the first part of the book and the prose of the second, in which he flits in and out in dream-like sequences. Here, at the end of his life, he is an aging man who cannot remember, perhaps the most serious critique for H.D., who identifies cultural amnesia as central to, as facilitator of, continual cycles of warfare. A constant theme of H.D.'s late work, particularly central to her well-known war epic *Trilogy*, the poet's role is to preserve and restore cultural memory, to dredge up the traces left in the palimpsest of history. In this sense, then, Claribel might be seen as usurping Shakespeare's position when, unmanacled, she offers a sprig of rosemary—rose of memory—to a fallen soldier, a casualty of the Crusades. It is memory, for H.D., that will heal civilization from war.

The recurrent scenes of the late Shakespeare's forgetfulness that periodically disrupt the literary critical essay of the second half of the book indict him as a participant in the erasure of cultural memory, as one who perpetuates cultural amnesia. In one revealing episode, Shakespeare struggles to remember lines from his *Antony and Cleopatra* in which Antony abdicates power in favor of love in a passage that follows directly a reference to William the Conqueror: *"Let Rome in Tiber melt—here is my—here is my—."* What he can't remember of Antony's speech is suggestive: "Let Rome in

Tiber melt, and the wide arch / Of the ranged empire fall! Here is my space. / Kingdoms are clay." In his final days and hours, H.D.'s Shakespeare cannot remember that "[k]ingdoms are clay," that love is more important than empire and kingdom. Thus, another critical context within which to view *By Avon River* is H.D.'s concern with English imperialism, an issue that aligns her with other late modernists whose writings begin to turn in the 1930s and 1940s toward issues of nation and politics. Her focus on *The Tempest* in particular means that the text might well be read in terms of what Douglas Mao and Rebecca Walkowitz have recently dubbed "the transnational turn" in "new modernist" studies.[119]

H.D.'s "turn"—a term Mao and Walkowitz borrow from Jed Esty's landmark monograph on late modernism[120]—was not tinged with the nostalgia of so many of her compatriots, however. The poetry and prose of *By Avon River* condemn English imperialism. H.D. may have characterized her book "as a sort of sign-post and tribute to Angleterre,"[121] but her love of her adopted home-country is not blind. When she remembers the Elizabethan period, she praises its poets but condemns the politics and policies of its court, its violence, and its riches. War and imperialism are inextricably tied, H.D. concludes, for both derive from the same source, nationalism: "That lure of foreign places, was really love of home, their own native boundaries. The urge would be satisfied for a time by wars in England. When a sort of transitional peace fell upon the prince and barons, it was time to leave."[122] As Francis Bacon writes in a poem H.D. includes in her analysis, it may well be that "[w]e're worse in peace."[123]

As Chedgzoy suggests, Claribel's marriage speaks directly "to the question of the white woman's pivotal role in the imperial project."[124] H.D.'s critique of imperialism goes further than her commentary on arranged marriages, however. Shakespeare in "Good Frend" is not only the playwright who neglects a key female character, Claribel, but also a poacher. In the first poem of the sequence, "The Tempest," H.D. lingers over a purported incident from Shakespeare's youth, his poaching of Sir Lucy's deer. As H.D.'s speaker approaches Shakespeare's tomb, the hallowed tone is disrupted when she steps on a gravestone for the Lucy family and recalls the tale of the young Shakespeare's theft of a deer, a crime that eventually led to his flight to London: "Sir Thomas Lucy caught him at it. . . . Poaching. . . . poaching?" From here, H.D. shifts swiftly from deer poaching to plagiarism, citing his sources for *The Tempest* in the pamphlets about the wreck of the *Sea Venture* in Bermuda, "taken out of the news-sheet." But it is not just the story of *The Tempest* that he "poaches" for his own purposes: "He stole everything, / There isn't an original plot / In the whole lot of his plays." To earn "[a] little success with the old Queen," he works "by patching up / Other men's plots and filling in / With odds and ends he called his own."[125]

As the nationalist propaganda of the war years makes clear, Shakespeare is an icon, standing in for England in times of strife, and thus Shakespeare's poaching can be read as England's imperialism. "Much sweet was plundered, / Stacked and stored," H.D. remarks in "Rosemary" in a stanza about Shakespeare's elaborate garden at New Place.[126] Shakespeare's estate at Stratford was an ostentatious purchase, the second largest house in his hometown at the time, a veritable mansion by Renaissance standards. Shakespeare's apparent obsession with the garden is a persistent motif in this text, not just in the poem but also in the prose, as his musings on the garden's design erratically interrupt her literary critical essay on his contemporaries, drawing her attention away from his rival poets. He is, metaphorically if absent-mindedly, sowing the seeds of the medieval aubades for future generations. And his constant thoughts about flowers do feminize him—constructing him as androgynous and thus not a threat to her own aesthetic autonomy, as Friedman has observed. But H.D. may also be critiquing his materialism, a materialism she expressly critiques in "Good Frend," when Claribel admires the Poor Clares' dedication to poverty. Shakespeare's grave is itself a tribute to his wealth, for he bought for himself and his family the prime sites at the altar of Trinity Church and protected that site with verse that curses anyone who dares to move him from his exalted position, verse that appears as epigraph to "Good Frend."

The theme of Shakespeare as poacher resurfaces in the second half of the book, as what she terms "Shakespeare's indifference to originality" echoes throughout her account of his peers.[127] While the young Ben Jonson was diligently reading, she notes dryly, Shakespeare "boasted in later life of other exploits," including his theft of Lucy's deer.[128] Though it is today unclear who influenced whom, H.D. indicates no less than three times the links between Michael Drayton's *Nymphidia* and Shakespeare's Oberon and Queen Mab in *A Midsummer Night's Dream*.[129] To emphasize further that Shakespeare lifted those characters from Drayton, she exercises some artistic license in two suggestions: first, that Drayton and Sir Lucy may be cousins, further strengthening their connection as victims of Shakespeare's theft (in fact, it is Drayton's patron who is Lucy's cousin); and, second, that Drayton showed Shakespeare a book of pansies that inspired his construction of his garden at New Place, an event Shakespeare fails to remember (in fact, pansies figure importantly in both *A Midsummer Night's Dream* and the *Nymphidia*).[130]

Given the degree of attention that Lucy's deer and the garden receive, in both halves of *By Avon River*, these suggestions cannot have been made lightly. Moreover, Drayton is not the only poet to be victim to Shakespeare's poaching. "There are many lyrics of Shakespeare's which might well be attributed to Fletcher," she writes, and Fletcher, she claims, "had outlined [*Romeo and Juliet*] for [Shakespeare] from the Italian folio."[131] *The Merchant of Venice*, she alleges, draws on Marlowe's *The Jew of Malta*, the latter, to her mind, the better play.[132]

Elizabeth I launched formally England's imperial project, as H.D. makes clear in "Good Frend" when she stresses *The Tempest's* sources in narratives of England's expansion into the New World. The Elizabethan era, then, is inevitably tied to imperialism and the amassing of wealth pilfered from other parts of the world. Opening with Raleigh's embittered condemnation of the court, "The Guest" is unrelenting in its critique of monarchical politics, of kings and queens who compel poets to pander to their whims or risk imprisonment—like Raleigh—in the Tower. That Raleigh's explorations contributed a great deal to Elizabeth's imperialist aims is not a coincidence. Indeed there are moments in the second half of *By Avon River* that read less like a literary critical essay on Shakespeare's contemporaries and more like a laundry list of poets wronged by the State. Sidney died fighting Elizabeth's war, Spenser's manor was burned to the ground, Raleigh and Essex were beheaded, Dyer ends a life of service to the Crown in poverty, Nashe and Waller were imprisoned, Southwell died a martyr, Herrick is exiled, Davison is disgraced. But "Shakespeare retired to Stratford."[133]

With considerable irony, H.D. remarks that "An accomplished courtier is, of necessity, a poet."[134] In the Elizabethan period, these roles are blurred. "We have imagined only one true way of recalling these, our poets," she writes, but she wants to read beyond the parameters of traditional literary criticism, beyond the canonical figures she begins with—Shakespeare, Sidney, Marlowe—but also beyond the literary into the political realm. Though she quotes liberally from their poetry, her commentary (like Braithwaite's) consistently describes these men in their public or military function, and their poetry invariably recounts their unjust suffering in the earthly realm and their readiness for a spiritual end. She traces webs of influence between literary figures that are based more in politics than in the arts. It is the court—the corrupt court—that holds these networks together. These poets were "steeped in the policies and politics of the time."[135] Poet after poet is exiled, excommunicated, executed. It is not just Shakespeare's but Raleigh's corpse that haunts "The Guest."

When H.D. writes of Shakespeare that he stands aside, that "[w]e can not imagine him shut up in the Tower," her intuitive observation is surely doubly valenced.[136] Is Shakespeare to be condemned for complicity with the court or commended for negotiating and sidestepping such a treacherous field? There was no escape from politics for the poet-playwright, she insists, when she reminds us that the new Elizabethan theater is written over the theatrical spaces of Henry VIII's palaces, spaces still faintly visible in the lush fabrics, the banquets, the candelabras of Elizabethan play sets. The history of English imperialism, she avers, can be seen in these play sets: "Why is this forgotten?" she asks; the church plundered the Orient, then, "[t]he church was plundered by the palace; the palace became the background for new ritual," so that the theater itself "was overlaid with the memory of secret plunder."[137] What distinguishes Shakespeare from his contemporaries, she points out in selection after selection of their poetry, is their choice of heavenly reward over earthly treasure.[138] While Shakespeare retires to his spacious home and plans his garden, other poets remind their readers that "Heaven is our heritage, / Earth but a player's stage."[139]

When *By Avon River* appeared in 1949, H.D. was not yet finished with Shakespeare. Though she writes in her memoir *Compassionate Friendship* in 1955 that "I am not jealous of Shakespeare anymore," her interest in his work has not waned.[140] She never wrote another book about Shakespeare, but she continued to read his poetry and plays avidly, marking passages of interest and annotating books about him. H.D.'s copy of Knight's 1955 study of Shakespeare's sonnets, *The Mutual Flame*, for instance, is thoroughly marked in her hand, noting passages in particular that deal with Shakespeare's bisexuality, with Achilles in *Troilus and Cressida*, with the Essex rebellion, and with Elizabeth's Virginia expeditions.[141] She writes in her 1955 memoir *Compassionate Friendship* of her "passion for his work" as she reads it alongside her epic *Helen in Egypt:* "he burns through my scenes, my scenario like an incandescent burner." She took notes as well in her copy of *Shakespeare's Sonnets*[142] and her edition of *Shakespeare as Poet*, a compilation of quotations from Shakespeare's plays,[143] and there is evidence that she revisited *The Tempest* with other themes in mind.

When Robert Herring suggests to her in 1945 that with the character of Beatrice in *Much Ado About Nothing* Shakespeare may have picked up "where Dante let off"—bringing the deific Beatrice "down to earth"—this may have provided the spark for a new endeavor.[144] By 1948, she is at work translating Dante's *La Vita Nuova*—which explores his love of Beatrice—furthering her knowledge of the tradition of courtly love and reigniting her interest in worshipped female icons. Initially, she tells Bryher that she wishes to do a "By Arno River" about Dante to pair with her Shakespeare book, but two years later she describes a more complex project to George Plank based on her "wild theory and idea, of linking up the Italian plays, names, references, etc. in Shakespeare with certain obscure passages of Dante."[145]

It is perhaps with Richard Aldington, though, that she talks the most about her enthusiasm for continued study. "I am very anxious to get this Dante thing into line with my Shakespeare, AVON book," she writes to Aldington in 1949, "It is notable that Dante spent his exsile [*sic*] in the Shakespeare Italy, Verona, Venice."[146] Aldington, in fact, becomes a research assistant of sorts, responding to her queries about Renaissance literature and history—concerning such topics as the circumstances around the sinking of the Spanish Armada, books on Marlowe and Jonson, disagreements about the Shakespeare canon, and the origin of blank verse—and he mails her a compilation of Elizabethan writings on life and culture.[147] In 1953, at Küsnacht, a rest home in Switzerland, H.D. helps to facilitate a Shakespeare club of sorts, staging readings of the plays with her multinational consort of friends and her German doctor, Erich Heydt. Even as she moved on in the late 1940s and 1950s—writing more about such topics as English history and art, Prague and religious persecution, the mythological Helen in Egypt—she continued to read and reread Shakespeare. Had she lived longer, perhaps, we would have a sequel to *By Avon River*.

Notes

1. "If one has taken joy and comfort from a country, one does not want to leave it when there is trouble about," H.D. writes poet Marianne Moore in 1944 of her decision to remain in London. Caroline Zilboorg, ed., *Richard Aldington and H.D.: The Later Years in Letters* (New York: Manchester University Press, 1995), 74. In Bryher's *Days of Mars: A Memoir, 1940–1946* (New York: Harcourt Brace, 1972), Bryher records that she plead with H.D. to return to the safety of her birthplace, America, but H.D. staunchly refused, 6. "It was the Puritan element, a matter of conscience and principle," Bryher explains, "that had now kept Hilda in London. 'It was here that people first read my poetry,' she said, 'I am staying with them.' . . . It is the poets who are the leaders of the people. She could have left us easily, but she stayed," 115, 116. H.D. writes Plank as early as November 24, [1938], that she could quite easily heed Bryher's advice and "with a turn of the wrist" use her birth certificate to flee London for the States, "[b]ut all my memories and my emotional status seems [*sic*] here." George Plank Papers, Yale Collection of American Literature, Beinecke Rare Book and Manuscript Library, New Haven, Connecticut.

H.D. did leave London several times during the war, but she did not travel outside of London as often as Bryher did, even though they had close friends in Cornwall and Derbyshire anxious to receive them. In *Within the Walls* (Iowa City: Windhover Press, 1993), H.D.'s memoir of the Blitz that overtook London from the fall of 1940 to the spring of 1941, she writes that Bryher urges her to leave town in the spring of 1941 when another Blitz was anticipated, but H.D. insists, "I do not want to go to Cornwall or to Eckington, for that matter," 13. Indeed, Bryher complains to May Sarton in a letter dated April 19, 1941, "I wish H. would go away, but she wont [*sic*]." May Sarton Papers, Berg Collection of English and American Literature, New York Public Library, Astor, Lenox, and Tilden Foundations. The day after the second wave of bombings occurred in 1944—featuring the fly-bomb, new German weaponry—H.D. emphatically resists Bryher's urging that they go immediately to Cornwall, reportedly declaring that Hitler would not scare her away: "'Leave Lowndes now because of That Man? Never!'" Bryher, *Days of Mars*, 133.

In the midst of the Blitz, H.D. tells her cousin Gretchen Wolle Baker on February

14, [1941?], that she doesn't regret her decision: "As a matter of fact, I am glad to have had the time here. It has all been most revealing and exciting and people have been so wonderful." H.D. Papers, Yale Collection of American Literature, Beinecke Rare Book and Manuscript Library, New Haven, Connecticut. In a later letter dated February 20, [1944], she suggests to Baker that the experience has been a healing one, a psychological necessity: "You must remember that I have had TWO wars and the first one rather cut me away from family etc. and now in my ripe middle-age, I have begun to go back and weave in the jagged ends."

2. The letter to artist and illustrator George Plank is dated July 9, [1949]. George Plank Papers. It is quoted in Susan Stanford Friedman, "'Remembering Shakespeare Always, But Remembering Him Differently': H.D.'s *By Avon River*," *Sagetrieb* 2.2 (1983): 47. It is Friedman who notes that H.D. "liked to carry *By Avon River* in her purse or pocket for re-reading and memorizing during the period when the ideas for *Helen in Egypt* began to take shape" in the early 1950s.

3. This letter to Plank is dated June 4, [1944]. George Plank Papers.

4. Horace Gregory, "The Moment of Revival," review of *By Avon River*, by H.D., *Poetry* 75.4 (1950): 224.

5. This letter to Pearson is dated June 24, 1950. Norman Holmes Pearson Papers, Yale Collection of American Literature, Beinecke Rare Book and Manuscript Library. Part of the quote is cited in Friedman, "'Remembering Shakespeare Always,'" 55.

6. H.D., *By Avon River*, 57.

7. Ibid., 78.

8. Kate Chedgzoy, *Shakespeare's Queer Children: Sexual Politics and Contemporary Culture* (Manchester: Manchester University Press, 1995), 109.

9. H.D., *By Avon River*, 71.

10. Ibid., 75.

11. Denis de Rougemont, *Love in the Western World*, trans. Montgomery Belgion (New York: Pantheon, 1940; 1956).

12. According to a letter from H.D. to her friend Viola Jordan dated April 19, [1945], H.D. had been to Stratford just once previously, before the war. Viola Baxter Jordan Papers, Yale Collection of American Literature, Beinecke Rare Book and Manuscript Library, Yale University.

13. This letter to Viola Jordan is dated May 18, [1945]. Viola Baxter Jordan Papers. She echoes this characterization of the trip in a letter to Baker on August 2, [1945], when she refers to it "as a sort of pre-peace celebration." H.D. Papers.

14. This letter from Herring is dated [1938?], but mentions H.D.'s *Trilogy* (ed. Aliki Barnstone [New York: New Directions, 1998]), *Tribute to Freud* (New York: New Directions, 2009), V-E Day, and their trip to Stratford; it was thus probably written in 1945. H.D. Papers.

15. Bryher, *Days of Mars*, 150.

16. Ibid., 151.

17. Ibid., 152.

18. H.D. writes Bryher on September 11, [1948], about her intent to dedicate the book to her: "You made it possible. . . . Stratford and all it meant in 1945, the Crown of my English life and going on into Avon, also due to you." Bryher Papers, General Collection, Beinecke Rare Book and Manuscript Library, Yale University, New Haven, Connecticut.

19. She tells Jordan that she "fell in love with the place" (letter dated May 18, [1945]; Viola Baxter Jordan Papers), and she writes to Baker from Stratford, "I so fell in love with the place that I booked months back, a room here" (letter dated August 2, [1945]; H.D. Papers).

20. It was difficult to secure lodging for the entire summer because of the popularity of Stratford's summer theater season among Londoners. Moreover, as Bryher explains, "the regulations forbade hotels to keep guests more than four days," so H.D. had to move frequently from one inn to another. *Days of Mars*, 162.

21. Bryher's letter to H.D. about their anniversary is dated July 15, 1945. H.D. Papers.

22. The Royal Shakespeare Company performed several Shakespeare plays that summer at the Shakespeare Memorial Theatre: *Much Ado about Nothing, The Merry Wives of Windsor, Othello, Twelfth Night, Antony and Cleopatra, Henry VIII*, and *Romeo and Juliet*. H.D.'s letters record her attendance at all but *Antony*, and she writes in particular of her impressions of *Twelfth Night, Much Ado, Henry VIII*, and *Romeo and Juliet*. See letters to Bryher throughout the summer of 1945 (Bryher Papers) and to Viola Jordan, dated September 3, [1945] (Viola Baxter Jordan Papers).

23. In the holograph version of "The Guest," H.D. initially includes orchids in Shakespeare's garden. H.D. Papers. She strikes through these passages, perhaps because "[o]rchid was a foreign word." She appears to be intent on capturing, in colloquial terms, native English flora. H.D. spent enough time in the gardens of New Place to feel accepted by the locals; she writes to Bryher on July 24, [1945], "I have learned a lot about New Place Garden. One woman, a friend of a gardner [*sic*], said they did not encourage tourists coming there—it was meant for Stratford people & a few outside people who *really cared*. I felt very flattered to be accepted as one of the inner circle. Yes—I belong here!" Bryher Papers.

24. This letter to Bryher is dated July 23, [1945]. Bryher Papers. Other letters that touch on her search for a house include letters to Bryher dated July 24, [1945] and August 13, [1945] (Bryher Papers), and a letter from Bryher to H.D. dated September 24, 1945 (H.D. Papers). She writes to Plank on August 7, [1945?], "I want a *place* on Avon." George Plank Papers. On August 11, she writes him that she was considering a particular cottage in Shottery, just west of Stratford, but it was too expensive.

25. See letters to Bryher dated [July 17, 1938] and [August 24, 1938]. Bryher Papers. In the first letter, H.D. finds *Henry VIII* "a frightful film," but helpful to her task of "trac[ing] the queens." "I have been deep in Henry VIII and Hampt. Court literature," she continues, commenting that she was intrigued by the links between early American and early English history and that she found the "religious muddle . . . most fascinating." She asks Bryher for "a good popular-ish vol. on Queen Bess."

26. See letters to Bryher dated March 23, [1940], and August 13, 1940. Bryher Papers. Billie Melman, *The Culture of History: English Uses of the Past 1800–1953* (Oxford: Oxford University Press, 2006), describes *The Sea Hawk* as a "swashbuckling melodrama" in which "the Nazis turned up in this Elizabethan romance, with the fleet standing between the German tyrant and his dream of world conquest." Flora Robson, as Elizabeth I, delivers a "stirring 'Churchillian' oration 'when the ruthless ambition of a man threatens to engulf the world,'" 23.

27. G. Wilson Knight, *The Olive and the Sword: A Study of England's Shakespeare* (New York: Oxford University Press, 1944). As discussed below, H.D.'s feelings about Knight are mixed, though her pencil marks in his 1955 book, *The Mutual Flame* (London: Methuen, 1955), show that his willingness to discuss Shakespeare's bisexuality appealed to her; see Diana Collecott, *H.D. and Sapphic Modernism 1910–1950* (Cambridge: Cambridge University Press, 1999), chapter 7, for more on Knight and sexuality. In a letter to George Plank, H.D. recalls the moment when she first discovered *The Olive and the Sword*: she was "enchanted," it was "a revelation" (May 12, [1955]). George Plank Papers. But, as a letter from Herring in early 1950 indicates, her reading is not entirely laudatory: "I'm glad you got the Wilson Knight book. My reactions are exactly yours. I think one *can* get too deep in what he is doing,—and lose W. S. in the process. . . . He is finding himself in Shakespeare, and though that is very good, he is losing Shakespeare in the process." H.D. Papers.

28. George Garrett, "That Four-Flusher Prospero," *Life and Letters Today* 16.7 (1937); reprinted in *Shakespeare Survey* (London: Brendin, 1937).

29. William S. Braithwaite, *The Book of Elizabethan Verse* (London: Chatto and Windus, 1908). Collecott, *H.D. and Sapphic Modernism 1910–1950*; Friedman, "'Remembering Shakespeare Always'"; and others miss the importance of this text, though the error is entirely understandable given that H.D. herself gives it an erroneous title in "The Guest." It is undeniably her source text for the other Elizabethan poets. Not only does all of the verse she cites appear in this book but also her biographical data is taken from its appendix, usually verbatim and with quotation marks to denote that she is working from a source. Her checkmarks in the margins of Braithwaite's index of authors match the authors cited in her book, and a penciled note by Bryher in the front of the book reads, "When Hilda came back to Switzerland after the war, she asked me to send her any anthology of Elizabethan poetry in Kenwin—She read this book continuously before writing Avon River." H.D. Papers.

H.D. explains in a letter to George Plank (January 26, [1950]; George Plank Papers) that her sole source for "The Guest" was "one out-dated demodé, beloved Elizabethan Anthology" (letter dated January 26, [1950]; George Plank Papers). This is echoed in a letter to her former husband, British writer Richard Aldington, when she refers to having "only one rather old-fashioned Anthology beside me" (letter dated February 14, 1949; H.D. Papers). While it was not in fact the only book she had at her disposal—her insistent protestations perhaps indicating her embarrassment over a few factual errors in the text—it is clear that she relies exclusively on it for the many Elizabethan poets she discusses. After finishing "The Guest," H.D. writes Bryher that she would like her own copy of Braithwaite's anthology (November 2, 1946; Bryher Papers), but Bryher responds that she can keep the one she lent her (November 5, 1946; H.D. Papers); H.D. also asks that Bryher find an additional copy of the anthology to send to her typist, Miss Woolford, so that she may have it on hand while typing "The Guest."

Friedman, "'Remembering Shakespeare Always,'" rightly complains that H.D.'s explanation of her omission of Milton is done "unconvincingly and lamely," 69. Milton is not included in Braithwaite's anthology, however, so the omission makes sense in that light. In fact, the section on Milton was added to the text after she produced the first penciled draft of "The Guest," perhaps in response to the obvious question of his exclusion.

30. H.D. writes Bryher July 21, [1945], that she has located the Shakespeare Press. Bryher Papers.

31. In a letter dated [1945?], Herring jokes with H.D. that Bryher was so obsessed with the Elizabethans that she "bull[ied]" the two of them into sharing her interest. H.D. Papers. H.D. writes to Bryher of finding Knight's study of the history plays, *The Olive and the Sword*, but warns her that though "it puts the sequence easily for me," it may be "a bit too elementary for you . . . 'an advanced student'" (letter dated July 18, [1945]; Bryher Papers).

32. Bryher discusses her fascination with Raleigh (or "Ralegh," as she preferred the earlier spelling) in *Days of Mars*, 164–65. She also talks about her admiration for Marlowe, Beaumont, and Raleigh in a letter to May Sarton dated December 28, 1943: "Ralegh, to me, was one of the very finest of the Elizabethans, I would rank him, along with Marlowe and Beaumont. So modern is his use of metre." She refers to herself as a "Marlowe specialist" in another letter dated April 30, 1942. May Sarton Papers. Bryher composes a poem to "Young Rawley" in 1947 (see letter to H.D., December 11, 1947; H.D. Papers). This love of the Renaissance culminated in Bryher's 1953 historical novel, *The Player's Boy*, ed. Patrick Gregory (New York: Paris Press, 2006).

33. Bryher, *Days of Mars*, 100–106.

34. Ibid., 106.

35. Ibid., 181. The memoir implies that the trip is much later, but Bryher made this second pilgrimage to find Shakespeare's lodgings on February 18, 1945. A letter to poet May Sarton indicates that on this trip she finds "the approximate site but of course it was all desolation. . . . [c]olumns, grasses between paving stones and the shell of what had once been a church" (see letter to Sarton dated February 22, 1945; May Sarton Papers).

36. Though Bryher reports, "I do not know if she actually wrote [in Stratford] some of the poem, 'Good Frend'" (*Days of Mars*, 162), H.D. tells Aldington in a letter dated February 14, 1949, "The poems, it is true, I had done in London, after my Birthday Celebration at Stratford in April, 1945" (qtd. in Zilboorg, ed., *Richard Aldington and H.D.*, 135).

37. These letters from Bryher are dated September 29, 1946, and October 3, 1946. H.D. Papers.

38. H.D., "Good Frend: Part I, The Tempest," *Life and Letters Today* 53.116 (April 1947); and H.D., "Good Frend: Part II, Rosemary," *Life and Letters Today* 54.119 (July 1947). Only sections I–IV, VI, and VIII of "The Tempest" appeared in the April 1947 issue; "Rosemary" appeared in its entirety. H.D. expresses her disappointment to Pearson on September 21, [1947], that Herring had omitted "my favourite V and VII, about the *Sea Adventure*." Norman Holmes Pearson Papers.

Bryher assumed control of *Life and Letters Today*, formerly *The London Mercury* and *Life and Letters*, in 1935 and held it until 1950. She placed Herring at the helm, though she remained closely involved with the periodical. A number of poems, stories, and reviews by H.D., as well as her memoir about Freud, appeared in the journal between 1935 and 1950.

39. H.D. writes Pearson on October 22, 1946, that "my work on the lecture notes gave me an incentive, in the early part of 1946." Norman Holmes Pearson Papers.

40. H.D. writes Aldington on February 14, 1949, that "I am very happy about AVON, as I did it from a few of my 'lecture notes,' but with only one rather old-fashioned Anthology beside me" H.D. Papers. In preparation for her trip to Bryn Mawr, H.D. asked friends such as Plank, Pearson, Vita Sackville-West, May Sarton, Osbert and Edith Sitwell, Walter de la Mare, and many others for a list of "your favourite lyrics, short dramatic sections or even prose" as she wanted to give "the Bryn Mawr girls" a sense of what other people like as a way of connecting to what they like (see letter to May Sarton, January 7, [1946]; May Sarton Papers). The list was not restricted to poetry of the Renaissance era, and there is other evidence in letters that H.D.'s notes were not merely about the Elizabethans but about English poetry more generally. In fact, she appears to have begun reading the English canon in 1945—from the medieval period to the nineteenth century—a project she continues for several years; when she turns to the pre-Raphaelites in 1948, for instance, she writes Sarton that her reading in that period will "fill in" the lecture notes she

had begun writing and may yet deliver (see letter dated January 13, [1948?]). May Sarton Papers. The lecture notes are not extant.

41. Norman Holmes Pearson Papers. She responds on December 27, [1947], "I think BY AVON RIVER is a lovely suggestion."

42. Benét notes its "haunting music" and "acute intelligences." Moore lauds its "overtones of sound and meaning" and its "uninsisted upon implications."

43. The letter to Aldington is dated August 7, [1948]. H.D. Papers. The letter to Bryher is dated August 17, [1949]. Bryher Papers.

44. Floyd Logan, review of *By Avon River*, by H.D., *Fort Wayne News-Sentinel*, July 30, 1949.

45. Kenneth Rockwell, review of *By Avon River*, by H.D., *Dallas Daily Times Herald*, July 17, 1949.

46. H.A.P., review of *By Avon River*, by H.D., *Florida Magazine of Verse* 10.1 (1949).

47. Charles Wagner, "Books," review of *By Avon River*, by H.D., *New York Sunday Mirror*, July 3, 1949.

48. John Frederick Nims, "A Strange Little Tribute of Poet to the Bard of Avon," review of *By Avon River*, by H.D., *Chicago Tribune*, September 18, 1949.

49. David Daiches, "Shakespeare's World," review of *By Avon River*, by H.D., *New York Herald Tribune Weekly Book Review*, September 11, 1949.

50. A.V.S., "H.D. Pays Tribute to Bard in Poem, Perceptive Essay," review of *By Avon River*, by H.D., *New Haven Register* 3 July 1949.

51. Wagner, review of *By Avon River*, by H.D.

52. H.A.P., review of *By Avon River*, by H.D.

53. Gregory, "The Moment of Revival," 227.

54. Ibid., 228.

55. Ibid.

56. Martha Bacon, review of *By Avon River*, by H.D., *Saturday Review of Literature*, August 20, 1949.

57. Thomas Hornsby Ferrill, review of *By Avon River*, by H.D., *San Francisco Chronicle*, September 18, 1949.

58. J. Duncan Spaeth, review of *By Avon River*, by H.D., *Philadelphia Inquirer*, September 10, 1949.

59. Herbert Barrows, "The Lyrical World of Shakespeare," review of *By Avon River*, by H.D., *New York Times Book Review*, July 31, 1949.

60. Rolfe Humphries, review of *By Avon River*, by H.D., *The Nation*, July 9, 1949.

61. A.V.S., review of *By Avon River*, by H.D.

62. Anon., review of *By Avon River*, by H.D., *Times Literature Supplement*, December 2, 1949.

63. M. W., review of *By Avon River*, by H.D., *Canadian Forum* 29 (November 1949).

64. H.D., *Avon* (Berlin: Suhrkamp Verlag, 1955).

65. Each book in the Tausenddrucke series was limited to 1,000 copies, the first 50 of which were printed on vellum.

66. I am indebted to Paul A. Youngman, who generously helped me work through the German.

67. See letters from Urzidil to H.D. dated March 20, 1955, and April 9, 1955. Urzidil sent H.D. a draft of his essay and notes. H.D. Papers.

68. Urzidil, who worked for Voice of America, translated for H.D. the transcript of the broadcast and the reviews of the book. Quotations from the reviews that appear below are Urzidil's translations. H.D. Papers.

69. See correspondence between H.D. and Günther in the H.D. Papers.

70. See Urzidil's letter to H.D. dated July 11, 1956. H.D. Papers.

71. See letter to White dated August 25, [1956]. H.D. Papers.

72. Friedman, "'Remembering Shakespeare Always,'" 49.

73. Bryher, *Days of Mars*, 151, 153.

74. H.D., *By Avon River*, 55.

75. The letter to Bryher is dated September 7, [1940]. Bryher Papers.

76. H.D., *By Avon River*, 52–53. H.D. marked in pencil this passage in the introduction to her edition of *The Tempest*, ed. M. R. Ridley (London: Dent, 1935): "By far the most interesting and certain sources are the various pamphlets describing the adventures of the expedition of nine ships and five hundred colonists which set out in May of 1609 for the new colony of Virginia. The flagship, the *Sea-Adventure*, carrying the leaders of the expedition, Sir Thomas Gates and Sir George Somers, was wrecked on the Bermudas," xiv.

77. Neil Corcoran, *Shakespeare and the Modern Poet* (Cambridge: Cambridge University Press, 2010), 7.

78. Kathleen Crown, "Two Judith Shakespeares: Virginia Woolf, H.D., and the Androgynous Brother-Sister Mind," in *Virginia Woolf; Texts and Contexts*, ed. Beth Rigel Daugherty and Eileen Barrett (New York: Pace University Press, 1996), 82. This is true, of course, in other national contexts. When Edward VIII abdicates, for instance, H.D. writes Bryher from London that everyone is "quot[ing] Shakespeare by the yard, historicals and Anthony and C" (letter dated December 14, [1936]; Bryher Papers). But in the early 1940s, Shakespeare and his plays are deployed intentionally as propaganda for the war effort.

79. H.D. reports to her friend Silvia Dobson in a letter dated February 12, 1945, that it was "remarkably well done, considering." Silvia Dobson Papers, Beinecke Rare Book and Manuscript Library, Yale University, New Haven, Connecticut. Helen Hackett, *Shakespeare and Elizabeth: The Meeting of Two Myths* (Princeton: Princeton University Press, 2009), discusses the nationalist message of that film: "Audiences were invited to identify with the triumphant heroism of Henry and his troops, riding forth to victory despite massive odds against them. The rousing

message was that the national success of Henry's age, and of Shakespeare's, could be achieved again in the present," 204–5.

80. H.D., *By Avon River*, 84.

81. Knight, *The Olive and the Sword*, 31.

82. Ibid., 1–3, 88.

83. H.D., *By Avon River*, 75.

84. Gregory, "The Moment of Revival," 226.

85. The quotations are taken from two letters from Herring in 1945, though one is misdated. H.D. Papers.

86. The letter from Bryher is dated June 6, 1945. H.D. Papers.

87. The letter from H.D. to Bryher is dated August 5, [1948]. Bryher Papers.

88. Bryher, *Days of Mars*, 162–63.

89. For different variations on this argument, see Friedman, "'Remembering Shakespeare Always'"; Chedgzoy, *Shakespeare's Queer Children*; Raffaella Baccolini, "Remembering and Rewriting Shakespeare: H.D.'s *By Avon River*," in *Shakespeare e la sua eredità*, ed. Grazia Caliumi (Parma, Italy: Zara, 1993); Claire Conilleau, "'What's in a Name?': H.D.'s Re-vision of Shakespeare," *Transatlantica* 1 (2010), accessed December 1, 2013, URL: http://transatlantica.revues.org/4801?&id=4801; and Crown, "Two Judith Shakespeares." Baccolini describes the text as "the place of self-definition" for the woman writer, in which "the woman poet transforms Shakespeare from a threat to herself, because of his genius, to a possible source of inspiration," 247, 248. Shakespeare, in Baccolini's interpretation, becomes the "androgynous mother," 240. Crown reads *By Avon River* with Virginia Woolf's essay on Shakespeare's mythical sister, claiming that "[b]oth texts locate the androgynous ideal within the exclusively male figure of Shakespeare," though she ultimately finds H.D. rejecting androgyny, 82, 85. Both Friedman and Chedgzoy place this text in the context of other texts, such as *Tribute to Freud*, that address and reimagine powerful male figures.

90. Friedman, "'Remembering Shakespeare Always,'" 45.

91. Chedgzoy, *Shakespeare's Queer Children*, 108.

92. Friedman, "'Remembering Shakespeare Always,'" 48.

93. We can discern H.D.'s ambivalence about Shakespeare in subtle ways by comparing the holograph to the printed version. The first page of the original holograph employs the phrases "my Love" and "our Love" in place of "Shakespeare"; she has lined through these affectionate phrases and uses "Shakespeare" in the final version.

94. It is important to note, however, that H.D. was not exclusively interested in forgotten female characters. A letter to Bryher dated June 6, [1949], shows her excitement that "I found or thought I found another 'lost' character in the *Tempest*, the son of the usurping Duke of Milan, Antonio. He is mentioned only once. I like this idea of lost, hidden or invisible characters and am on the hunt for more of them,

having got-away, as it were with Claribel." Bryher Papers. Her copy of *The Tempest* shows her penciled marks beside endnotes that discuss what she terms "Invisible players—," including Francisco and Antonio's son.

95. H.D., *By Avon River*, 51–52. In H.D.'s personal copy of *The Tempest*, she has penciled marks and underscored all references to Claribel, including the lines indicating that Claribel is the heir to the throne: "Who's the next heir of Naples?" Antonio asks, to which Sebastian replies, "Claribel, / She that is queen of Tunis; she that dwells / Ten leagues beyond man's life" (act 2, scene 1). Interestingly, she also marks passages on Dido, the doomed Queen of Carthage who commits suicide when Aeneas leaves her to found Rome; this may suggest, for H.D., some darkness surrounding the fate of African queens and thus some urgency about liberating Claribel from the text.

96. Ibid., 52.

97. Ibid., 61.

98. Chedgzoy, *Shakespeare's Queer Children*, 113.

99. H.D., *By Avon River*, 60.

100. Ibid., 60, 67.

101. Friedman, "'Remembering Shakespeare Always,'" 59n27.

102. Orgel, introduction to *The Tempest* by William Shakespeare (Oxford: Clarendon University Press, 1987), 30–31.

103. H.D. also owned the pamphlet, *Shakespeare Survey*, that compiled Garrett's essay—"That Four-Flusher Prospero"—with two by William Empson, who was also a *Life and Letters Today* contributor. Robert Herring's epilogue to the volume argues with some urgency for interpretation of Shakespeare based in close reading. Interestingly, then, H.D. is probably reading from both New Critical and humanist approaches, the two principle warring factions in literary criticism of her day. See Terence Hawkes, "Take me to your Leda," in *Shakespeare and Politics*, ed. Catherine M. S. Alexander (Cambridge: Cambridge University Press, 2004), for a discussion of the battle between the Empson New Critical school and Knight's humanism. Richard Halpern, *Shakespeare among the Moderns* (Ithaca: Cornell University Press, 1997), shows, however, how Knight does draw to an extent on New Critical methodology, 38.

104. Garrett, "That Four-Flusher Prospero," 41, 38.

105. Ridley, ed., *The Tempest*, xix. She also marks, in her copy of *The Tempest*, references to Miranda as "princess" and as "Queen of Naples," illustrating the parallels she is drawing between Miranda, Claribel, and Elizabeth of Bohemia. Next to the latter reference, she has penciled "Claribel—/ sister—/ Queen of Tunis—."

106. H.D., *By Avon River*, 104.

107. Ibid., 21.

108. Here I disagree with Chedgzoy's otherwise cogent argument when she

asserts, "The troublesome marriage with the African king is here endowed with positive associations by being linked with the Song of Songs and with the plants celebrated in esoteric lore." *Shakespeare's Queer Children*, 111. My own reading is that any positive associations are disrupted by the allusion to arranged marriage.

109. H.D., *By Avon River*, 55.

110. Ibid., 55, 57, 61.

111. Ibid., 132.

112. Crown, "Two Judith Shakespeares," 81.

113. Friedman, "'Remembering Shakespeare Always,'" 66.

114. A.V.S., review of *By Avon River*, by H.D.

115. H.D., *By Avon River*, 121, 120. See Friedman, "'Remembering Shakespeare Always,'" for more on the importance of de Rougemont's book, *Love in the Western World*, which H.D. referred to as "MY BIBLE," 58. She read copies both in English and in the original French.

116. H.D. Papers.

117. Cary DiPietro, *Shakespeare and Modernism* (Cambridge: Cambridge University Press, 2006).

118. H.D., *By Avon River*, 54.

119. Douglas Mao and Rebecca L. Walkowitz, "The New Modernist Studies" *PMLA* 123.3 (2008): 737–48.

120. Joshua Esty, *The Shrinking Island: Modernism and National Culture in England* (Princeton: Princeton University Press, 2003). Esty discusses late modernism's "anthropological turn" away from aesthetics and toward nationalist politics and from the British Empire to old England.

121. See letter to Bryher dated July 15, [1951] (Bryher Papers).

122. H.D., *By Avon River*, 119. These lines resonate as well with Timothy Brennan's observation that "European nationalism itself was motivated by what Europe was doing in its farflung dominions. The 'national idea,' in other words, flourished in the soil of foreign conquest." "The National Longing for Form," in *Nation and Narration*, ed. Homi K. Bhabha (New York: Routledge, 1990), 59.

123. H.D., *By Avon River*, 111.

124. Chedgzoy, *Shakespeare's Queer Children*, 105.

125. H.D., *By Avon River*, 54.

126. Ibid., 59.

127. Ibid., 90.

128. Ibid., 83.

129. Ibid., 84, 126, 129. In the holograph, H.D. had initially described *Nymphidia* as "that somewhat tedious *reductio ad absurdum* of Mercutio's invocation to Queen Mab," but she strikes through it. H.D. Papers. She may have omitted this judgment

in the final version so as not to detract from the act of Shakespeare's plagiarism with a critique of Drayton's poem.

130. Ibid., 124, 131.

131. Ibid., 88–89, 128.

132. Ibid., 109, 126.

133. Ibid., 101.

134. Ibid., 77.

135. Ibid., 111.

136. Ibid., 109. Interestingly, the end of this sentence makes reference to Shakespeare's death as scandalous. In the holograph version, she defends Shakespeare from this "accusation," pointing out that dying at the age of fifty-two was not uncommon in this period, or was "almost a good, old age"; in the printed version, however, she omits this defense of Shakespeare. Earlier in the manuscript, she refers to the vicar who makes the "accusation" as "shameless," but lines through this characterization. H.D. Papers.

137. H.D., *By Avon River*, 116.

138. For another perspective, see Jeffrey Twitchell-Waas, "Seaward: H.D.'s *Helen in Egypt* as a Response to Pound's *Cantos*," *Twentieth Century Literature* 44.4 (1998). Twitchell-Waas writes, "In 'The Guest,' written in the immediate aftermath of World War II, H.D. suggests that much of the poetic genius of the Elizabethan age was stunted and dissipated because of various poets' engagement with the public sphere, whereas Shakespeare's genius achieved fulfillment because he resisted the lures of immediate history," 469. I see her view of Shakespeare's self-imposed isolation within the private sphere as more complicated.

139. H.D., *By Avon River*, 81.

140. H.D., *Magic Mirror, Compassionate Friendship, Thorn Thicket: A Tribute to Erich Heydt*, ed. Nephie J. Christodoulides (Victoria, BC: ELS, 2012), 120.

141. G. Wilson Knight, *Mutual Flame*. H.D. writes George Plank on March 29, [1955], that she is enjoying her reading of *Mutual Flame*. George Plank Papers.

142. *Shakespeare's Sonnets* (London: Richards, 1945). H.D. writes Plank on November 8, [1953], that she is rereading the sonnets. George Plank Papers. She writes Aldington on July 20, [1956], that she is rereading them yet again. H.D. Papers.

143. *Shakespeare as Poet: An Anthology*, ed. A. R. Entwistle (London: Thomas Nelson, n.d.).

144. This letter is dated [November? 1945?]. H.D. Papers.

145. The letter to Bryher is dated September 25, [1948]. Bryher Papers. The letter to Plank is dated January 26, [1950]. George Plank Papers.

146. The letter to Aldington is dated February 24, [1949]. H.D. Papers. There are several letters about Shakespeare, the Elizabethan era, and Dante between the two

from 1948–1956. This project is very much tied to her novel *White Rose and the Red*, for as she is studying the Pre-Raphaelites she becomes interested in the translation of Dante by Dante Gabriel Rossetti's father.

147. John Dover Wilson, *Life in Shakespeare's England* (London: Penguin, 1944).

A Note on the Text

This edition is based precisely on the only print edition to date, which was published by Macmillan Press in 1949. H.D. and Norman Holmes Pearson read proofs of that text, and she approved it for publication. No emendations, corrections, or regularizations have been made to this text. The list of authors and dates following "The Guest" was part of the printed book.

Drafts of the text are held in the H.D. Papers in the Yale Collection of American Literature at the Beinecke Rare Book and Manuscript Library. There were doubtless others, but H.D. reports in *Compassionate Friendship*[1] that upon completion of *By Avon River* she destroyed "a mass of preliminary notes" before beginning her novel *The Sword Went Out to Sea.*[2] There is no extant manuscript of "Good Frend." There are two typescripts of the three-poem sequence; the first, prepared by a typist, is corrected minimally by Pearson, while the second is the typesetter's copy. There are also galleys of the entire sequence prepared by *Life and Letters Today*, corrected minimally by H.D. The galleys are entitled "Good Frend" and lack a dedication.

There is a corrected pencil holograph copy of "The Guest" in a notebook. There are also two typescripts: the first, prepared by a typist, is corrected minimally by H.D., mostly to note the placement of section breaks in the text; and the second is typesetter's copy and bears minor corrections by Pearson. Additionally, there exists a list of editorial queries by Norman Holmes Pearson, with terse responses by H.D. written in the margins; in these responses, she resists his suggested changes to authors' birth and death dates as well as his critique of her characterization of Donne as a lifelong Catholic.

In the holograph, H.D.'s original title, "The Body's Guest," appears on the first page of composition; the word "Body's" has been struck through, and this title page is signed "H.D." As Susan Friedman explains in *Penelope's Web*, Hilda Doolittle used a range of pseudonyms during her career, including "H.D."[3] This signature in the notebook is significant in that, even in the compositional stage, she conceives of "The Guest" as a product of the poet known as H.D., and not of Delia Alton, the nom-de-plume she employs in writing the novels that follow completion of *By Avon River*. The note to Pearson, the paragraph explaining the omission of Milton, and the list of authors and dates do not appear in the holograph. On the final page of the notebook, beneath the dates that appear in the printed edition, H.D. has written, "All Saints Day," but this is not retained in the printed edition.

Notes

1. H.D., *Magic Mirror*, 99.

2. H.D., *The Sword Went Out to Sea: (Synthesis of a Dream), by Delia Alton*, ed. Cynthia Hogue and Julie Vandivere (Gainesville: University Press of Florida, 2007).

3. Susan Stanford Friedman, *Penelope's Web* (New York: Cambridge University Press, 1990), 35–46.

By Avon River

H.D.

GOOD FREND

Shakespeare Day, 23rd April, 1945

GOOD FREND FOR IESVS SAKE FORBEARE,
TO DIGG THE DVST ENCLOASED HEARE!
BLESTE BE Y̋ᴱ MAN Y̋ᵀ SPARES THES STONES,
AND CVRST BE HE Y̋ᵀ MOVES MY BONES.

23rd April, 1564

23rd April, 1616

For
BRYHER
Shakespeare Day
April 23, 1945

&

ROBERT HERRING
St. George Day
April 23, 1945

PART I

The Tempest

I

Come as you will, but I came home
Driven by *The Tempest*; you may come,

With banner or the beat of drum;
You may come with laughing friends,

Or tired, alone; you may come
In triumph, many kings have come

And queens and ladies with their lords,
To lay their lilies in this place,

Where others, known for wit and song,
Have left their laurel; you may come,

Remembering how your young love wept
With Montague long ago and Capulet.

II

I came home driven by *The Tempest*;
That was after the wedding-feast;
'Twas a sweet marriage, we are told;
And she *a paragon ... who is now queen,*
And the rarest that e'er came there;

We know little of *the king's fair daughter*
Claribel; her father was Alonso,
King of Naples, her brother, Ferdinand,

And we read later, *in one voyage*
Did Claribel her husband find at Tunis:

Claribel was outside all of this,
The Tempest came after they left her;
Read for yourself, *Dramatis Personae*.

III

Read for yourself, *Dramatis Personae*,
Alonso, Sebastian, Prospero,
Antonio, Ferdinand, Gonzalo,
Adrian, Francisco, Caliban
(Whom some call Pan),
Trinculo, Stephano, Miranda,
Ariel, Iris, Ceres, Juno;

These are the players, chiefly,
Caliban, a savage and deformed slave,
Ariel, an airy Spirit, Miranda,
The magician's lovely daughter,
The magician—ah indeed, I had forgot
Boatswain, Mariners, Nymphs and Reapers,

And among these, are other
Spirits attending on Prospero.

IV

Read through again, *Dramatis Personae*;
She is not there at all, but Claribel,
Claribel, the birds shrill, Claribel,
Claribel echoes from this rainbow-shell,
I stooped just now to gather from the sand;

Where? From an island somewhere . . .
Some say the *Sea-Adventure* set out,
(In May, 1609, to be exact)
For the new colony, Virginia;

Some say the *Sea-Adventure* ran aground
On the Bermudas; but all on board
Were saved, built new ships
And sailed on, a year later;

It is all written in an old pamphlet,
Did he read of her there, Claribel?

V

The flagship, the *Sea-Adventure*
Was one of nine ships; it bore
Sir Thomas Gates and Sir George Somers;
So the poet read, some say
Of the five hundred colonists;
(O the wind, the spray,
The birds wheeling out of the mist,
The strange birds, whistling from strange trees,
Bermuda); there was more than one pamphlet,
(The newspaper of his day),
He searched them all;
Gates, Somers—who were they?

Englishmen like himself, who felt the lure
Of the sea-ways—here we are in London—
A new court festival, a masque?
Elizabeth, our princess, is to wed
The Elector Palatine—who's that?
Frederick, I think. And where's the place—
Bohemia? I don't think so,
But anyhow it doesn't matter,
A foreign fellow is to wed our princess,
The grand-daughter of Scotland's Mary;
Occasion—compliment—another play!

VI

That was yesterday or day before yesterday;
To-day (April 23, 1945, to be exact),

We stand together; it always rains
On Shakespeare's Day, the townsfolk say,
But to-day, there is soft mist only . . .

Slowly, there are so many of us,
We pass through the churchyard gate,
And pausing wait and read old names
On the stones under our feet;
Look—there's a Lucy—O, the hunter's heart,
The hunter's stealth,
But listen to this,
He's caught at last—who?
John Shakespeare's lad—up to no good—
Sir Thomas Lucy caught him at it—
Poaching—(O feet of wind,
O soul of fire, so Lucy caught you
Stalking deer?)—poaching?

VII

He stole everything,
There isn't an original plot
In the whole lot of his plays;
They're scattered everywhere, hotchpotch;
A little success with the old Queen?

Well, yes—by patching up
Other men's plots and filling in
With odds and ends he called his own,
But now—he's gone back home,

And time he went;
He couldn't compete with the new wits,
New fashions—that last, he called *The Tempest*,
Was taken out of the news-sheet,
Stale news at that and best forgot,

The *Sea-Adventure* and that lot,
Gates, Somers—who are they anyway?

Or who *were* they? They'll come to no good,
(No one ever did) in that colony,
What d'you call it? Virginia?
Look at Drake, Raleigh.

VIII

Awkwardly, tenderly,
We stand with our flowers,
Separate, self-consciously,
Shyly or in child-like
Delicate simplicity;

Each one waits patiently,
Now we are near the door;
Till sudden, wondrously,
All shyness drops away,
Awkwardness, complacency;

Ring, ring and ring again,
'Twas a sweet marriage,
So they say, *my beloved is mine*
And I am his; Claribel
The chimes peel;

Claribel, the chimes say,
The king's fair daughter
Marries Tunis; O spikenard,
Myrrh and myrtle-spray,
'Twas a sweet marriage;

Tenderly, tenderly,
We stand with our flowers,
Our belovèd is ours,
Our belovèd is ours,
To-day? Yesterday?

PART II

Rosemary

BLEST BE Yᴱ MAN Yᵀ SPARES THES STONES.

I

My fingers knew each syllable,
I sensed the music in the stone,
I knew a rhythm would pass on,
And out of it, if I could stoop
And run my bare palm over it
And touch the letters and the words,
Reading the whole as the blind read.

My fingers knew each syllable,
As a lute-player with a lute,
Whose hand lies waiting on the frame,
Who knows the wires are taut and bright,
Who waits a gesture from a throne,
Or from a balcony, or down,
Among the crowd, from his own lady.

If I could touch the stone, I knew
That virtue would go out of it;
I plotted to efface myself,
To steal un-noticed to the rail,
To kneel and touch if but one letter;
I wondered if the script were worn
And dim and old, or if it shone,
With light and shadow on the stone.

But when I stood before the altar,
The stone had vanished as if under

Azure and green of deep-sea water,
Hyacinth-green and hyacinth-blue;
So once a discus idly thrown,
Had slain the Spring and yet forever,
That death had blossomed, for the power
Of Love transformed Death to a flower.

There were no letters anywhere,
But on each bud, each leaf, each spray,
The words were written that beneath
The laurel, iris, rosemary,
Heartsease and every sort of lily,
Speak through all flowers eternally,
Blest be $\overset{e}{y}$ man—that one who knows
His heart glows in the growing rose.

II

And still the bells sway,
My belovèd is mine
and I am his;
And still the bells say,

The king's fair daughter
Marries Tunis; O spikenard,
Myrrh and myrtle-spray,
'Twas a sweet marriage.

III

Say Claribel,
Say asphodel,
No flower of death,
But fragrant breath
Of life;

See everywhere,
Bright flower-de-luce,

Sword-flower and king-spear
For a truce;
       For strife

Is ended,
We ascended
From gloom and fear,
Not after death
       But now and here.

IV

Who hold him dear,
Bring woody stem
With leaf and flower,
The sweet herb,
       Rosemary,

Known from old time,
In sacred office,
To trim the bride,
To deck the shroud,
       Ros maris,

Dew of the sea,
Salt with sea-spray,
So was his music
Drawn from wood,
       Rosemary.

V

But not lute alone
Nor lyre-frame,
Carpenter square and tool
Were made from the tree,
       Rosemary;

Many, many the bees
Hummed in that tree,

Much sweet was plundered,
Stacked and stored,
     Rosemary;

O, what a house he built
To shelter all of us,
O what a plesaunce,
Planed by his rule,
     Rosemary.

VI

Time has an end, they say,
Sea-walls are worn away
By wind and the sea-spray,
Not the herb,
     Rosemary.

Queens have died, I am told,
Faded the cloth-of-gold,
No Caesar half so bold,
As the herb,
     Rosemary.

Rooted within the grave,
Spreading to heaven, save
Us by the grace he gave
To the herb,
     Rosemary.

VII

What rose of memory,
Ros maris,
From what sea of bliss!

VIII

Full fathom five
     and under

The sea-surge
              thunder,
       Rosalind and Rosaline
       With Juliet and Julia
       Join hands with Maria,
       Mariana and Marina,
       Katherine and Katherina
       And with many other bright
       Spirits;
           Iras,
           Iris,
           Isabel,
       Helen, Helena; Helenus
       With other princes leads the host
       From Arden, Navarre and Illyria,
       Venice, Verona and Sicilia;

Knowing these and others well,
Seeing these whom I have loved,
Hearing these—why did I choose
The invisible, voiceless Claribel?

IX

She never had a word to say,
An emblem, a mere marriage token,

Nor even trod a rondelay
Or watched a play within the play

With other ladies—and yet—
I wonder when the time was short,

And he had said farewell to court,
And pondered, fingering the script,

Can this then, really be the last?
If he remembered Claribel.

X

For still the bells sway,
My belovèd is mine
　　　　and I am his,
And still the bells say,

The king's fair daughter
Marries Tunis; O spikenard,
Myrrh and myrtle-spray,
'Twas a sweet marriage.

XI

I only threw a shadow
On his page,
Yet I was his,
He spoke my name;

He hesitated,
Raised his quill,
Which paused,
Waited a moment,

And then fell
Upon the unblotted line;
I was born,
Claribel.

XII

What's in a name?
Everything, life, death,
Infamy or fame.

It is enough,
I live forever,
He called me fair
In one short line.

XIII

I had no voice
To chide the lark at dawn,
Or argue with a Jew,
Be merciful;

I had no wit
To banter with a clown,
Or claim a kingdom
Or denounce a throne;

I had no hand
To snatch a dagger,
Or pluck wild-flowers,
For a crown.

XIV

I stand invisible on the water-stair,
Nor envy Egypt,
Drifting through the lilies;
I may go here or there,
Bargain for bracelets on the bridge in Venice,
Or buy ripe cherries in Verona's market;

Call me most proud who wait,
Even upon the very outskirts of the crowd,
                    At carnival,
Or stand among the strangers at the gate,
                    Watching a burial.

XV

And then I wondered . . .
When wandering by Avon's water,
Who best attended him,
Squire and page and jester from Arden,
Dim shapes or shapes seen and sensed clearly

And laughter heard and song and history,
Unrolled further into the past,
    Unrolled mysteriously
    Into the future;

    And then I wondered . . .
    What voice it was from Avallon,
    Calling that last April,
    Farewell, farewell,
    But only to pain, regret, disaster,
    O friend, farewell
    Is only to fear, despair, torture,
    Say not farewell,
    But hail, Master.
          Was it Ariel?
          Was it Claribel?

PART III

Claribel's Way to God

I

I met a Poor Clare with a chaplet
Of beads who muttered as she went,
And ran her fingers over it,
With much of *ora* and of *ave*.

She called the thing a rosary,
And when I asked her what she meant,
She said it was for Rose-of Mary,
Heaven-dowered, heaven-sent.

I asked the Clare why she was poor,
She said she was Saint Francis' daughter,
And dedicate to poverty,
Obedience and chastity.

There was some music in the thing,
That rattled on now of *pro nobis*,
And Rose-of-Mary minded me
Of the *ros maris*.

And so I got a woodcarver,
To hew me out just some such beads,
But mine were made of rosemary,
And fashioned and strung differently.

II

I met a friar in a hood,
And asked him who Saint Francis was,

He said, a holy man and good,
He preached to wolves and even men,

He talked and whistled to the birds;
I asked the friar, where and when?
The friar said, O, that was after
He gave away his cloak and then,

His shoes; I said, but how
Could he endure the frost and snow?
The friar said it was no durance,
But joy to do his Lady penance.

I asked, who could this lady be?
The friar said, simplicity
And purity and holy love,
And her sweet name was Poverty.

And of her Lord, Sir, who is he?
The friar said, God and God's Son,
The spoken and the written Word,
These Three ... but One.

III

I, too, was Clare but Clare-the-fair,
Claribel, not a Poor Clare,
For I was much too well endowed,
Yet ignorant, I would entreat

A learned scholar or a prelate,
To show me what I did not know,
To tell me what I dared not ask
The Poor Clare or the wandering friar.

I met a prelate at the gate,
His robe was rich with ornament,

He had a strong body-guard before,
And many servants followed after;

I followed with them to the door;
One with his halberd waited there,
He looked with awe at my attire,
Stood at attention when I spoke,

I pray your Lord a word with me;
He bowed before the Queen of Tunis
And said I'll wait before the dais
And name you to His Holiness.

IV

He must have seen nobility
Embroidered on my sleeve, for I
Was swiftly ushered through the crowd;
The prelate greeted me—my daughter?

He raised two fingers and I bowed;
I said, I come to ask of God;
He said, ah fair, ah worthy lady,
This passion for philosophy

Becomes you well, and many follow
The lure of Rhetoric and I hear
The court is all for argument,
Plato, Plotinus, Origen.

Proclus, Ficinus—I presume
You follow Plato, shun the Stoics?
And without waiting for an answer,
The Arian heresy creeps back,

Look to Jerome and Augustine,
Ambrose and Cyprian when in doubt;
He nodded to the servitor,
He raised two fingers and I bowed.

V

I wandered much in Italy,
To find the answer; in Assisi,
I saw a picture of a poor friar,
Francis himself, the mountain wolf,

The birds in branches in a row;
I saw his sandal and a cloak,
Worn and thread-bare that was his;
I begged admission to the Clares,

And a long time, brewed rue and thyme
And stuffed rose-petals in tall jars,
And all the jars were marked with names,
Orris, marjaram, jasimine.

I told the Mother, I must leave,
For still my rosary was wrought,
Differently from the other Clares,
And strung and fashioned unlike theirs,

For other names and other prayers;
For though I learnt what *ora* meant,
And knew *pro nobis* was for us,
Their *aves* were not for my rosemary.

VI

I wandered near, I wandered far,
And met with wondrous courtesy;
They thought me one of them—only
One seemed to stare and wonder.

The others thought that I had lived,
The others thought that I had died,
They never seemed to sense or know
That I was a mere marriage token,

Who never had a word to say;
But he, it seemed, regarded me,

As if myself, I were the play,
Players and a great company.

He said, *I died, I die again,*
But this time, shrived and satisfied;
I said, wait sir; for I would know,
Where you have been, where you will go.

He said, I went to Acre and back,
But now I learn, the screw and wrack
Are torturing my brother Templars;
Was it for this—the Sepulchre?

VII

I was in Venice once again,
Where ships were docked and wounded men
Lay on their pallets, or on straw,
Thrown down before the Ducal Palace

And in Mark's square and Piazetta
And all along the crowded Riva;
Under an arch, he lay alone,
Like a crusader cut of stone;

A lantern cast its shadow on
The cross, emblazoned on his tunic,
Now it is night again, he said
Come Lady, say what you will say,

Are we condemned and damned, we brothers,
We followers of the Holy Cross?
I said, sir, this is rosemary,
I am no priest, a nursing-sister

Has little time for argument;
I never followed what they meant
By schism and by heresy,
But this will take your pain away.

VIII

I laid the spray upon his tunic,
He said, ah Mary, nay, not Mary,
But Wisdom, the Supernal Light;
The trouvères hid in the aubade,

Worship of light, the Arabs told
A tale of passion and of beauty,
Disguised as Lover and as Lady,
To hide the ineffable Mystery;

In Persia, too, and we of Acre
Worshipped the same, pledged to one God;
I said, the Clares were very good,
And gave me this robe for the robe,

I laid aside, for though I could
Not tell their rosary nor their *aves*,
They praised me much for that I knew
The lore of every plant that grew.

He said, *your robe is very white,*
Bend down; he said, *are these the eyes?*
He drew me close, I heard his voice,
But once—this side of Paradise.

IX

Consolamentum here and now,
I heard as my lips touched his brow;
To him alone, I told my secret,
Sir, I am nothing but a name,

Claribel; Brightly-fair, he said,
O clearly beautiful, thou Spirit;
So he alone among them all
Knew I was other than I seemed,

Nor nursing-sister nor a queen,
And he it was that broke the spell,

For as he said, farewell, farewell,
An echo from across the water,

Answered from bell-tower and cathedral;
The lantern flickered and went out,
And yet the buds of the *ros maris*
Shone like dew fallen on his cross.

He said, I died, I die again,
But this time shrived and satisfied,
And as the bell from San Giovanni
Answered San Marco, the dawn came.

X

Though still San Marco pealed and rang,
The pavement seemed to melt away,
Though still I heard Giovanni answer,
I found I knelt in Avon meadow,

I found I stood by Avon river,
But Ariel was there before;
And as he sang farewell, farewell,
My chaplet told its *ora, ave*

To Ariel's song, *farewell, farewell*
Is only to pain, disaster; farewell
Is only to fear, despair, torture,
Say not farewell, but hail, Master!

And then but one chime pealed so sweetly,
I thought it Mary-of-the-Lily,
But it was Avon's Trinity;
And suddenly, I saw it clear,

And suddenly, I saw it fair,
How Love is God, how Love is strong,
When One is Three and Three are One,
The Dream, the Dreamer and the Song.

THE GUEST

Go, Soul, the Body's guest,
Upon a thankless arrant,
Fear not to touch the best;
The truth shall be thy warrant;
Go, since I needs must die,
And give the World the lie!

To
BRYHER
from
Seehof
Küsnacht

My thanks are due to Norman Holmes Pearson for revision of the poems and some of the dates, quoted in The Guest. *In certain instances I have retained earlier traditional dates, since disputed or disproved, and I have also endeavoured to preserve the living tradition, though sometimes at variance with the discoveries of modern scholarship.*

R EMEMBERING SHAKESPEARE always, but remembering him differently. Reach from your bed in dark night, half in a dream or delirium. What do you seek? Your hand, touching the bed-table, remembers the telephone—but that was in your own room in London. You are somewhere else; you want something? There are no friends near. You murmur a number, 1-5-6-4 and follow it with another, 1-6-1-6. But that is no telephone number.

1-5-6-4. This is the year that Christopher Marlowe was born in Canterbury. This is the year that William Shakespeare was born at Stratford-on-Avon. With a slight alteration, a mere matter of ten years, we have 1-5-5-4. Philip Sidney was born exactly ten years before Shakespeare and Marlowe. Some say this Christopher became an actor, after leaving Oxford, some that he went with Sidney to the wars. Small wars but wars in the Low Countries and with The Huguenots in France. Sir Philip Sidney witnessed the Massacre of Saint Bartholomew. Later "when Queen Elizabeth sent English troops to help the Dutch in their struggle for freedom," he "fell fighting at Zutphen, in September, 1586."

"He remains the most conspicuous figure of chivalry among English personalities."

Let us step back that ten years.

Fulke Greville, Lord Brooke of Beauchamp Court, Warwickshire, lived for those days to the considerable age of seventy-four. His friend, Sir Philip Sidney, was thirty-two, that September. They were both thirty-two, that September. But after forty-two years of separation, the honourable member of the Privy Council had one last word to say. He would have engraved on his tombstone, this: "The Friend of Sir Philip Sidney."

Now another step backward, not far, 1553. This is the date of the birth of Edmund Spenser, in London.

It was due to the influence of Sir Philip Sidney that Spenser received advancement as secretary to the Lord Lieutenant of Ireland, and a grant from the Crown. His castle and manor were later burnt and plundered.

Edmund Spenser came home with his wife and children, where it is said he died, "in extreme indigence and want of bread."

Subtract one more number. 1552 is the date of the birth of Sir Walter Raleigh. He was born in Devonshire. "He served five years in France with the Huguenots" and later in the Netherlands. In 1579, he with his half-brother, Sir Humphrey Gilbert, planned their first trip to America. He was beheaded October, 1618.

We have come back to Stratford. It is just two years since William Shakespeare died at New Place, April 23, 1616.

Christopher Marlowe, born in the same year, died at the age of twenty-nine, stabbed in that mysterious tavern brawl, outside London.

We have, in the more complete anthologies of *Songs and Lyrics* from the Elizabethan poets and dramatists, more than one hundred names. Not one is negligible. I have mentioned eight of these, seven men and one woman. Queen Elizabeth is commonly the only woman listed among the more than one hundred Elizabethan lyrists.

> Blow, blow thou winter wind,
> Thou art not so unkind
>   As man's ingratitude;
> Thy tooth is not so keen,
> Because thou art not seen,
>   Although thy breath be rude.
>
> Freeze, freeze thou bitter sky,
> That dost not bite so nigh
>   As benefits forgot:
> Though thou the waters warp,
> Thy sting is not so sharp
>   As friend remembered not.

We have imagined only one true way of recalling these, our poets. A cursory glance at Sidney's *Arcadia*, a more careful reading of Spenser's *Faerie Queene*, a re-reading of Fletcher's *Faithful Shepherdess* and an intensified study of *Tragedies, Comedies* and *Historical Plays* of William Shakespeare, will not do it. Let us begin with Sir Edward Dyer, 1540. He was a friend of Doctor John Dee, adviser and astrologer of the Queen. Sir Edward rose to fame as treasurer of the realm in the heyday of Elizabethan grandeur. He came to grief, as he forsook Doctor John Dee and his confederates at Prague, explaining bluntly to the Queen that her hopes of future alchemical treasure were founded on a fraud. He was no mean poet.

He died in 1607, in poverty.

> My mind to me a kingdom is;
>   Such present joys therein I find,
> That it excels all other bliss
>   That earth affords or grows by kind:
> Though much I want which most would have,
> Yet still my mind forbids to crave.

Edmund Spenser returned home to die; Sidney met his death through reckless chivalry; Marlowe, an even more romantic end, in that mysterious tavern brawl; Raleigh, the legendary figure of romance, was beheaded in the Tower; Sir Edward Dyer, like Edmund Spenser, died in poverty and disgrace; and though "The Friend of Sir Philip Sidney" lived, for Elizabethan times, to the astonishing age of seventy-four, Fulke Greville, Lord Brooke is said at the end to have been stabbed by one of his own servants. We have named seven of these. Of William Shakespeare, alone, can we visualize a chair drawn up before an open window, an apple-tree in blossom, a friend or two and children. There was Elizabeth and, with her, Judith. Hamnet, Judith's twin, is not forgotten.

We do not know what he is thinking. Queen Elizabeth has been dead now, thirteen years. Sir Walter Raleigh is still alive, he has two years yet to live, eating his heart out in the Tower. An accomplished courtier is, of necessity, a poet.

> Go, Soul, the Body's guest,
>   Upon a thankless arrant,
> Fear not to touch the best;
>   The truth shall be thy warrant;
>   Go, since I needs must die,
>   And give the World the lie!

Say to the Court, it glows
    And shines like rotten wood;
Say to the Church, it shows
    What's good and doth no good;
      If Church and Court reply,
      Then give them both the lie.

We wander through a labyrinth. If we cut straight through, we destroy the shell-like curves and involutions. Where logic is, where reason dictates, we have walls, broad highways, bridges, causeways. But we are in a garden.

Philomel, with melody
Sing in our sweet lullaby;
Lulla, lulla, lullaby, lulla, lulla, lullaby;
    Never harm,
    Nor spell nor charm,
Come our lovely lady nigh;
So, good night with lullaby.

And ladysmocks all silver white
Do paint the meadows with delight.

Ladysmocks? They lie pale lavender across the unmown strip of grass. The place is new; New Place, they call it. He is planning the Knotte Garden. Shall there be wildflowers in it? Mary-buds, by all means. They will gather harebells soon. Some say they were left, like the rosemary-dust that powders his woven-wool shawl, by the Conqueror. *Let Rome in Tiber melt—here is my—here is my—* But we are thinking of the Knotte Garden. How design it? Judith has gone away. Now where is Hamnet? *To-morrow and to-morrow and to-morrow. Out, out brief candle.* But it was not very brief. There were long waits between. *From you have I been absent in the spring.* Not this spring, certainly.

When daisies pied and violets blue,
And lady-smocks all silver-white,

> And cuckoo-buds of yellow hue
> Do paint the meadows with delight . . .

But *white* and *delight* had happened before, and *hue* and *blue* everywhere. But *hue* was different, that time.

> From you have I been absent in the spring,
> When proud-pied April, dressed in all his trim—

but proud-pied—it was daisies pied, a moment ago. Pied? Dappled, two-coloured, part-coloured, two-souled. Where was the advantage in that, O *master-mistress of my passion?* It was *daisies smell-less but most quaint* now. He would no longer . . . *white—delight?*

> Nor did I wonder at the lily's white
> Nor praise the deep vermilion in the rose,
> They were but sweet, but figures of delight,
> Drawn after you, you pattern of all those.

But who was the pattern of all those? A child tugged at the knotted edge of his grey shawl. Another child was laughing, but it wasn't Hamnet. He looked at her-his face. They were both his children, but Judith with her hair tucked over her ears, was no Juliet. Judith was Hamnet. Hamnet was Judith. And he had left them at the bridge and spurred his horse through Oxford for an idle fantasy. Perfection dwelt in two separate. There was no *master-mistress of my passion.* It was late now. But Judith understood what he wanted with the garden.

> Mary-buds begin
> To ope their golden eyes.

Yes, marigolds. But king-cups were not suitable for the garden. Like deadmen's-fingers, they dug deep. Deadmen's-fingers? He had some time avoided their country name. The flowers grew on a long stem, more than half of which was white-green under the leaves. The flower resembled the harebell but was a different colour, blue and violet; he called them both long-purples.

But Mary-buds were closing. Was it evening? That bell, the misereri? *I am sick, I must die.*

The bells were from London.

Thomas Nash was born three years after Shakespeare. He died fifteen years earlier; he was thirty-four. Like Marlowe and Raleigh, his life was suspect. He had spent some time in prison. It was 1600, when he wrote *Summer's Last Will and Testament*. He died a year later.

> Adieu, farewell earth's bliss!
> This world uncertain is,
> Fond are life's lustful joys,
> Death proves them all but toys;
> None from his darts can fly:
> I am sick, I must die,
>   Lord have mercy on us!
>
> Rich men, trust not in wealth,
> Gold can not buy you health;
> Physic himself must fade;
> All things to end are made;
> The plague full swift goes by;
> I am sick, I must die.
>   Lord have mercy on us!
>
> Beauty is but a flower,
> Which wrinkles will devour:
> Brightness falls from the air;
> Queens have died young and fair;
> Dust hath closed Helen's eye;
> I am sick, I must die.
>   Lord have mercy on us!

Strength stoops unto the grave:
Worms feed on Hector brave;
Swords may not fight with fate:
Earth still holds ope her gate.
Come, come, the bells do cry;
I am sick, I must die.
                    Lord have mercy on us!

Wit with his wantonness,
Tasteth death's bitterness,
Hell's executioner
Hath no ears for to hear
What vain art can reply;
I am sick, I must die.
                    Lord have mercy on us!

Haste therefore each degree
To welcome destiny:
Heaven is our heritage,
Earth but a player's stage,
Mount we unto the sky;
I am sick, I must die.
                    Lord have mercy on us!

Thomas Nash is known as the companion of Robert Greene, George Peele and Christopher Marlowe. Robert Greene, his inseparable companion, was seven years older and died nine years earlier, again suspect. They were possibly all secret-service agents. Accomplished scholars, Nash and Greene like Marlowe had travelled widely in France and Italy. Nash, we may conclude, died of the plague. Robert Greene escaped it by some eight years. His death, like Marlowe's, however, has remained a mystery. George Peele lived to the age of forty. He, too, is accused of haunting low riverside taverns and even, indirectly, of having met his death in one of them, possibly by poisoning. Marlowe's exploits are apt, in popular esteem, to overshadow the careers of the less robust members of, possibly, a sort of secret-service group working in the service of the Queen, probably working dangerously as counter-espionage agents.

But their lives like their deaths are overshadowed by that other agent of Queen Elizabeth. Sir Walter Raleigh was only twelve years older than the most important member of this group. Christopher Marlowe died at twenty-nine. Raleigh was sixty-six when he wrote, that last evening in the Tower:

> Give me my scallop-shell of quiet,
> My staff of faith to walk upon,
> My scrip of joy, immortal diet,
> My bottle of salvation,
> My gown of glory, hope's true gage;
> And thus I'll take my pilgrimage.
>
> Blood must be my body's balmer;
> No other balm will there be given;
> Whilst my soul, like quiet palmer,
> Travelleth toward the land of heaven;
> Over the silver mountains,
> Where spring the nectar fountains.
>
> There will I kiss
> The bowl of bliss;
> And drink mine everlasting fill
> Upon every milken hill.
> My soul will be a-dry before;
> But after it will thirst no more.

Ben Jonson's name is bracketed, as a rule, with that of Michael Drayton and of Shakespeare. From Sir Walter Raleigh to Ben Jonson is an easy transition. They were both, taken all in all, solid men. Sir Walter of the Devonshire landed gentry looked out from Plymouth, toward more land. Ben Jonson, a Scotsman, traditionally of poor parents, born in London, sought to attain a lost inheritance. He wrote plays solely, he said, to gain a livelihood. He was eight years younger than Shakespeare and twenty years younger than Raleigh. Yet he seems, in a way, a bridge between these two.

His was an old head on young shoulders, but he never, in any sense of the word, lost that head. We feel in some way, that there was no Mary Arden in his background.

There was, no doubt, a deposed Catholic mystic in Ben Jonson's make-up. It accounts for his processions of Queens, who might have been, in the earlier Tudor period, mediaeval saints. His majestic pageants were removed, however, from the real realm of fantasy; the people of his play were abstract. They were Virtues, for the most part, or Latinized figures from a Renaissance series, a wall-painting where Vanity is trod down by Modesty, and Rhetoric joins hands with Poetry. They are the images or abstractions of the humanists, gorgeously arrayed in folds of painted raiment. *Queen and Huntress, chaste and fair*, stands in white. She is this Cynthia of their eternal preoccupation. The mind of the Tudor Englishman could loyally transfer his ancestors' allegiance to the Queen of England. What the heart lost, the mind gained thereby.

We can not imagine Ben Jonson other than preoccupied with the classics. He was a bookish child, we may be sure of that, with few books. Books were the prized possession of aristocrats, for the most part, or were treasured in the small out-posts of monasticism, in and around London. We can imagine Ben Jonson bargaining with a Greyfriar. Tacitus and Livy, to us, are dry and lifeless; Plautus and Terence, worse. Yet Ben Jonson, I should imagine, would have given literally, his soul for more Latin and more Greek. The child at Avon, on the other hand, boasted in later life of other exploits. With moon-light on the snow, he sought the forest of Sir Thomas Lucy. Whose was the fairer Huntress? She, Cynthia, is said with her arrows, to give madness.

Michael Drayton was born the year before Shakespeare. Drayton was a Warwickshire lad. Drayton's name has been recorded with Ben Jonson's, in the notable page of a certain victor of Stratford, who has gained immortality by a spiteful entry in his private diary. It was April, 1616, when William Shakespeare of New Place, thought wistfully of gilly-flowers, clove-pinks or, as some called them, sops-in-wine. There was to be a hedge of holly and someone would graft, he knew, low to the ground, to be the better seen there, a branch of mistletoe. Best graft it to the espalier, apple or pear or plum; fruit-wood would take mistletoe. *Blow, blow thou winter wind. Thou art not so unkind*—it was cold now.

This is the entry from the private diary: "Shakespeare, Drayton, and Ben Jonson had a merry meeting and it seems drank too hard, for Shakespeare died of a fever there contracted."

Michael Drayton is perhaps best remembered by his stirring ballad, *Agincourt*. Whether or not his King Henry was inspired by the "perfect King," the reprobate friend of Falstaff and Sir Pierce of Exton, turned reformer in *Henry V*, is beside the point.

> Fair stood the wind for France
> When we our sails advance
> Nor now to prove our chance
>   Longer will tarry;
> But putting to the main,
> At Caux, the mouth of Seine,
> With all his martial train,
>   Landed King Harry.
>
> Upon Saint Crispin's Day
> Fought was this noble fray,
> Which fame did not delay
>   To England to carry.
> O when shall English men
> With such acts fill a pen?
> Or England breed again
>   Such a King Harry?

Drayton's *Agincourt* stands by itself, with or without Shakespeare's *Henry V*, just as his *Virginian Voyage* will be remembered by many who have never heard of *Nymphidia*, except as the original of Shakespeare's later Oberon and Queen Mab.

John Webster is admittedly one of the greatest of the English dramatists, yet the date of his birth is usually indicated by a question-mark. His death is given as 1630. Perhaps, in a way, this is significant, for Webster was obsessed with the mediaeval concept of death. With him, it is indeed *vanitas vanitatum*. He is concerned with unburied men as well as with buried ones. I myself would conclude that John Webster was fairly young at the time of the Great Plague. I believe he was at an exceptionally sensitive and impressionable age, when the plague swept London. We are given no indication of the place of his birth. Was he a London child, who was found destitute, beating his fists against a locked-door—locked from without by the grim Watch? I imagine him somewhere near Saint Paul's. The plague-pits had destroyed his land-marks. It may have been a kindly Watch who locked him in.

His name is Webster, his name is John. He beats and beats on the firm oak, with his small fists. In the room behind him, lies one of whom he was later to write:

> Strew your hair with powders sweet
> Don clean linen, bathe your feet,
> And—the foul fiend more to check—
> A crucifix let bless your neck:
> 'Tis now full tide 'tween night and day;
> End your groan and come away.

But the groan had long since ended. He could only remember her concern. There was a faint fragrance lingering in the air, though the charcoal burner in the dark room behind him, had turned ash, two days ago. The tallow-dips had given out before that.

> All the flowers of the spring
> Meet to perfume our burying.

Thomas Dekker with Thomas Middleton was known to be a friend and collaborator of John Webster. Thomas Middleton again, has a question-mark after the date of his birth, though it is conjectured that he was born about 1570. Dekker's is also given as about 1570.

Logically then, we might reason that John Webster would be little more than thirty when the plague swept London. But again, we do not know where Webster was born. Thomas Dekker was "one of the celebrated wits of the reign of James I." Thomas Middleton "of whom little is known," becomes "Chronologer to the City of London shortly before his death." And John Webster himself, "a member of the Merchant Taylor's Company."

Substantial men, we might say, these three, or else favourites of a corrupt Court. I visualize Thomas Middleton as grey-haired and worthy of the honour bestowed shortly before his death. But perhaps Chronologer to me, conjures up an image of vast respectability, a reputable and not-too-old Father Time, in fact. But it is better to follow one's own clues and have of each of these poets, a living and personal memory, rather than grow weary and confused with disputable facts about them.

Thomas Middleton's dramas are drawn after the same grim pattern as Webster's most famous one, *The Duchess of Malfi.* If we are confused about Middleton's authenticity, it is no small wonder. Beside his own plays, he is known to have contributed whole scenes to well-known works of William Rowley, Philip Massinger, John Fletcher and Ben Jonson.

But the name of Thomas Dekker is lighted as by flambeaux: on the one hand, *Sweet Content,* on the other, *Sorrow.*

> Art thou poor, yet hast thou golden slumbers?
>   O sweet content!
> Art thou rich, yet is thy mind perplex'd?
>   O punishment!
> Dost thou laugh to see how fools are vex't
> To add to golden numbers golden numbers?
>   O sweet content! O sweet, O sweet content!
>
> Can'st drink the waters of the crispèd spring?
>   O sweet content!
> Swim'st thou in wealth, yet sink'st in thine own tears?
>   O punishment!
> Then he that patiently want's burden bears,
> No burden bears, but is a king, a king!
>   O sweet content! O sweet, O sweet content!

O, Sorrow, Sorrow say where thou dost dwell?
 In the lowest room of Hell.
 Art thou born of human race?
 No, no, I have a furier face.
Art thou in city, town or court?
 I to every place resort.
O, why into the world is Sorrow sent?
 Men afflicted best repent.
  What dost thou feed on?
   Broken sleep.
  What takest thou pleasure in?
   To weep,
 To sigh, to sob, to pine, to groan,
 To wring my hands, to sit alone.
O when, O when shall Sorrow quiet have?
 Never, never, never, never,
 Never till she finds a grave.

As Thomas Middleton's exact value is difficult to assess, so to an even greater degree, is that of Philip Massinger. Perhaps one line may better place him, than argument as to how much of his reputation is due to his intimate friendship with John Fletcher. It is enough that he stands by *The Blushing Rose and Purple Flower.* We do know that Philip Massinger "was at one time page in the household of the Earl of Pembroke," and that "some fifteen plays are to his credit."

We may judge that Philip Massinger was a later friend of John Fletcher. It must be remembered that it was Francis Beaumont who lured the older man into writing. John Fletcher was five years older than Francis Beaumont, and we may wonder what terror or superstition kept Fletcher's imagination tied down, dispersed or in prison, during those earlier years. Why did he not write sooner? Or why did he write at all? As it happens, the name John Fletcher now takes precedence of that of his generous patron, the younger brother of Sir John Beaumont, who was himself a poet. John Fletcher collaborated, it is true, with Philip Massinger but it was possibly the death of his friend, Beaumont, that caused him to seek a substitute for that loss. "Also attributed to William Shakespeare" has been frequently written after John Fletcher's name.

Beaumont, his intimate friend, and William Shakespeare both died in 1616.

> Roses, their sharp spines being gone,
> Not royal in their smells alone,
>   But in their hue;
> Maiden pinks, of odour faint,
> Daisies smell-less, yet most quaint,
>   And sweet thyme true;
>
> Primrose, first-born child of Ver;
> Merry spring-time's harbinger,
>   With hare-bells dim;
> Oxlips in their cradles growing,
> Marigolds on death-beds blowing,
>   Larks'-heels trim.
>
> All dear Nature's children sweet
> Lie 'fore bride and bridegroom's feet,
>   Blessing their sense!
> Not an angel of the air,
> Bird melodious, or bird fair,
>   Be absent hence!
>
> The crow, the slanderous cuckoo, nor
> The boding raven, nor chough hoar,
>   Nor chattering pye,
> May on our bride house perch or sing,
> Or with them any discord bring,
>   But from it fly!

Francis Beaumont was thirty-two years old when he died. Shakespeare was fifty-two. John Fletcher lived nine years longer. He attained the unique honour, among the one hundred lyric poets, roughly attributed to the Elizabethan age, of being, from time to time, confused with William Shakespeare. There are many lyrics of Shakespeare's which might well be attributed to Fletcher, who was only fifteen years younger. We wonder where it was that the son of Richard Fletcher, the future Bishop of London, and the then not so famous rival of Christopher Marlowe, first met. Gentle Shakespeare is so common a phrase that we have ceased to think about it. But the word, gentle, seems equally appropriate to the retiring scholar, John Fletcher, who needed the more robust young aristocrat, Francis Beaumont, to give him the assurance that perhaps, the gentle Shakespeare also lacked. We have come back to Court with Pembroke's page, Philip Massinger and with the brother of Sir John Beaumont.

The son of the then obscure Richard Fletcher and the grammar school boy from Stratford did not feel at home there.

As to Francis Beaumont, it is he, in retrospect, whose important name becomes a shadow. *Luce's Dirge* from *The Knight of the Burning Pestle*, might have been written by either John Fletcher or William Shakespeare.

> Come, you whose loves are dead,
>   And, whiles I sing,
>   Weep and wring
> Every hand, and every head
> Bind with cypress and sad yew;
> Ribbons black and candles blue
> For him that was of men most true!
>
> Come with heavy moaning,
>   And on his grave
>   Let him have
> Sacrifice of sighs and groaning;
> Let him have fair flowers enow,
> White and purple, green and yellow,
> For him that was of men most true!

And yet, on reconsideration, there seems a distinctly un-Fletcherian flavour about the light touch. No doubt, some sort of *Dirge* was necessary, at this moment, for the occult disasters, attendant on the bold experiments with crucible and astrolabe. There was the historical precedent of the sudden leap to fame and the more precipitate fall to infamy, of Doctor John Dee. But we do not feel that Francis Beaumont was in any way involved with the philosopher's stone or the transmutation of base metal into gold. The Queen had been dead ten years when the two of them put the finishing touches to *The Knight*. It was no longer necessary to follow the vagaries of the Court—or at least now, there were other fashions at the Court of King James. Francis Beaumont we feel, in any case, was an independent entity. This poem shows it. With a delicate yet robust touch, he strives for something different. He is not great enough to be trivial. He would never fill in a line with so immature a device as *lulla, lulla, lullaby* or:

> Then heigh ho, the holly:
> This life is most jolly.

I have said that *Luce's Dirge* might have been written by Beaumont's collaborator, John Fletcher or by Shakespeare. I was wrong. There is not Fletcher's even temper in it. There is not Shakespeare's indifference to originality. *Out, out brief candle* could never have been blue, and flowers, *white and purple, green and yellow* would have been, by no alchemy, but by a simple process of association, *daisies pied and violets blue* or else *the marigold that goes to bed with the sun*.

If we conclude that John Webster was roughly a contemporary of his collaborators, Middleton and Dekker, we realize that the date of his birth was probably within less than a decade of that of John Donne. Certainly, Webster and Donne had much in common, chiefly the terror of death. If Thomas Nash gives us

> Come, come the bells do cry;
> I am sick, I must die,

we must conclude that his contemporaries were obsessed with the same prescience. Thomas Nash, it is generally believed, died of the plague in 1601. The others, whose ages varied, were none the less, living under the same conditions. John Donne, at any rate, went through some startling transformations. From the strong Catholicism of his mother and probably of his childhood, he turned to an exaltation of the flesh. But this is the same John Donne who in his more solid middle-years proclaimed from the pulpit of Saint Paul's his doctrine of the body's dissolution. His gruesome classics are unparalleled in their minute details of physical disintegration; he invokes and almost conjures out of the tomb, for our precise edification, the decayed or worse, decaying and cast-off garment of the soul. His sermons were all of death, but like John Webster, it is the death of the body that obsessed him. We have visualized John Webster as a child. I see John Donne at some period of his youth in monastic garb, one of a procession with charcoal sticks, dried herbs and pick and spade.

The *Dirge* of Francis Beaumont which we have just quoted, like the exquisite lines sung by the fool in *Twelfth Night*, have (for all of *poor corse* and *bones*), nothing of death about them.

> Come away, come away, death,
>   And in sad cypress let me be laid;
> Fly away, fly away, breath;
> I am slain by a fair cruel maid.
> My shroud of white, stuck all with yew,
>   O prepare it!
> My part of death, no one so true
>   Did share it.
>
>   Not a flower, not a flower sweet,
> On my black coffin let there be strown;
>   Not a friend, not a friend greet
> My poor corse, where my bones shall be thrown:
> A thousand thousand sighs to save,
>   Lay me, O, where
> Sad true lover never find my grave
>   To weep there!

Richard Crashaw comes somewhat later. He was born in 1613, three years before the death of Shakespeare. His early lyrics follow the pattern of *Supposed Mistress* and *Shepherd's Hymn*. But his youthful conflicts are soon settled by full allegiance to Rome. A favourite of Queen Henrietta

Maria, "he died soon after he became beneficiary of the Basilica Church of Our Lady of Loreto." His poem to Saint Teresa contains some of the most luminous and ecstatic lines in English poetry.

> Love, thou art absolute, sole Lord
> Of life and death.

The Flaming Heart is dedicated to the Saint of Avila. Teresa with Seraph and darts, has usurped the place of the earlier Love with his arrows. The poet, like the Saint, has transferred his allegiance from earthly martyrdom to heavenly. Love is, in any case, a martyrdom. It still remains a question, however, whether the poet in retreat at Loreto, was by that "beneficiary," the greater martyr than the tortured being who in 1600, cried out

> Haste therefore each degree
> To welcome destiny.

Thomas Nash, we may presume, might also have found refuge in a monastery. The same might be said of any of his contemporaries. Some may have taken refuge in the country, others may have wished to return to London, but have been refused admittance. In any case, the mark of the plague was on them.

There is no doubt, however, that the "beneficiary" made the greater poet of Richard Crashaw.

> Live in these conquering leaves: live all the same;
> And walk through all tongues one triumphant flame;
> Live here, great heart; and love and die and kill;
> And bleed, and wound, and yield, and conquer still.
> Let this immortal life where'er it comes
> Walk in a crowd of loves and martyrdoms.
> Let mystic death wait on't; and wise souls be
> The love-slain witness of this life of thee.
> O sweet incendiary! show here thy art,
> Upon this carcass of a hard cold heart;
> Let all thy scattered shafts of light, that play
> Among the leaves of thy large books of day,

Combined against this breast at once break in,
And take away from me my self and sin.

There was no religious conflict in George Herbert. The younger man escaped the divided allegiance of John Donne. The court bestowed on this younger brother of the poet, Edward, Lord Herbert of Cherbury, no "beneficiary." This "pure and saint-like" being took over the modest living of an English country parish. Yet in the cool recess of that remote place, he produced sonorous, ritualistic poetry which rivalled that of the Roman convert at Loreto and the still Romanized Dean of Saint Paul's.

> I struck the board and cried, No more;
> I will abroad.
> What, shall I ever sigh and pine?
> My lines and life are free, free as the road,
> Loose as the wind, as large as store.
>   Shall I be still in suit?
> Have I no harvest but a thorn
> To let me blood, and not restore
> What I have lost with cordial fruit?
>   Sure there was wine
> Before my sighs did dry it; there was corn
> Before my tears did drown it.
> Is the year only lost to me?
> Have I no bays to crown it?
> No flowers, no garlands gay? All blasted?
>   All wasted?
> Not so, my heart; but there is fruit,
>   And thou hast hands.
> Recover all thy sigh-blown age
> On double pleasures; leave thy cold dispute
> Of what is fit and not; forsake thy cage,
>   Thy rope of sands

Which petty thoughts have made, and made to thee
Good cable to enforce and draw
  And be thy law,
While thou didst wink and wouldst not see.
  Away: take heed,
  I will abroad.
Call in thy death's-head there: tie up thy fears.
  He that forbears
  To suit and serve his need
  Deserves his load.
But as I raved and grew more fierce and wild
  At every word,
Methought I heard one calling, *'Child!'*
And I replied *'My Lord!'*

  John Ford was a little older than George Herbert. Although he stands high in the ranks of post-Shakespearian dramatists, I personally prefer him because he is said to have written the music for *Guests*. This exquisite poem might have been written by George Herbert, although it appears in the later editions of Elizabethan Song Books, as Anonymous or is labelled simply, Christ Church MS. It would seem for this reason, to belong to an earlier period, but the sentiment is wholly of the later group, the so-called post-Shakespearian lyrists, who were born toward the end of the sixteenth century.

Yet if His Majesty, our sovereign lord,
  Should of his own accord,
  Friendly himself invite,
And say, 'I'll be your guest to-morrow night,'
How should we stir ourselves, call and command
All hands to work! 'Let no man idle stand.

'Set me fine Spanish tables in the hall,
  See they be fitted all;
  Let there be room to eat,

And order taken that there want no meat.
See every sconce and candlestick made bright,
That without tapers they may give a light.

'Look to the presence; are the carpets spread,
    The dazie o'er the head,
    The cushions in the chairs,
And all the candles lighted on the stairs?
Perfume the chambers, and in any case
Let each man give attendance in his place.'

Thus, if the king were coming, would we do,
    And 'twere good reason too;
    For 'tis a duteous thing
To show all honour to an earthly king,
And after all our travail and our cost,
So he be pleased, to think no labour lost.

But at the coming of the King of Heaven
    All's set at six and seven:
    We wallow in our sin,
Christ can not find a chamber in the inn.
We entertain him always like a stranger,
And, as at first, still lodge Him in the manger.

Richard Rowland's *Our Blessed Lady's Lullaby*, by the merest chance, is not anonymous. He too is associated with Christ Church College, Oxford, and it might be even more apposite to say that he might have written *Guests*. He was born the same year or the year after Shakespeare, but, an ardent Catholic, he left Oxford, set up a press in Antwerp and took the name of his Dutch grandfather. The English Jesuit, Robert Southwell was born a few years earlier. He returned to England, after some years as Prefect in Rome. He died a martyr at Tyburn, 1595, after an imprisonment of three years. *The Burning Babe* caused Ben Jonson to say, "he would have been content to destroy his own writings if he would have written this poem."

As I in hoary winter's night
    Stood shivering in the snow
Surprised was I with sudden heat
    Which made my heart to glow;
And lifting up a fearful eye
    To view what fire was near,
A pretty babe all burning bright
    Did in the air appear.

✣ ✣ ✣

With this He vanish'd out of sight
    And swiftly shrunk away,
And straight I callèd unto mind
    That it was Christmas Day.

Francis Quarles, also of Christ Church, though somewhat later, was another martyr. He was cupbearer to that same Elizabeth of Bohemia, for whom Shakespeare wrote *The Tempest*. Later, the Commonwealth took his estate, but what "sent him to his grave" was the sacrilege committed on his books.

My soul, sit thou a patient looker-on;
Judge not the play before the play is done:
Her plot has many changes; every day
Speaks a new scene; the last act crowns the play.

Of William Strode we know nothing whatever, except that he was a contemporary of Francis Quarles. His *Music*, however, gives him a place with this group.

O, lull me, lull me, charming air!
    My senses rock with wonder sweet;
Like snow on wool thy fallings are;
    Soft like a spirit's are thy feet!
        Grief who need fear
    That hath an ear?
        Down let him lie,
        And slumbering die,
And change his soul for harmony.

Sir John Beaumont, Francis Beaumont's older brother, is usually neglected because of the younger man's affiliation with John Fletcher and hence, by association, with Shakespeare. But John Beaumont's *Of His Dear Son, Gervase* belongs to the devotional poetry of this time.

> Dear Lord, receive my son, whose winning love
> To me was like a friendship, far above
> The course of nature or his tender age;
> Whose looks could all my bitter griefs assuage;
> Let his pure soul, ordained seven years to be
> In that frail body which was part of me,
> Remain my pledge in Heaven, as sent to show
> How to this port at every step I go.

Phineas Fletcher, like John Beaumont, is apt to be ignored, because of his older cousin. His lyric however, *Drop, drop slow tears* must not be forgotten.

> Drop, drop slow tears,
>   And bathe those beauteous feet
> Which brought from Heaven
>   The news and Prince of Peace:
> Cease not, wet eyes,
>   His mercies to entreat:
> To cry for vengeance
>   Sin doth never cease.
> In your deep floods
>   Drown all my faults and fears;
> Nor let His eye
>   See sin, but through my tears.

His brother, Giles Fletcher, was even less fortunate. He took orders but was said to have died of grief because of the lack of sympathy shown him by his parishioners.

It was to Drummond of Hawthornden that Ben Jonson said that he would rather have written the one poem, *The Burning Babe*, than have produced all his own elaborate and beautiful Pageants and Masques. William Drummond was a Scotsman like himself. Drummond's sonnets are supposed to be among the best in the language. Personally, though William

Drummond is not classed among the purely religious or devotional poets, I prefer his sonnet sequence, *Flowers of Sion*. John the Baptist cries out:

> 'All ye whose hopes rely
> On God, with me amidst these deserts mourn;
> Repent, repent, and from old errors turn!'
> —Who listen'd to his voice, obey'd his cry?
> Only the echoes, which he made relent,
> Rung from their flinty caves, *'Repent! Repent!'*

Henry King, Bishop of Chichester, was also a friend of Ben Jonson's and a conventional writer of sonnets. But perhaps he is best represented by his *Exequy*:

> Sleep on, my Love, in thy cold bed
> Never to be disquieted!

James Shirley belongs to this group of religious writers. George Herbert was born in 1593, James Shirley in 1596. Shirley was also intended for the Church, but he avoided exile from court and city. *Is the year only lost to me?* cries George Herbert from his country parish. But James Shirley capitulated. Rome and Queen Henrietta Maria claimed him. He was "the last of the great group of dramatists who immediately followed Shakespeare." But conflict must have run in the blood of this Englishman, for he does not attain the unity either of Richard Crashaw at Loreto, nor that of George Herbert in his country parish.

> The glories of our blood and state
>   Are shadows, not substantial things;
> There is no armour against Fate;
>   Death lays his icy hand on kings:
>   Sceptre and Crown
>   Must tumble down,
> And in the dust be equal made
> With the poor crooked scythe and spade.
>
> Some men with swords may reap the field,
>   And plant fresh laurels where they kill:

But their strong nerves at last must yield;
　　They tame but one another still:
　　　Early or late
　　　They stoop to fate,
And must give up their murmuring breath
When they, pale captives, creep to death.

The garlands wither on your brow;
　　Then boast no more your mighty deeds;
Upon Death's purple altar now
　　See where the victor-victim bleeds.
　　　Your heads must come
　　　To the cold tomb;
Only the actions of the just
Smell sweet and blossom in their dust.

Although Robert Herrick unquestionably belongs to this group, the son of the prosperous London goldsmith seems to have had no religious conflicts of any sort. Like George Herbert, his early lyrics were written from a country parish, but there is no hue and cry:

　　Away: take heed,
　　I will abroad.

Robert Herrick was quite content at Dean Prior, Devonshire. We may imagine the young bachelor riding in leisurely manner, through those fields.

　　Fair daffodils we weep to see
　　　You haste away so soon;
　　As yet the early-rising sun
　　　Has not attain'd his noon.
　　　　Stay, stay
　　　Until the hasting day
　　　　　Has run
　　　But to the evensong;

And having prayed together, we
Will go with you along.

He has time and leisure and attractive duties. The country has not yet
been ravaged by death. Robert Herrick travels out of his parish, but not far.
There are violets growing along the hollows.

Welcome, maids of honour,
You do bring
In the Spring
And wait upon her.

She has virgins many,
Fresh and fair;
Yet you are
More sweet than any.

You're the maiden posies,
And so graced
To be placed
'Fore damask roses.

Yet, though thus respected,
By-and-by
Ye do die,
Poor girls neglected.

But there are other girls who must not be neglected. They are the daughters of the princely Manor Houses within the circuit of a day's ride. Their sympathies are naturally with the Court, but Robert Herrick out-does Pembroke's page and Sir John Beaumont's brother, in knowledge of the world. If he neglects Julia, she will recover. It is true, Electra, Œnone and Anthea may command him anything. In the end, they do command him. He takes his stand with the Royalists.

Bid me to live, and I will live
Thy Protestant to be;
Or bid me love and I will give
A loving heart to thee.

For his Royalist sympathies, he is ejected from his parish and returns to London. For years, we hear nothing of him. James, Charles, the Commonwealth and Charles II follow one another. But where is Robert Herrick?

Sir Walter Raleigh hurled his invective at the Court of King James:

> Say to the Court, it glows
> And shines like rotten wood.

Shakespeare retired to Stratford. In the character of Prospero, he confesses in the Epilogue to *The Tempest*:

> Now my charms are all o'erthrown,
> And what strength I have's mine own.

It is generally accepted that this play was written as Shakespeare's farewell to Court. In it, however, there is no hint of bitterness or rivalry. If he is to be elbowed out, he will at least, give at the last, a demonstration of good manners. Robert Herrick has never been compared to Shakespeare, and there was no question of rivalry or competition. Actually, most of his poems appeared anonymously. It was only in later life, that he himself collected them. He was almost sixty, when he issued his own poems, under the title *Hesperides*.

Robert Herrick lived to the age of eighty-three. He was restored to his Devonshire parish two years after the return of Charles II. He was then seventy-one.

Two names are inevitably associated with that of Robert Herrick.

> Bid me to live and I will live
> Thy Protestant to be

is repeated, a theme with variations, by Richard Lovelace and by Edmund Waller. It is true that these lesser poets were born some time after the death of Elizabeth, but they reflect Sir Philip Sidney and Robert Herrick, without imitating them. Richard Lovelace, in a marked degree, suggests Robert Herrick, in his *Althea from Prison* and his *Lucasta* poems. The very names might have been of Herrick's choosing, and yet the familiar lines are his own.

> Tell me not, Sweet, I am unkind
>   That from the nunnery
> Of thy chaste breast and quiet mind
>   To war and arms I fly.
>
> True, a new mistress now I chase,
>   The first foe in the field;
> And with a stronger faith embrace
>   A sword, a horse, a shield.
>
> Yet this inconstancy is such
>   As you too shall adore;
> I could not love thee, Dear, so much
>   Loved I not Honour more.

Edmund Waller was likewise imprisoned during the wars. His name and reputation, like that of Richard Lovelace, rest solely on one poem.

> Go, lovely Rose—
>   Tell her that wastes her time and me,
>   That now she knows,
> When I resemble her to thee,
> How sweet and fair she seems to be.
>
>   Tell her that's young,
> And shuns to have her graces spied,
>   That hadst thou sprung
> In deserts where no men abide,
> Thou must have uncommended died.
>
>   Small is the worth
> Of beauty from the light retired:
>   Bid her come forth,
> Suffer herself to be desired,
> And not blush so to be admired.

> Then die—that she
> The common fate of all things rare
> May read in thee;
> How small a part of time they share
> That are so wondrous sweet and fair.

As a contrast to Lovelace and Waller, there is Sir John Suckling. He joined the army of Gustavus Adolphus, returned with one hundred horse and fought with the Scotch and Royalists. His career was one of "wild and reckless dissipation" and it is said, "fleeing from England, he put an end to his life in Paris." His life and poetry are the reverse of

> Bid me to live and I will live
> Thy Protestant to be,

and

> I could not love thee, Dear, so much
> Loved I not Honour more.

Of Love and Honour, he wrote:

> Some bays, perchance, or myrtle bough
> For difference crowns the brow
> Of those kind souls that were
> The noble martyrs here:
> And if that be the only odds
> (As who can tell?), ye kinder gods,
> Give me the woman here!

His friend, Thomas Carew, cupbearer to Charles I, however, though reported to be "fonder of roving after hounds and hawks" than of plays and poetry, yet contradicts this with his exquisite *Song*:

> Ask me no more where Jove bestows,
> When June is past, the fading rose;
> For in your beauty's orient deep
> These flowers, as in their causes, sleep.

Ask me no more if east or west
The Phoenix builds her spicy nest;
For unto you at last, she flies,
And in your fragrant bosom dies.

Henry Constable was about Shakespeare's age. His lyrics, notably *Diaphenia*, appear in various song books.

Diaphenia, like to all things blessèd
When all thy praises are expressèd,
　　Dear joy, how I do love thee!
As the birds do love the spring,
Or the bees their careful king:
　　Then in requite, sweet virgin, love me!

Sir William Davenant, a reputed godson of Shakespeare, was a friend of the king's cupbearer, Thomas Carew and the "wild and reckless" Sir John Suckling. He is best known by his *Song*:

The lark now leaves his wat'ry nest,
　　And climbing, shakes his dewy wings.
He takes this window for the East,
　　And to implore your light he sings—
Awake, awake! the morn will never rise
Till she can dress her beauty at your eyes.

Sir Henry Wotton, born four years after Shakespeare, again owes his reputation to one poem. He had travelled in France and Italy on various diplomatic missions, during the reign of Queen Elizabeth. Venice and the German states claimed him, when James became king. *The Tempest* was written to celebrate the marriage of James' daughter, Elizabeth, later known as Elizabeth of Bohemia or the Winter Queen. It was to this unfortunate princess that Wotton in later years, dedicated his life.

You meaner beauties of the night,
    That poorly satisfy our eyes
More by your number than your light,
    You common people of the skies;
What are you when the moon shall rise?

You curious chanters of the wood,
    That warble forth Dame Nature's lays,
Thinking your passions understood
    By your weak accents; what's your praise
When Philomel her voice shall raise?

You violets that first appear,
    By your pure purple mantles known
Like the proud virgins of the year,
    As if the spring were all your own;
What are you when the rose is blown?

So, when my mistress shall be seen
    In form and beauty of her mind,
By virtue first, then choice, a Queen,
    Tell me, if she were not designed
Th' eclipse and glory of her kind.

Another Elizabeth recalls a like devotion. The unfortunate favourite, Robert Devereux was beheaded, like Raleigh. The Earl of Essex was only thirty-four at the time of his death. *A Passion of My Lord of Essex* was enclosed in a letter from Ireland, to the Queen. This other "passion" might well have been indited from the Tower, as was Raleigh's *Go, Soul, the Body's guest.*

Her thoughts and mine such disproportion have;
All strength of Love is infinite in me;
She useth the 'vantage time and fortune gave
Of worth and power to get the liberty.
Earth, sea, heaven, hell, are subject unto laws,
But I, poor I, must suffer and know no cause.

Francis Davison escaped death at the beginning of the reign of Elizabeth, but he was "disgraced for carrying her warrant for execution of Mary Stuart to the Council." *My only star* might have been written by Essex from the Tower.

> O cruel tiger!
> If to your hard heart's center
> Tears, vows, and prayers may enter,
>   Desist your rigour;
> And let kind lines assure me,
>   Since to my deadly wound
>   No salve else can be found,
> That you that kill me, yet at length will cure me.

Essex was executed two years before the Queen's death. Seventeen years later, two years after the death of Shakespeare, Sir Walter Raleigh will feverishly conclude:

> So when thou hast, as I
>   Commanded thee, done blabbing,—
> Although to give the lie
>   Deserves no less than stabbing,—
>   Yet stab at thee that will,
>   No stab the soul can kill!

With Thomas Campion, we return to Paradise. He was born three years after Shakespeare and died four years after. He is classed with Herrick and Shakespeare as one of the three outstanding English lyric poets of all time. His words like Herrick's and Shakespeare's, sing themselves, yet in Campion's case, we possess the actual Song Books or Books of Aires, with the words and music, running along together, both written by the poet. It is possible that Thomas Campion wrote many of the airs for Shakespeare's lyrics. He, like Ben Jonson, follows the classic tradition. Few realize that Ben Jonson's familiar *Drink to me only with thine eyes* is a transcription from the Greek. It is possible that this familiar melody was written by Thomas Campion.

Perhaps Campion's most successful Latin rendering is that of Catullus' *Vivamus mea Lesbia, atque amemus*. Yet the darkness of the Latin poet's hopelessness in the face of death, is somehow turned to light, when Thomas Campion translates:

> But, soon as once set is our little light,
> Then must we sleep one ever-during night.

The same thing may be said of *In imagine pertransit homo*.

> Follow thy fair sun, unhappy shadow!
>   Though thou be black as night,
>   And she made all of light,
> Yet follow thy fair sun, unhappy shadow!
>
> Follow her, whose light thy light depriveth!
>   Though here thou liv'st disgraced,
>   And she in heaven is placed,
> Yet follow her whose light the world reviveth!
>
> Follow her, while yet her glory shineth!
>   There comes a luckless night
>   That will dim all her light;
> And this the black unhappy shade divineth.
>
> Follow still, since so thy fates ordainèd!
>   The sun must have his shade,
>   Till both at once do fade;
> The sun still proved, the shadow still disdainèd.

George Chapman belongs to the more conventional school of classic tradition. He is, of course, best known for his translation of Homer. He completed the *Hero and Leander*, left unfinished by Christopher Marlowe. He was born five years before Marlowe and Shakespeare. The song, *Muses that Sing* might have been written by George Chapman for one of the unfinished *Hero and Leander* sections.

> Abjure those joys, abhor their memory,
> And let my Love the honoured subject be
> Of Love, and honour's complete history;
> Your eyes were never yet let in to see

> The majesty and riches of the mind,
> But dwell in darkness; for your god is blind.

For your god is blind can not be said of Thomas Campion.

> Follow still, since so thy fates ordainèd!
> > The sun must have his shade,
> > Till both at once do fade;
> The sun still proved, the shadow still disdainèd.

For through the words, there is a lyric pulse that transmutes the mere syllables into a universal language. The sun and shadow merge. The eternal symbol of union becomes a sound of silver rain, as a light hand completes the stanza with a run of improvised notes, not contained in the original Book of Aires. The Paradise of Dante was actually the property of the humanists. The inspirational tenderness of *Come away, come away, Death* and *Fair Daffodils, we weep to see* transcends the death which they invoke. With Marlowe and Sir Walter Raleigh, there is death indeed, in spite of heroic defiance:

> Yet stab at thee that will,
> No stab the soul can kill!

Shakespeare, Campion and Robert Herrick do not need Dante's geometric circle within circle, to show the way from Hell to Paradise. If Hell was implicit in court and city, there were flowers to sweeten the stench of death. There were flowers to heal and flowers to be *strown . . . on my black coffin.* For these three, the lead that enclosed the body of the fortunate, was of no importance. *Come, come, the bells do cry, I am sick I must die* recalled other memory than that of the Black Watch.

Christopher Marlowe of "the mighty line" was undoubtedly an actor. He was *Tamburlaine the Great* and *Doctor Faustus.*

> Is this the face that launched a thousand ships,
> And burnt the topless towers of Ilium

is spoken aloud. It is declaimed in public or in the semi-privacy of a suspect tavern, with full knowledge of the ash upon the hearth-stone, the empty jug on the table and the crooked slant of an ill-fitting shutter. If there was no one to listen, still Kit Marlowe would declaim to the empty bench, drawn up before the ale-drenched table. *Helen make me immortal with a kiss* could be spoken to the dark wench who ordered him to bed, or to the lad who waited for the wits and gallants after the play, to scatter orange peel, so that he might have the possible chance of half an orange or the luck to find a loose coin in the strewn rush. Christopher Marlowe is known as "the first great dramatist in English literature." He is said to have influenced Shakespeare in his early plays. But Shakespeare as an actor in the Blackfriars Playhouse accepts only minor roles, or later, you might say, no role at all, as the ghost in *Hamlet* or Adam, Orlando's old retainer in *As You Like It*. We can not imagine the swash-buckling Marlowe, if he had appeared at all, accepting other than the main role. But Marlowe acted himself to death and so did Walter Raleigh.

But music like dream, transcends time and space. Marlowe's *The Jew of Malta* and *Edward II* recall *The Merchant of Venice* and the pageant of kings, *John*, *Richard II*, *Richard III*, *Henry IV* and *Henry V*. Through them, another, from a less illustrious town than Canterbury, pleads for an island.

> This royal throne of kings, this scepter'd isle,
> This earth of majesty, this seat of Mars,
> This other-Eden, demi-paradise,
> This fortress built by Nature for herself
> Against infection and the hand of war,
> This happy breed of men, this little world,
> This precious stone set in the silver sea,
> Which serves it in the office of a wall
> Or as a moat defensive to a house,
> Against the envy of less happier lands,
> This blessèd plot, this earth, this realm, this England.

But when infection had completed its devastation and when this throne of kings was no longer royal, William Shakespeare, unlike Christopher Marlowe, unlike Walter Raleigh, stands aside. We can not imagine him shut up in the Tower, and if accusation was brought against him, it was merely of "a merry meeting" and "fever there contracted." Thomas Campion lived to be almost exactly the same age, and Robert Herrick may be said, in his own person, to have prolonged the Elizabethan age, on through what later critics call the Jacobean, the Caroline, the Commonwealth and the Restoration. He died at the age of eighty-three, toward the end of the seventeenth century.

It may be noted that we have touched on the poetry of the minor Royalist poets, Lovelace, Waller, Suckling and Thomas Carew, and have not even mentioned the giant Commonwealth or Puritan poet, John Milton. It has been contended that his muse is not Elizabethan, but it is not for that reason that we have been forced to exclude him. He stands alone, we do not even compare these lesser poets with him, nor is there any minor constellation to reflect his light. The inclusion of John Milton would unbalance this sequence and if we included him, we would exclude the others. It has been our intention to recall echoes of the great period by way of its minor satellites, rather than the heroic verse of this outstanding figure.

John Lyly is another of the great group. *Euphues* is remembered because of *euphuism*, a word coined from the name of the hero of Lyly's extravagant *Anatomy of Wit*. It is said that both Shakespeare and Ben Jonson wrote parodies on Lyly and his intention to re-make the English language. We find Shakespeare's parody in *Love's Labour's Lost* and Jonson's in *Every Man Out of His Humour*. But John Lyly, the poet lives, though Lyly the exponent of rhetoric, is shelved and un-read save by experts and historians.

> What bird so sings, yet so does wail?
> O 'tis the ravished nightingale.
> *Jug, jug, jug, jug, tereu!* she cries,
> And still her woes at midnight rise.
> Brave prick-song! Who is't now we hear?
> None but the lark so shrill and clear;
> How at heaven's gate she claps her wings,
> The morn not waking till she sings.
> Hark, hark, with what a pretty throat
> Poor robin redbreast tunes his note;
> Hark how the jolly cuckoos sing

Cuckoo! to welcome in the spring!
Cuckoo! to welcome in the spring!

Thomas Heywood is reputed to be the author of two hundred and twenty plays, of which only twenty-three have survived. He dealt chiefly with country scenes and country people.

Pack clouds, away, and welcome day!
  With night we banish sorrow.
Sweet air, blow soft; mount, lark, aloft
  To give my Love good-morrow!
Wings from the wind to please her mind,
  Notes from the lark I'll borrow;
Bird, prune thy wing, nightingale, sing:
  To give my Love good-morrow!
  To give my Love good-morrow!
    Notes from them all I'll borrow.

Francis Bacon, like John Lyly, was steeped in the policies and politics of the time. He has been called one of the greatest of philosophers. He wrote essays, *Counsels, Civil and Moral*, the *Advancement of Learning*, and a translation of *De Augmentis Scientiarum*. The following poem is a transcription from the Greek.

The world's a bubble; and the life of Man
  Less than a span:
In his conception wretched—from the womb
  So to the tomb!
Curst from his cradle, and brought up to years
  With cares and fears.
Who then to frail mortality shall trust
But limns on water, or but writes in dust.

Our own affection still at home to please,
  Is a disease;
To cross the sea to any foreign soil,
  Peril and toil;
Wars with their noise affright us; when they cease
  We're worse in peace.

What then remains, but that we still should cry
For being born, or, being born, to die?

This is one theme of the Elizabethan age. Webster and Middleton are outstanding examples of the black wave of terror and depression that swept over the island, as a result of the dissolution of the monasteries and the seven years, spent by Mary in seeking to restore them. Following the fires of martyrdom and the reeking stench of the unburied, was an aftermath or after-birth of Hell. I have spoken of Dante. Webster, Middleton, Nash, Lodge, Donne plunged lower into the *Inferno*. There was a *Purgatorio*, however, implicit in the *Duchess of Malfi* and a *Mad World my Masters*. Dante, like Sophocles, drew on the abstract. Webster, Middleton, Dekker, Ford, Massinger and a host of others, portrayed, in a renaissance setting, parables that represented unbearable actuality. What they themselves had not seen, was common gossip of the older generation. From this mad world, there was no escape.

There was one escape. Dante found it in a dream. But Dante's dream is un-dreamlike in texture. He may have heard the bells of *Santa Maria Maggiore* or the *Trinita*, above the bridge, where he stood and saw the uncovered bier of a stranger, unveiled like the Simonetta of Botticelli. Or he may have followed the funeral procession of a girl, known to him personally. The girl, in any case, remains an abstraction, a myth. But with Webster, the girl is, as I have said, someone known intimately. If her face is uncovered, it is better that we hide our eyes and summon the young monk who loiters behind the others. His name is John Donne.

Of necessity, he with pick and spade, must consider this *poor corse*.

Where I am clad in black
The token of my wrack,

writes Thomas Lodge. He is of this period.

After death, when we are gone,
Joy and pleasure is there none.

Thomas Lodge, the physician, may be classed with John Donne. If help came at all, it was usually too late. And the love of the humanitarian and the healer breaks before the sight of endless agony and piteous decay.

Accurst be Love, and those that trust his trains!
    He seemeth blind, yet wounds with art,
    He sows content, he pays with smart,
    He swears relief, yet kills the heart,
    He calls for truth, yet scorns desart.
Accurst be Love, and those that trust his trains!
Whose heaven is hell, whose perfect joys are pains.

I have mentioned Sir Edward Dyer, as my earliest poet. But I would like to step back a generation to Sir Thomas Wyatt, who died nine years after the Queen was born. A trusted courtier of Henry VIII, he touches his lute as a troubadour. It is customary to compare the art of Sir Thomas Wyatt to that of the Latin poet, Horace. But Horace was a master of fine mosaic or a chiseler of marble. The courtier-poet must be musician rather than engraver; he was called upon to compose the music as well as the words of his poems. Every gentleman at the Court of Henry VIII, was, like the king himself, musician and poet. Music and poetry were not yet disassociated.

    My lute awake! perform the last
    Labour that thou and I shall waste,
       And end that I have now begun;
    And when this song is sung and past,
       My lute be still, for I have done.

The praise of love, as a convention, was no longer tenable. It had come to England with Eleanor of Aquitaine, the mother of Richard Lion-Heart.

    O Richard, O mon roi,
    L'univers t'abandonne,

was sung outside the prison-tower, where the Saracens held the prince captive. But the prison-tower was nearer home now. I wonder, when Ben Jonson wrote the *Masque of Queens*, if he was influenced by those state processions, the Play of the people of the town of London. They had no other Play, then.

Samuel Daniel with his brother John, the musician, produced Masques which at one time threatened the popularity even of Ben Jonson. There were also the Masques of the Inner Temple, to which William Browne gave, for a time, new life. But the Masque was, like the conventional Shepherd and Shepherdess pastorals of Edmund Spenser and of his predecessor, Nicholas Breton, growing set and stylized. The Court was threatened by an outside factor. There was the new Globe Theatre to be considered. Certain plays could be cut to fit both Court and theatre, or extraneous dialogue could be added to a more or less complete comedy or tragedy. There was more than one set of conventions to be considered now. The bargeman and the beggar who loitered on the water-steps, had other spectacles beside the Royal Processions from Greenwich Palace to London. The Tower had had its fill of tragedy. Now tragedy found a place upon the boards, new planed, of the Globe Theatre.

> Fear no more the heat o' the sun,
>   Nor the furious winter's rages;
> Thou thy worldly task hast done,
>   Home art gone and ta'en thy wages:
> Golden lads and girls all must,
> As chimney-sweepers come to dust.

Home art gone—there was the mulberry-tree. Taffeta and damask had never held such colour. He had heard of a white mulberry that had turned purple, at the blood spilled of Grecian lovers. It had been necessary, he remembered, to enliven the history with mummery for the pit. But the gallants had not sat, dour-faced at this intrusion of the grotesque, into what happened to be originally intended as a tribute to *Cynthia*. *Cynthia* now, could be tricked up with a lantern, and *Wall* was a good part. Bottom the Weaver, as well as the hectoring row of courtiers, could criticise and condemn a *Midsummer Night's Dream*. There had been some awkwardness but the uncouth lad who scraped up the rushes had been induced to substitute for the decorous but unconvincing Thisbe of the first set of players. They were on and off the stage now. There was no *Wall* between.

Fear no more the frown o' the great;
    Thou art past the tyrant's stroke;
Care no more to clothe and eat;
    To thee the reed is as the oak;
The sceptre, learning, physic, must
All follow this and come to dust.

Still, there was hunger for fine damask, for purple hangings, for the anodine of incense, for the assurance of beatitude and the lost Host. The love of beauty had been satisfied by the dim, flower-stained light that fell, whether on a black velvet cloak or upon the sackcloth of a row of penitents. From the stench of life in the narrow, fulsome alleys, there was then, escape. It might be a cathedral unbarred, or a sacristy at the bridge-head. Even if death were waiting, for a moment, there was security. The Saints could be cajoled or bribed, or even tempted by a promise of new altar cloth or a cup of silver. Death was a known entity, not only the skeleton on ropes that the older courtiers remembered in the *Miracles* of the Coventry *Corpus Christi*, or of Westminster, nearer home. He himself was not infallible.

The mind may compromise but the heart can not. Brilliant casuistry and subtle diplomacy in the end, made that compromise. But the English heart was not satisfied. The jewelled plate, the flower-stained windows had been marred by agents other than the assessors of the Crown. Priceless gems, it is true, can not intimidate the Spirit of God, but they can heal and console the Spirit of Man. The beauty displayed was, as it were, the dowry, brought by the Church, in the ceremony of betrothal. The Wedding took place at all hours of the day and night. This pledge was assurance of reunion after death. As God's Anointed, the King stood second only, in the hearts of loyal Englishmen. When the king broke faith, it was as if God had left them.

The mind might compromise, it was forced to do so. The heart could not. But compromise was necessary.

We hear much of the sign-boards, set up in the Globe Theatre, this is a palace, this is the throne-room, this is the ante-chamber of His Excellency.

We are apt to forget that many of the original masques and plays were acted in the palace itself, in the throne-room or in the ante-chamber. The decor, the decorations, the ornate imported mirrors, the purple hangings, the dais steps, the embroidered tapestry were all there. Why is this forgotten? The plays of Shakespeare had scenery waiting for them. Portia's caskets are produced by the Lord Treasurer, perhaps they are alms boxes from some magnificent cathedral. For the Capulet banquet, the scene is already laid. The musicians have only to tune up, in the gallery. Sumptuous plate and linen, looted from the Cardinal's palace, was shared alike by Montague and Capulet. Juliet's tomb was, no doubt, magnificently draped in violet. The candle-sticks recalled another canopy, another burial. The church was plundered by the palace; the palace became the background for new ritual. Although we hear so much of the mean equipment of the Globe Theatre, it must be remembered that, in the eyes of the producer at least, the place was overlaid with the memory of secret plunder. Death could yet be cajoled and men made happier.

We reach here, the high-water mark of human achievement. The Deity is seldom mentioned by William Shakespeare. It has been noted that in the famous speech of Henry V before Agincourt, he calls upon Saint Crispin and noticeably, except through the similarity of assonance, avoids direct appeal to the World's Saviour. Malvolio in *Twelfth Night*, who some think is a parody of Francis Bacon, others, a dissenting Puritan, addresses his champion as Jove. Princes of the church, before and after battle, discourse learnedly, it is true, on the rhetoric of religion. But these tirades or exhortations are in character, in costume, you might say. The dramatist himself remains discreetly non-committal. He is as abstract as Aeschylus, yet he speaks personally. He is diplomatic, yet he leaves us in no doubt as to how the scales of Justice will tilt. Sophocles' hero re-emerges as the Prince of Denmark. Aristotle's old truism, *katharsis* or cleansing, as the purport of all high tragedy, is obvious, yet the cleansing does not focus solely on the soul. The mighty penance of beholding in another's fate, the possible disaster, attendant on one's own headstrong pride, is conceded. We must find out for ourselves, what makes our neighbour's fault outrageous to us, and how our perversity hides from us our own sin. But sin is a word that is almost absent from the vast wealth of word and phrase found in the idiom of William Shakespeare.

Fear no more the lightning-flash,
    Nor the all-dreaded thunder-stone;
Fear not slander, censure rash;
    Thou hast finished joy and moan;
All lovers young, all lovers must
Consign to thee and come to dust.

All lovers young—lovers are always young. There is no sadness in this song. We know from the beginning, that the child, Fidele is not dead, but will re-emerge as the woman Imogen. To the devout Catholic, this assurance would not be necessary. To the devout Christian, unwilling to renounce the hope, implicit in his religion, there was now only subterfuge or disillusion. Into the great vacuum, left by the flame that had hung alike over Catholic and Protestant martyr, there rushed with the whirlwind of the Pentecost, this host, drunk with new wine. It was the wine of the Spirit, certainly. Formerly, those condemned to life, equally with those condemned to death, knew the way out of and into darkness. If there was doubt or indecision, it could be countered by the logic of the church. There was no logic, no reason now. There was no safety. Mary had sought to avenge the martyrs of her mother's faith. Elizabeth again, had re-animated her father's frenzy against the monasteries and hospitals, re-established by her sister, Mary. Who would come next?

This was the question in the minds of Webster, Middleton, Dekker, Ford, Massinger and that host who stood in the black shadow of the charred city. They answered it. It has been noted that many of these extravagant tragedies had a renaissance or Italian setting. Rome is never the scene of these many plays. When Shakespeare addresses Rome, it is the Rome of political faction, antedating the long drawn out religious faction. But Venice, Milan, Verona, Sicily, Naples are annexed. *Let Rome in Tiber melt* was spoken by Marc Antony, but the poet was possibly thinking of the ruin wrought in his own country, by other Caesars and other Antonys and by the lure of other Cleopatras. This historical play comes late. His English kings have had their say, during the life-time of the great Queen. Now Shakespeare goes back into time, to Egypt and to Ancient Britain.

But Egypt and Ancient Britain, legendary or historical, have boundaries. The English kings who preceded them in the sequence of historical plays, stood equally, for all their roses white and red, upon solid ground. There had been no poets since Chaucer. He might have appeared in a scene from *Henry V* or *Henry VI*. He seems as legendary as a character in a play. We have *Richard III*, and there is no poet in it, nor incidental song and minstrelsy. The reign of Henry VII produced John Skelton, standing alone, an English poet with a scattering of unimportant, imported French about him. Henry VIII himself a musician, encouraged song and poetry, but it was indigenous to the Court. There is Thomas, Lord Vaux, as well as Henry Howard, Earl of Surrey and Sir Thomas Wyatt. From the universities, we have Nicholas Grimald and John Heywood, the Oxford dramatist who became Court jester. But theirs was the stylized, exquisite music that was first introduced by the Provence troubadours, imported as we have said, by England's fifth queen, the mother of Richard I. It had taken four hundred years for the Provençal lyrist to establish his identity, but Eleanor's *School of Love* found strange pupils at the Court of Henry VIII.

> Now cease, my lute! this is the last
> Labour that thou and I shall waste,
> And ended is that we begun;
> Now is this song both sung and past—
> My lute be still, for I have done.

For a short space, the lute was still indeed. Edward VI and Mary had no plays, written for them or about them. For ten years there is a gap in time. Edward VI, a ward under the protection (or its opposite) of various Court officials, might almost have been that other Edward who with his brother Richard was deposed and done away with in the Tower. The shadow of the Tower grows blacker, though we thought we had moved out of its compass, with the death of Henry VIII. But the death of Edward VI is still a mystery, unlike that of his predecessor Edward V, and his brother Richard. Mary Tudor is the first queen of England, in her own right. How far the atrocities committed in her name were actually of her connivance or due to the power of Rome, will also remain a mystery. Now, terror took the place of sanctuary. The Cathedral door was still unbarred, but its crypt held prisoners, swept into that dark vault, with no knowledge that they were suspect, as they knelt at the altar-rail, either wrapt in contemplation or for purposes of policy.

For ten years the fate of England and the world hung in the balance. William of Normandy was affiliated with the Latins. The Court and wealthy land-owners followed the custom and religion of the conqueror. But beneath the solid tyranny of the first king of England, there was that native culture of Caedmon and Cynewulf, the Christian Saxon poets. Their names recall *King Lear* and again, *Cymbeline*. They ante-dated Normandy by some five hundred years. They again had succeeded the first Latins by roughly five hundred years. Behind William, there was one thousand years of animosity. Though the first William was affiliated with Rome, it was not the Rome of the conqueror Caesar.

It was as if the ten years of Edward VI and Mary had broken the crust, hardened by time, of a not yet extinct volcano.

Beneath the lava and ashes of Norman conquest, a living world lay buried. It had seeped up from time to time, since the days of William. It had drawn the best of his warriors away from England. The Holy Wars were an excuse for travel, more than an excuse, a necessity. That lure of foreign places, was really love of home, their own native boundaries. The urge would be satisfied for a time by wars in England. When a sort of transitional peace fell upon the prince and barons, it was time to leave. So Richard Lion-Heart with his train of princely ruffians leaves England. Later the same predominant instinct seizes a restless people. Incited again by an Italian precedent, Drake and Raleigh follow the example of the Venetians, John and Sebastian Cabot, and the great Magellan.

The volcano was seething. Flame and fire had undermined the Pope's authority. If that could be defied, and now (in the reign of Elizabeth), with impunity, then anything could happen. The process was partly unconscious but rebellion was at work here, and the carefully wrought, balanced sequence of dramatic action, on and off the stage, became independent of authority.

It is one thing to cast off authority, it is another thing to cast off love. As authority waned, love grew. Rome was like a great bee-hive, but we are apt to forget that at the time of Caedmon, Rome was only one of several centres of equal power and authority. Augustine came to England from Africa, and the Church of Africa, at that time, stood equal with the Church of Rome. Simon de Montford, the William of his day, had made his final inroads against the Church of Provence. The Inquisition had destroyed the cult of Our Lady, as an embodiment or rather personification of the Church Spiritual, but the Lady banished from the churches of Provence, found refuge elsewhere. The troubadours, wandering along the flowering highways, carried with them the lute that Thomas Wyatt, some three hundred years later, touched for the last time, at the Court of Henry VIII. For Eleanor, remembering her own girlhood and the fleeting smile of a lost lover in Provence, had tempered her exile in the bitter north, by endeavouring to introduce into the brutish throng of that alien baron, Henry II, some shadow of the memory of games, played in earnest and vows spoken in the phrase and rhythm of the early church. The *School of Love* was related to another and now also dispersed religion, the cult of the original kings of Britain and of Brittany. The Round Table, as is now recognised, is a symbol of the last Supper. Eleanor herself was, no doubt, unaware of this, but the reign of the Plantagenets was marked by a later flowering of the "lost" religion. It was not only the genista or the golden gorse, that burst into a flame of blossom, it was the *courtezia* of love, as well as the *aubade* of the musicians and poets of Provence. That influence became a sort of courtly convention; it is implicit in the plays, *John* and *Richard II*, which deal with the third and with the last of the eight Plantagenet kings. With the sensitive, wavering Richard II, the golden flower is trodden underfoot, in the hundred years' frightful conflict over roses, white and red.

These are Shakespeare's kings. They may be England's, but that sometimes seems irrelevant and unimportant. Without these plays and the later comedies and tragedies, England, in the light of the world's culture, would rank at best, as a sort of bulwark of material strength, *this fortress built by Nature for herself*. It is the weakness, not the strength of England that defies time. It is the death in poverty, of Edmund Spenser, returned, a failure, from Ireland; it is the recklessness of Sir Philip Sidney, whose *your need is greater than mine* has become proverbial; it is Sir Walter Raleigh who with his last breath, gives the lie to pomp and circumstance; Kit Marlowe with *if all the pens that ever poets held*; Thomas Nash, a voluntary witness that *the plague full swift goes by*; Ben Jonson with his sublimization of the black-draped barges at the foot of the Tower stairs, in his *Masque of Queens*, and of John Donne's

> One short sleep past, we wake eternally,
> And Death shall be no more; Death, thou shalt die;

it is Sir Henry Wotton with his hopeless devotion to Elizabeth of Bohemia, and Essex in the Tower, fighting and defiant, like Raleigh, to the end.

Simon de Montford had sworn to exterminate the last, living member of the Church of Provence. He succeeded in driving the worship of Love into the high-ways and by-ways of Europe. But Rome itself was not immunized. It was the Kathars of Provence who first inaugurated the system of wandering mendicants. Although the out-cast laid aside his sandals and robe, his transformation was but superficial. As he wandered, a troubadour, from castle-fortress to castle-fortress, he was (unknown to the lords of Aquitaine and Provence), spreading the germs of deadly heresy, the worship of beauty. This worship, forced to renounce the official language of the Church, disguised itself in terms of earthly passion. But this passion was never requited. In other words, the love of the troubadour was love of the Spiritual. This love could not be satisfied on earth. Later, it became formalized into the code, set forth in the *Morte d'Arthur*. The knight wore his lady's favour, but it was understood that that lady was set apart, a convention or ideal to which he was dedicated. So subtle was the influence of the mendicant, cast out of the Church of Provence, that a further transformation, or a turn in the road, brings him to Assisi. Francis was brought up, as all the young noblemen of his time, on tales of knightly valour and the poems of these same troubadours. Renouncing wealth and privilege, he takes to himself the rough garment of sack-cloth. Francis brings back the cult of Our Lady Poverty to Rome.

Later, the Saint of Avila, also brought up on tales of knightly valour, leaves her dowry and her palace, and in the end, gathered her novices about her and lays the foundation of the new order of Carmelites, as Francis had done of the Franciscans. It will be noted that Francis overcame insuperable difficulties before his cult of Our Lady Poverty proved acceptable to the Holy Father at Rome, and that Teresa was actually, during the writing of her great book, under the suspicion and, at one time, the interdict of the Inquisition.

The poet is always suspect. In spite of himself and all his good intentions, he comes to no good. We have seen how the germs of this deadly heresy flourished in England. These heretics were the more the martyrs, in that they themselves were unconscious of the source of their inspiration. Reason, as I have said, was well within the intellectual range of each one of them. But love was stronger. The power of love built up a kingdom. When his trust in Church and Court fell, in the bitter dissensions begun by Henry VIII, the suspect instinctively began to prepare for himself his recompense. It was the children of the martyrs who fulfilled the unconscious longing of the older generation.

Two roads were open to these heretics or poets. There was the way of stark reality and there was escape from that reality. There was one door always open, but they looked fearful and diminished, straight through the portals of Death, and saw what was or was not there. It was no longer possible to accept dogma or even inspiration from another, as to the steps down to Hell or those leading up to Heaven. They must see for themselves and they did see. As the boundaries of the known world, so the boundaries of the unknown were extended. This was a spiritual necessity.

> Wit with his wantonness
> Tasteth death's bitterness,

but the bitterness was not the idea of absolute extinction. The lesser and the greater poet alike met in the unanimous acceptance of one article of faith.

> For in that sleep of death what dreams may come
> When we have shuffled off this mortal coil,
> Must give us pause.

The dream was greater than reality. Out of it, they built a city, comparable to Augustine's *City of God*, or a fortress as formidable as the *Castle* of Teresa. Francis himself might have learned much from the blossoms of Robert Herrick or the *lilies of all kinds* of that *Winter's Tale*. The spiritual inheritance, substantially absorbed by Rome, was not lost. It had been carried, not in iron chests guarded by the vanguard of a conquering army, but it had blown on the wind, as the jongleur, the jester, the beggar wandered, himself suspect, from court to court. He gathered sometimes as he went, strange flowers, it is true, but the seeds of the faith, in the end, blown by the tempest or carried in the dowry-chest of the girl from the south, took root.

An exotic flower—it blossomed only in the queen's tiring-room or later, in the king's banquet-hall. Then it was hewn down. But the roots of that flower still flourished and sent out thorny branches. In France, the popularity of the *Roman de la Rose* was at its height, when Richmond proclaims, at the end of *Richard III*,

We will unite the white rose and the red.

Theoretically, the Tudors bore the red and the white rose, in the heraldic wreath around the lions and lilies. But Henry VIII proved the fallacy of this presumption, for Mary re-animated the old dissension, and to Elizabeth, all roses were one colour.

If we presume symbolically, that the white rose is a symbol of spiritual love, it is obvious that the red rose is not only a symbol, but an actual image of the heart. The blood-red blossom is also symbol of the martyr's death. The white rose, drained of its life-blood, is not a symbol only, but a phantom as well, and a phantom more real than the incontinent world of cathedral and of court. *Death thou shalt die* was spoken by one of the arch-heretics, whether officially a Catholic or of the disinherited Church of England makes no difference. There were no boundaries, and though actually each might walk in hourly fear of the opposing faction, there was, in the innermost circle of the heretical church, no schism and no dissension.

Official death was more likely to track down the fortunate. Marlowe was early recognized as a dramatist and he was as well, as has recently been established, a secret agent of no mean ability. I have said that he acted himself to death and that the same is true of Raleigh. Spenser was selected or favoured by the Lord-Lieutenant of Ireland for diplomatic reasons; Ben

Jonson, having had his childhood blighted by poverty, devoted himself to producing those processions of animated abstractions. These four outstanding heretics were marked down, from the first, for disaster. Though Ben Jonson's disaster was perhaps unrecognized, it is none the less obvious. His success was attained at the price of renouncing genius for talent.

Thomas Nash, we may imagine, was not so much a victim of circumstance, as of voluntary dedication, *The plague full swift goes by*, and Webster, a child or youth, sees death in its most abhorrent aspect of gradual or partial decay. To the observer, whether physician like Thomas Lodge or grave-digger like John Donne, there can be no possible compromise. The dedicated may rush to the altar-rail for absolution, or he may seek out a place in the Inn.

He may have, indeed he must inevitably have passed through the same charnel-house which Juliet in her ravings, reproduces for us and the traditional grave-digger in *Hamlet* offers us, in the death-head of poor Yorick. *Alas, poor Yorick*—the memory of this earthly skull served at the end as a reminder to this cautious citizen of Stratford to be careful of his last belongings: *Good Frend, for Iesus sake forbeare.*

He was sitting with Michael Drayton and Ben Jonson after dinner, one spring evening. These were old friends. Drayton was one year older. Was he perhaps a cousin or friend of one of the younger Lucys? He is known to have been connected with the neighbouring Warwickshire nobility. The lad may have secretly hunted with Michael Drayton and some of the younger Lucys. The older Lucys would have kept to themselves, their own rule and convention would have excluded the son of John Shakespeare and Mary Arden from their hunting-parties.

Ben Jonson is still younger. There is eight years difference in their ages. Ben Jonson in his avid pursuit of learning—of books—had condescended to take part in one of his own, not too successful productions. He paid the young man what he could but regretted, from the first, that he could teach him nothing. Ben Jonson's brilliant mind, however, had been recognized. He himself and Fletcher had had many set-backs. It seemed nothing could intimidate Ben Jonson. He sat there, solid yet easily swayed by the passing whims of Court and fashion. He did not ask Jonson the news, this time. Drayton went on talking.

Long-purples grew beside the Avon. Some called the flowering spray of willow-herb, long-purples. But that was not what he meant when he hesitated, trying to remember what Mary had first called the others. They were not harebells. He held the stems toward her. She never called them deadmen's-fingers, he knew that. He couldn't remember what she had called them. He saw the fire reflected in the row of pewter plates. Then he was back in the kitchen and smelt wood-smoke and spice, and the delicate fragrance of the flowers with the too-long green-white stems that he held toward Mary Arden. There were mistakes like that. And the rhymes had sometimes caused dissension in the green-room. Not like Marlowe, they said. No, he wasn't like Marlowe, nor was he much like the others. Fletcher was more tolerant—but take Ben there. Michael hardly counted. Michael remembered exploits, when moonlight on the snow bewitched his arrows. Michael had admired him for his archery, and that early infatuation had spoiled his later judgments. But taken all in all, he hadn't done so badly. There was the new house and the garden.

The wind was blowing from the Cotswolds. Lear had wandered among those scattered boulders, and from a hillock, he had watched till *Birnam wood be come to Dunsinane*. When it did come, he heard a shout, *Hail king! for so thou art*. The old king was raving and blind, but that was earlier. Or was it later? Malcolm did not have the last word, however. Perhaps he should have cut the act, after Macbeth's *to-morrow and to-morrow and to-morrow*. The rest of the scene was unnecessary, but there was always that space between the end and the departure of the players. That had to be filled in. Each actor wanted to return and make his presence felt, after the play was actually over. But Prospero had had the last word. Yes, that was a tempest. He remembered how he had lost his way, stumbling over the stony ground. The casement rattled and the fire sent out a cloud of smoke, as a late guest brushed past them. He opened the door and the cold wind rushed in; Michael was still talking.

It was an old controversy. Was or was not the Grecian right in the assumption that certain unities were necessary? Unity of time, space and so on. But he had long since despaired of these same unities. It was hardly a matter of unities, it was holding the audience that concerned him. As to time and place—there was *Tamburlaine*. There was no break there. *Tamburlaine the Great* needed no Touchstone nor any Twelfth Night fool, with *Come away, come away, Death* to distract an audience. Whether or not that play ended to be enlivened by unities broken and shattered, was really beyond his knowing. But Ben knew the answer to these things. There was Aristotle and the final word, *katharsis*—that was Greek certainly.

> And sighed his soul toward the Grecian tents
> Where Cressid lay that night.

The *Merchant* lacked unity, there was no doubt about that. It was Marlowe's *Jew* that had given him the idea, but the Jew of Venice did not succeed as the *Jew of Malta* had done. Ben Jonson was right there.

Juliet was still worse. It was two plays really. One play was over when Mercutio cried,

> They have made worms' meat of me.

It had started as a romance, but as the Jew spoiled the unity of the *Merchant*, so some alien voice had shouted down the lovers' triumph. He had tried to intimidate them, or rather Mercutio had, by delaying the action (or trying to delay Romeo), by a long poem that should have been left out, or at best or worst, gone into the *Dream*. It was Drayton's idea really—Oberon and *Midsummer Night's Dream*. There was no room for deadmen's-fingers or long-purples there.

We know there was *courtezia*. There was as well, the *aubade* which Juliet tried in vain to nullify. Love fulfilled was powerless against the old forces of unconscious longing for ultimate union. All worldly gifts must be offered—the gift of wealth and leisure, in the case of Francis, the gift of convention and the world's commendation, in the case of Teresa. The soul, blindly seeking, had found haven or sanctuary in the Office of the Mass, and the mind, tortured and disintegrating, was lulled by the anodine of countless *Aves* and *Pater Nosters*. Even when the body was ill-clothed, there were the wonders of the dowry of the Saints to be gaped at, and the candle-sticks and costly vestments of the servers. The world was clothed in satin and rich velvet; one might even brush against a sable or an ermine border. One beheld an assembly in this drawing-room that one would never, under any circumstances, be permitted to mingle with, elsewhere. There were now open cathedral doors, but with all the effort to re-establish the Latin ritual in its English trappings, there was something lacking. It was not for nothing that Simon de Montford had plundered the Holy Land of Provence. Not all the rhythm and metre was the property of the wandering mendicant, or at least, it did not remain so. Into the pagan litanies of Rome, there crept a tender, wistful note. The *Fioretti* vied with the porphyry and marble of Diocletian, and the Child, with the discarded myths of Capitoline Jupiter.

The Child was the symbol of ultimate union.

Juliet was a child, really. Controversy as to the marriageable age of girls in Renaissance Italy does not alter that. In fact, Juliet was two children, though one of them was doomed. Both of them were doomed, finally, for how could one of them live without the other?

Parental authority had killed Juliet. She died that morning when he left her. Friar Lawrence, gathering his herbs, was Francis come to life, in his sandals and brown habit. He could delay the final dissolution by a few days, no longer. The Church, the Bride of Provence (or Verona) lay decked in her renaissance marriage garments and crowned with flowers. She is lying in her bride-bed, and parents and household pass before her; they genuflect or kneel, till finally Friar Lawrence himself takes over responsibility.

He will steal this Bride of Provence from her father's very palace.

Montague and Capulet (the eternal faction) have both been forced to relinquish the claim to spiritual inheritance. There will be a new life, another renaissance, when the bridegroom returns from Mantua. We have only to wait. Friar Lawrence, Francis and the gentle Shakespeare wait with us. But events beyond their control, take over the play and the lovers are united, as only they could be, beyond the grave. Romeo returns too soon or too late. Juliet wakes too soon or too late.

The fire is going out. Ben Jonson and Michael Drayton are still arguing. There was that *katharsis*. The body of society, the body of life could not be healed. There was only one solution, but though he had intended to follow the plot as Fletcher had outlined it for him from the Italian folio, the story had misled him. He had, however, taken the main events. But unlike Marlowe's *Tamburlaine*, this lesser tragedy had been interrupted. It was not only that Mercutio became too important in the first part, and so cut the play in half. The play faltered in any case. Juliet's nurse intruded. The parents were bodiless, abstractions like Ben Jonson's. Paris, the worldly suitor, was unconvincing. He did not really love her. He would never have died at her tomb, fighting the legitimate bridegroom.

> All lovers young, all lovers must
> Consign to thee and come to dust.

All lovers young—lovers are always young. But the child Fidele, in *Cymbeline*, is not two children but one—so later, William Shakespeare. Imogen is Fidele, just as Rosalind is Ganymede. Juliet is herself only, but she seeks for ultimate fulfilment in another. But according to the old creed and canon of the Kathars, that was not possible. Now we have come back to Eleanor of Aquitaine and the *School of Love*.

What he taught, he taught unconsciously. The ache and urge for the ideal had been thwarted. No doubt, what was lost by Mary was gained by Elizabeth. But still, through Elizabethan poetry, there is this obsession with the lost Virgin. The moon, a symbol of chastity, was associated with the Mother of God. Now Cynthia herself must be invoked, in the guise of Queen Elizabeth. But there were younger adepts. To them, no doubt, there was another schism. We hear nothing of this, but the playwright shows his rebellion in the unevenness of the Venetian story, and even more so

> In fair Verona, where we lay our scene.

They were children, huddled together in Judith's bed. Capulet found only one of them. The nurse was wailing, in her tiresome fashion. Friar Lawrence explained it afterwards, but it was too late. The unities of time and place had been disregarded. Michael had a theory, it was, as was usual with him, compound of moon-beams and of cob-webs. He had always re-written his stanzas and re-worked them. Now he was returning to his old *Nymphidia*. There, he had assembled his elves and fairies, his ant, his bee, his Hobgoblin in the manner of an old wives' tale. Now he remembered *Agincourt* and how, after the fall of the curtain, his own audience had for-gotten him and called for Michael Drayton. It was like that. But *Henry V* was a success all told. It may have been Michael's ballad that had made it so. He watched Juliet sleeping.

Would she ever wake up and if she did, who would tell her about Ham-net? *But that the dread of something after death*—that was later, but it was Juliet's fear. The lines were overlaid with the horror of the old plague. But she would wake up. Or perhaps she would not wake up. Or she would wake and find Hamnet dead, and refuse to live without him. Michael said it was Queen Eleanor who brought the song to England. A French queen. But Michael said she was Richard's mother. Which Richard? Not Rich-mond's rival? No, there were three before Richard III, if you count the child. There was the other Edward but that was all long after. How had he gone? But that was Mary's brother. Mary? He smelt the saffron cakes, as she drew them from the oven. He held the flowers toward her. He had forgotten what she called them—not deadmen's-fingers, anyway.

He thought they were talking about Aristotle and the *katharsis*, the healing implicit in those unities. But it was Queen Eleanor and Provence and a ritual that had to do with Mary. No, it wasn't Mary. It was, it seemed, the Church Spiritual. It was the Bride of God these Kathars, as Michael called them, worshipped. But wasn't every church that? He couldn't follow any further. They were all heretics. Was he recalling the old days of the boy Edward and his sister, Mary?

But it was not Agincourt now that roused him. It was the thought of the island before Henry. But that was another Henry, the third, Michael was insisting. He hadn't really interrupted. The fire had gone out, and the wind from the door cut through his shoulder-blades. He shifted his chair, a hint they should be going. It was the worship of beauty, Michael was concluding, that William and the barons had clamped down. But hadn't the French brought in beauty? Michael was patient with him. France was not all Normandy, Michael was saying to him.

Of course, he knew that.

Cynthia had not satisfied him. Moonlight on the snow had spoiled him for any other. He was glad to get back to Stratford.

> Never harm,
> Nor spell nor charm
> Come our lovely lady nigh.

She spoke of grapes, the vine, remembering Antony and the purple sails. But that was not Imogen, it went back further. Her claim on Caesar had been disregarded. Antony by her jealousy had been goaded to death. Then she died. But she died splendidly, although she feared the mockery of the players, after the victory of the new Triumvirs. Actium. Now he was back with the old dilemma. Suppose she woke up and found him, or suppose she woke up and didn't find him. *What's this? A cup, closed in my true love's hand?* Would it have been better, after all, to have had her die first? Michael went on talking.

Antony had died first. But that was another cup. Antony was so much younger. But that happened three years before her death and then, Cleopatra was much older. There was really no comparison. Poor Essex. Raleigh had succeeded him, but under another tyrant. His *Virginia* was enough of a compliment to last a life-time—her life-time. That was Michael's too. *The Virginian Voyage.* He would have been off with them, but he had discovered his own island. England?

We are such stuff as dreams are made on and if actively, we are restricted, we escape. It was so, from the beginning. Their Warwickshire vines were too low-growing, they said, but the small berries were sweet. He held the goblet to the light but the tapers reflected too many pictures in the glass. The flagon was empty.

Francis Bacon talked endlessly. Mantua, Padua, Vienna, Sicily, Ravenna, Venice, Verona—he stared at him. The face, lean and brown, the thin fingers, the hollow at his temples—his hands again. Italy! *Let Rome in Tiber melt*, but it wasn't Rome he thought of. The Venetian goblet was filled with white wine. He did not touch it. He watched the hand that moved so eloquently, and the shadow of the hand. He noted the cuff, pleated with a thread of dark-wine silk, and a knot of the same colour at the wrist. His beard was trimmed to an even finer point than usual. He spoke in firm, fine measure. He spoke as he looked, a courtier and a gentleman. What he said had an assurance that was English, the English of the schoolmen. It was not the language of the ordinary courtier. Most of them had gone. Francis Bacon had delayed him. He was a man of about his own age, yet he seemed infinitely older. He had had the advantage of Trinity and Cambridge. There was something he and Raleigh had in common. He knew what it was. Deliberately, he turned the long-stemmed chalice in his own somewhat shorter, stronger fingers. The glass stem would snap, if he were not careful. The glass was gold and the wine was gold, yet neither quite matched the yellow flame of candles. The words of Francis Bacon were deliberate, diplomatic. He understood them. He was quite prepared to under-score the dialogue, so that as usual, the players came within the range of Cynthia's shining. He did not have to be told to do that, nor was even a diplomatic hint necessary. He kept his archer's gaze on the fine, dark features. He must not look at the chalice nor the gold wine. Mantua, Padua—he steadied his arm. He tightened the bow-string. But he would wait.

The vine-stem did not snap—he meant the wine-stem. He meant the stalk of the wine glass. But he was looking at another. He had managed with Hippolyta, the Amazon, the Virgin Huntress—all that mixed up with Michael's Titania and Oberon. These things were not difficult. But he was looking at Ben now. It was not that he regretted his refusal of the offer. His French was adequate. Francis Bacon had stipulated nothing. Another gentleman was needed. The glass stem had not broken. There was John Shakespeare's concession, of course—a Swan and an Arrow with suitable Latin, was a protection. But it was no protection—why did he remember now? Michael had more than made up for the Lucy insult.

Still he looked at Francis Bacon, and though he saw arcades and the sun falling on a shallow lagoon through the arch of a bridge, and a marble column frightened him with an ecstasy, too great to be borne—though they were not there, he felt them, *things in heaven and earth*—and knew that the flowers would be different and the flowers would be the same, like the tiny pansy border in the illuminated book that Michael showed him, from his father's library—though he felt, rather than heard their voices and the resonance of them echoing, as they could never do in England, his glance did not waver. No, he thanked Francis Bacon for his offer.

He had died first, the cup of death clasped in his hand. There was still a stain of purple in the wine glass, he himself held. They had stopped talking. He remembered that other golden wine and the chalice, like the cup of a day-lily. The day came too swiftly, for the day brought darkness, the darkness of knowledge. They were huddled together in Judith's bed, as he remembered them last together, though that was after he left London. That is, he remembered, as he drove his tired horse through Oxford, on the way back. He remembered them huddled together. They were cold. Did he speak harshly to Hamnet? He could not remember. He remembered words out of his own play,

> Or bid me go into a new-made grave
> And hide me with a dead man in his shroud.

That was the child, Juliet, Judith. He himself had prophesied the whole thing. If he had not written the play, it never would have happened.

Now he saw why he had not gone with Francis Bacon, as one of the minor courtiers, on the Queen's business. The Queen's business was waiting beyond Oxford. He hardly understood the implication or the impact of what he felt. It was a thing sensed, not thought. But there were words for it. Michael had just said something that had stirred a memory. It was Judith, it was Juliet, it was Queen Eleanor. It was a plum-coloured sleeve and the shadow of a thin hand and the feel of the glass stem between his thumb and finger. It was the sense of the moment when the slender stem would snap—and waiting. It was keeping back something. They had all, always kept back something. The metres ran on, recklessly or bound or ruled rather, like Campion's music. But something snapped. It was not the Venetian glass stem. He had come home because he loved Judith.

September 19
November 1
1946

The following dates of birth and death have been used in
the structure of *The Guest*.

Bacon, Francis	1561–1626
Beaumont, Francis	1584–1616
Beaumont, John	1583–1627
Breton, Nicholas	1545?–1626?
Browne, William	1591–1643
Campion, Thomas	1567–1620
Carew, Thomas	1598?–1639?
Chapman, George	1559?–1634
Constable, Henry	1562–1613
Crashaw, Richard	1613?–1649
Daniel, John	?–1625
Daniel, Samuel	1562–1619
Davenant, William	1606–1668
Davison, Francis	1575?–1619?
Dekker, Thomas	1570?–1641?
Devereux, Robert	1567–1601
Donne, John	1572–1631
Drayton, Michael	1563–1631
Drummond, William	1585–1649
Dyer, Edward	c.1540–1607
Fletcher, Giles	c.1588–1623
Fletcher, John	1579–1625
Fletcher, Phineas	1582–1650
Ford, John	1586–1640?
Greene, Robert	1560?–1592
Greville, Fulke	1554–1628
Grimald, Nicholas	1519–1562

Herbert, Edward	1583–1648
Herbert, George	1593–1633
Herrick, Robert	1591–1674
Heywood, John	c.1497–c.1580
Heywood, Thomas	1575?–c.1650
Howard, Henry	1517?–1547
Jonson, Ben	1572–1637
King, Henry	1592–1669
Lodge, Thomas	1558?–1625
Lovelace, Richard	1618–1658
Lyly, John	1554?–1606
Marlowe, Christopher	1564–1593
Massinger, Philip	1583–1640
Middleton, Thomas	1570?–1627
Nash, Thomas	1567–1601
Peele, George	1558–1597?
Quarles, Francis	1592–1644
Raleigh, Walter	1552–1618
Rowlands, Richard	1565–1620
Rowley, William	1585?–1642?
Shakespeare, William	1564–1616
Shirley, James	1596–1666
Sidney, Philip	1554–1586
Southwell, Robert	1561–1595
Spenser, Edmund	1553?–1599
Strode, William	1599?–1645
Suckling, John	1609–1642
Vaux, Thomas	1510–1556
Waller, Edmund	1606–1687
Webster, John	1580?–1630
Wotton, Henry	1568–1639
Wyatt, Thomas	1503–1542

Editor's Notes

Please note that biographical information on Renaissance poets is drawn largely from Garrett A. Sullivan Jr. and Alan Stewart, eds., *The Encyclopedia of English Renaissance Literature* (Malden, Mass.: Blackwell, 2012). Readers are advised to consult this source for more comprehensive information. I have also included for each figure passages on which H.D. drew for biography in William S. Braithwaite's *The Book of Elizabethan Verse* (London: Chatto and Windus, 1908).

Good Frend

Notes to pages 47–49

Shakespeare Day, 23rd April, 1945. The birth and death of Shakespeare are celebrated on April 23. This specific date in 1945 marks H.D.'s first pilgrimage to Stratford-on-Avon.

Good frend. . . . my bones. H.D. transcribes the epitaph inscribed on Shakespeare's tomb at Trinity Church in Stratford-on-Avon. The title of the verse part of the book, "Good Frend," is taken from the first two words of this epitaph.

23rd April, 1564 / 23rd April, 1616. The two dates beneath the epitaph are Shakespeare's birth and death dates respectively.

For BRYHER . . . April 23, 1945. H.D. dedicates this volume to the two people who accompanied her to Stratford at the close of World War II, her lifelong companion, Bryher, and their close friend, Robert Herring, who edited *Life and Letters Today* after Bryher assumed leadership of the periodical. The specific designations are apt. Bryher was an avid reader of Renaissance plays and poetry, and Herring had been at work on an experimental verse play about St. George, drafts of which he shared with H.D. By stressing the common date of Shakespeare Day and the English national holiday, St. George's Day, H.D. draws a connection between the literary and the political in commemorating the deaths suffered by England in World War II. St. George's emblem, a red cross on a white background (or a red rose on a white lapel), was first adopted by Richard the Lionheart, an English monarch who will play a significant role in "The Guest." See note on **Richard Lion-Heart** on page 164.

PART I. The Tempest

Notes to pages 51–55

The Tempest. "Good Frend" responds to this play by William Shakespeare, first performed in 1611. H.D.'s marked copy of *The Tempest*, ed. M.R. Ridley (London: Dent, 1935), is the edition she used when she composed the poem. She also owned a set of the complete works, and in H.D.'s *The Sword Went Out to Sea: (Synthesis of a Dream) by Delia Alton*, ed. Cynthia Hogue and Julie Vandivere (Gainesville: University Press of Florida, 2007), 56, her autobiographically based protagonist is presented with an illustrated, fairy-tale version of *The Tempest* by a character based on Ezra Pound.

lilies. Lilies recur throughout this poem, and in other contemporaneous texts by H.D., in a number of guises. In *Majic Ring*, ed. Demetres P. Tryphonopoulos (Gainesville: University Press of Florida, 2009), the lily appears prominently and frequently as the French heraldic *fleur-de-lys* and the sacred Egyptian *nénufar*, or water lily. In *Trilogy*, ed. Alike Barnstone (New York: New Directions, 1973), 7, the "lily-head / or the lily-bud" crowns Hermes' caduceus, and in *Within the Walls* (Iowa City: Windhover Press, 1993), 5, she embroiders the *fleur-de-lys* on a tapestry. The Virgin Mary, who figures in "The Guest," is often depicted carrying a lily in medieval and Renaissance art; H.D. alludes to this below. The lily is featured in Song of Solomon 2:16 ("My beloved *is* mine, and I *am* his: he feedeth among the lilies"), also referenced below. H.D.'s close friends, Cole and Gerald Henderson, gifted her with Fred Stoker, *A Book of Lilies* (London: King Penguin, 1943), 9, 12, which discusses the lily's association with the Virgin Mary and its use in heraldry. She would have also been interested in Stoker's comments on its use in wartime to heal soldiers, so as a symbol it brings together violence (through heraldry) and healing; for its military significance, see also note on **flower-de-luce** on page 139. A Shakespeare play from which H.D. took the names Hermione (for several of her autobiographical characters) and Perdita (for her daughter), *The Winter's Tale*, refers to "lilies of all kinds, / The flower-de-luce being one"; "lilies of all kinds" appears on page 139 of "The Guest." In Stratford in the summer of 1946, H.D. made a list of various flowers, including the "fleur-de-luce" and the "lily-white," in her copy of A. R. Entwistle, *Shakespeare as Poet* (London: Thomas Nelson and Sons, 1929).

Remembering how your young love wept / With Montague long ago and Capulet. The reference is to Shakespeare's *Romeo and Juliet*, one of the plays H.D. saw performed in Stratford in the summer of 1945. The play was directed by Robert Atkins, and it starred David Peel and Moira Lister in the title roles. About the performance, she writes Bryher in a letter dated June 8, [1945], "dear Fido, I have seen the *only* possible Juliet, at long last bar-none, not even Bergner. I was shivering with apprehension, but someone had a bright idea—a *child*, all-but! . . . Romeo, very young, too! It is supposed to be something special—and *came off*! Much better than Guilgood & Peggy A.—no comparisons. . . . Crowded house & such enthusiasm! All the original charm was there. I was afraid it might not be, but it *was*!" Bryher Papers, General Collection, Beinecke Rare Book and Manuscript Library, Yale University, New Haven, Connecticut. Here H.D. compares the performance favorably to the 1935 production of the play at the New Theatre in London, in which John Gielgud and Peggy Ashcroft starred in the titular roles, and she refers to Bryher's friend and one-time love interest, the Jewish Austrian actress Elisabeth Bergner, who had played Juliet in 1928 at the Berliner Theatre.

'Twas a sweet marriage . . . at Tunis. The italicized portions of this passage are taken from act 2 of *The Tempest* and refer to the marriage of Claribel to the King of Tunis. In H.D.'s copy of *The Tempest*, she has underscored these lines. Alonso and Ferdinand are characters in *The Tempest*, and Tunis is modern-day Tunisia.

Claribel. A character referenced in Shakespeare's *The Tempest* who does not appear in the play.

The flagship . . . Somers. H.D. misnames the *Sea Venture*, part of an expedition of England's Virginia Company that was bound for Jamestown in 1609 but shipwrecked in the Bermudas. In her copy of *The Tempest*, H.D. marks this passage from the introduction, which also misidentifies the ship: "By far the most interesting . . . sources are the various pamphlets describing the adventures of the expedition of nine ships and five hundred colonists which set out in May of 1609 for the new colony of Virginia. The flagship, the *Sea-Adventure*, carrying the leaders of the expedition, Sir Thomas Gates and Sir George Somers, was wrecked on the Bermudas; but all on board were saved, built ships on the island, and reached Virginia in the next year, whence the accounts of their adventures were sent to England," xiv.

Elizabeth . . . Frederick. James I of England arranged the marriage of his daughter, Elizabeth, to Bohemia's Frederick V, Elector Palatine, in an effort to politically stabilize Europe, but the Thirty Years War erupted only two years after they wed, and the couple lived in exile in Holland for the rest of their lives. All of the English monarchs since are descendants of this Elizabeth, known as the "Winter Queen." Borne by H.D.'s grandmother, Elizabeth is a name that recurs throughout H.D.'s post–World War II writings, including *The Mystery*, ed. Jane Augustine (Gainesville: University Press of Florida, 2010) and *Vale Ave* (New York: New Directions, 2013). She read for Elizabeth, the Queen Mother, in 1943 and avidly collected articles on the coronation of her daughter, Elizabeth II. See also note on **You meaner beauties . . .** on page 158.

Bohemia. Area of central Europe in what is now the Czech Republic. When Elizabeth married Frederick V, it was under Austrian rule.

Mary. Mary Stuart, or Mary I of Scotland, known as Mary, Queen of Scots. She reigned over Scotland from 1542 to 1567. Both Mary and Elizabeth I had claim to the English throne, and Elizabeth I signed Mary's execution order in 1587. Mary Stuart was the mother of James IV, who after the death of Elizabeth I became James I, the first Scottish King of England.

April 23, 1945 . . . Shakespeare's Day. See note on page 135.

the churchyard. The reference is to Trinity Church in Stratford, the parish church where Shakespeare's tomb lies.

Lucy. H.D.'s speaker sees the tomb of Sir Thomas Lucy, who legendarily caught a young William Shakespeare poaching deer on his land.

John Shakespeare. William Shakespeare's father, a merchant glover in Stratford.

old Queen. Elizabeth I of England. See note on page 143.

The *Sea-Adventure* . . . Somers. See note on **The flagship . . .** on page 137.

Drake, Raleigh. Sir Francis Drake and Sir Walter Raleigh each led voyages to the New World at the behest of the English monarchy during the Renaissance. Raleigh will play a key role in "The Guest," in which his imprisonment and execution by James I is recounted.

my beloved is mine / And I am his. Lines from Song of Solomon 2:16: "My beloved *is* mine, and I *am* his: he feedeth among the lilies." Variations on these lines also appear in a poem by Francis Quarles that appears in Braithwaite's anthology; see note on **Francis Quarles** on page 154.

The king's fair daughter. See note on *'Twas a sweet marriage* on page 137.

spikenard, / Myrrh and myrtle-spray. Referred to several times in the Bible, fragrant spikenard and myrrh figure in Song of Solomon. Myrrh, which means *bitter*, appears in H.D.'s *Trilogy* as one of the gifts of the Magi. Myrtle is commonly used in English wedding bouquets.

Our belovèd is ours. See note on *my beloved is mine* on page 138.

Part ii. Rosemary

Notes to pages 56–63

Rosemary. The title of part II of "Good Frend" is an herb H.D. makes great use of in her late writings because it is associated with both memory and healing. It is also used, as H.D. notes in this poem, in both weddings and funerals. Rosemary is worn on England's Remembrance Day, commemorating World War I.

Blest be . . . stones. See note on **Good Frend** on page 135.

So once a discus . . . to a flower. The reference is to Hyacinth, a spring fertility god, who was accidentally slain by his lover, Apollo, during a game of discus. Apollo transformed Hyacinth's blood into a flower.

lily. See note on **lilies** on page 136.

Blest be y̆ man. See note on **Good Frend . . .** on page 135.

My belovèd is mine / and I am his. See note on page 138.

The king's fair daughter. See note on *'Twas a sweet marriage* on page 137.

spikenard, / Myrrh and myrtle-spray. See note on page 138.

'Twas a sweet marriage. See note on page 137.

Claribel. See note on page 137.

asphodel. Part of the lily family, H.D. named one of her early 1920s novels after this flower, which was associated with the ancient Greek underworld and planted near graves. Thus, this section of the poem juxtaposes plants associated with birth and marriage with death. H.D. imagines ascending from the underworld of war, reborn into a world of peace.

flower-de-luce, / Sword-flower and king-spear. The flower-de-luce is the fleur-de-lis, or lily, associated with the French monarchy before it was adopted by England's Edward III as an imperializing gesture claiming England's right to France. Here it is linked to other flowers whose names evoke militarism and the monarchy. See also note on **lilies** on page 136.

Ros maris. A sea rose, literally (as H.D. indicates) "dew of the sea." As in *Trilogy*, H.D. plays with the language to suggest rosemary, rose of Mary, and "rose of memory." See also note on **rosemary** on page 138.

plesaunce. This term refers to the knot in the popular knot gardens popular in Renaissance times. See also note on **Ladysmocks . . . harebells soon** on page 145. Earlier definitions of plesaunce stress the garden's aesthetic rather than useful properties.

Full fathom five. Ariel's song in act 1 of *The Tempest*, sung when Ferdinand first appears on stage. Braithwaite includes these lines in his anthology, entitling the song "A Sea Dirge." H.D. marked this song in her copy of the play.

Rosalind . . . Helena. Female characters from several Shakespeare plays. Rosalind is from *As You Like It*, a favorite play of H.D.'s youth. From *Romeo and Juliet*, Rosaline Capulet is, like Claribel of *The Tempest*, a character who never appears on stage; Romeo is in love with Rosaline before he sees Juliet. Juliet is from *Romeo and Juliet*, Julia from *The Two Gentlemen of Verona*. Maria appears in *Twelfth Night*, Mariana in *Measure for Measure*, and Marina in *Pericles*. Katherine is in *Henry VIII*, while Katherina is in *Taming of the Shrew*. Iras is one of Cleopatra's attendants in *Antony and Cleopatra*, Iris is a Roman goddess who appears in *The Tempest*, and Isabel is in *Measure for Measure*. Helen appears in *All's Well That Ends Well*, Helena in *A Midsummer Night's Dream*.

Helenus. Priam's son in Shakespeare's *Troilus and Cressida*.

Arden . . . Sicilia. Settings of several Shakespeare plays.

What's in a name? From a well-known speech by Juliet in Shakespeare's *Romeo and Juliet,* act 2: "What's in a name? that which we call a rose / By any other name would smell as sweet."

To chide the lark at dawn. From another speech of Juliet's in act 3 of Shakespeare's *Romeo and Juliet.*

Or argue with a Jew, / Be merciful. A reference to Portia in Shakespeare's *The Merchant of Venice.*

To banter with a clown. A reference to Rosalind in Shakespeare's *As You Like It.*

Or claim a kingdom. A reference to Katherine in Shakespeare's *Henry V.*

Or denounce a throne. A reference to Hermione in Shakespeare's *The Winter's Tale,* the play from which H.D. draws the name of many of her autobiographical characters in her fiction and the name of her daughter, Perdita.

To snatch a dagger. A reference to Lady Macbeth in *Macbeth.*

Or pluck wild-flowers / For a crown. A reference to Ophelia in *Hamlet.*

lilies. See note on page 136.

Venice. Setting of Shakespeare's *The Merchant of Venice* and *Othello.*

Verona. Setting of Shakespeare's *Romeo and Juliet* and *The Two Gentlemen of Verona.*

Avon's water. The Avon River flows through Stratford, Shakespeare's birthplace.

Arden. Setting of Shakespeare's *As You Like It.*

Avallon. Mythical island where King Arthur died. In her correspondence with H.D., Bryher often refers to England as Avallon.

Ariel. A character in Shakespeare's *The Tempest.*

PART III. Claribel's Way to God

Notes to pages 64–70

Poor Clare. Dedicated to poverty, the Poor Clares are a Franciscan order of nuns dating from the early thirteenth century, founded after the death of St. Clare, a wealthy Italian who joined the church, giving up all of her possessions, upon hearing St. Francis of Assisi preach. Clare and Claribel are obviously another instance of H.D.'s characteristic wordplay, but it is also true that H.D. would have seen the Altar of St. Clare on one of her many visits to the Victoria and Albert Museum in South Kensington.

ora. Ora, which is Latin for pray, is a word in the traditional Ave Maria prayer.

ave. Ave, which means hail, is a word in the traditional Ave Maria prayer.

Rose-of-Mary. H.D. plays on the words rosary and Rose-of-Mary, linking rosemary to the Virgin Mary, who will figure in "The Guest." See also notes on **Rosemary** and **Ros maris** on pages 138 and 139.

Saint Francis. St. Francis of Assisi was a Catholic friar and saint born in the twelfth century. The patron saint of animals, he was known for preaching to animals, which H.D. notes in later references to wolves and birds. See also note on **Poor Clare** on page 140.

pro nobis. In the traditional Ave Maria prayer, *ora pro nobis* is Latin for pray for us.

ros maris. See note on page 139.

rosemary. See note on page 138.

Claribel. See note on page 137.

Queen of Tunis. Claribel. See note on page 137.

Plato . . . Stoics. H.D. lists Plato and four Neoplatonists. The first four are classical Greek philosophers; the last is a Roman philosopher. The ancient Greek philosophical school of Stoicism emphasized logic, morality, and willpower over the emotions, and, as H.D. notes, rejected the idealism of Plato.

The Arian heresy . . . Cyprian. The nontrinitarian Arians believed that because Christ was created by God, he was separate from, and thus subordinate to, God. The early Christian Church deemed this notion heretical. In a passage H.D. marked, Denis de Rougemont's *Passion and Society,* trans. Montgomery Belgion (London: Faber and Faber, 1940), 163, locates this belief in the songs of the troubadours, who couched tributes to the Virgin Mary in songs of courtly love, an idea expounded upon in "The Guest." Jerome, Augustine, Ambrose, and Cyprian were prominent figures in the early Christian church who rejected Arianism. Ambrose, Augustine, and Jerome were three of the first four Fathers of the Church, while Cyprian was a North African bishop who died a martyr in Carthage.

Assisi . . . Clares. See notes on **Poor Clare** and **Saint Francis** on pages 140 and 141.

I went to Acre . . . Sepulchre. This passage refers to the medieval Crusades, which figure significantly in this poem as well as in "The Guest." The Crusades were campaigns led by Catholic Europe between the eleventh and thirteenth centuries into the Holy Land. A city in what is now Israel, Acre was a key site during the Crusades, conquered several times by various forces. Given her comprehensive knowledge of Greek mythology, H.D. may also have been aware that Acre is where Heracles found curative herbs to heal his wounds; Claribel heals the fallen Crusader in this part of the poem with an herb. The Templars were a Christian military organization during the time of the Crusades who settled in Acre after losing Jerusalem. The Church of the Holy Sepulchre, located in Jerusalem, is thought to be built on the site where Christ was crucified, buried, and resurrected. Protection of this site was one of the motivations behind the First Crusade.

I was in Venice. . . . crowded Riva. These are all landmarks in Venice, Italy, which H.D. visited many times.

Mary . . . The trouvères hid in the aubade. French troubadours of the medieval period performed aubades, or morning songs of love. In "The Guest," H.D. traces the origin of English lyric poetry to these figures, who she claimed disguised hymns to the Virgin Mary as songs of courtly love. This understanding of the troubadours derives, as Friedman argues, from H.D.'s reading of Denis de Rougemont. In his *Passion and Society* he argues in passages H.D. marked that "The *Church of Love* was reproduced in *countless sects* more or less secret and more or less revolutionary, and their close similarity of feature testifies to a common origin and to a tradition faithfully preserved," 169 (emphasis is H.D.'s).

the Clares. See note on **Poor Clare** on page 140.

Consolamentum. H.D.'s interest in groups deemed heretical by the Catholic Church extends to the nontrinitarian Cathars, the target of the Albigensian Crusades and the original Inquisition. The Consolamentum was a Cathar sacrament, a ceremony that cleansed the believer from sin, typically when near death. De Rougemont's books link the Cathars to the troubadours who disguised their love for the Virgin Mary in songs of courtly love, a subject of "The Guest."

the bell from San Giovanni / Answered San Marco: San Giovanni e Paolo and Basilica di San Marco are Venetian churches.

Ariel. See note on page 140.

Mary-of-the-Lily. See note on **lilies** on page 136.

The Guest

Notes to pages 71–74

Go, Soul . . . the World the lie. The epigraph for "The Guest" is a poem attributed to Sir Walter Raleigh, frequently anthologized as "The Lie" but entitled "The Soul's Errand" by Braithwaite. Lines from this poem recur throughout "The Guest."

To BRYHER from Seehof Küsnacht. H.D. dedicates the prose section of *By Avon River* to Bryher. She refers to the Swiss clinic at which she recovered after her illness at the end of the war.

My thanks are due . . . modern scholarship. H.D. also thanks the American who would become her literary executor, Norman Holmes Pearson, who acted as her agent for this manuscript. Correspondence at the Beinecke Library reveals that H.D. and Pearson argued over the dates assigned to various poets discussed in "The Guest." H.D. held firm to her own dates, and her position is articulated below: "it is better to follow one's own clues and have of each of these poets, a living and personal memory, rather than grow weary and confused with disputable facts about them."

Notes to pages 75–76

Christopher Marlowe. A popular Elizabethan poet and playwright in his day, Marlowe was born to a poor shoemaker in 1564, was educated at Cambridge, and died in 1593. Marlowe's life is the stuff of legend, much of which has been called into question by recent scholars. Marlowe's best known dramatic works include *The*

Jew of Malta, Tamburlaine, Edward II, and *Doctor Faustus.* Here H.D. paraphrases Braithwaite: "Some say after leaving school he became an actor in London and others that he went with Sidney to the wars in the Netherlands," 793.

Philip Sidney. An Elizabethan courtier, thinker, and poet, Sidney lived from 1554 to 1586. He wrote on a wide range of topics, and his best known literary works include *A Defence of Poesy,* the *Arcadia,* and *Astrophil and Stella.* H.D., though, focuses on Sidney's military service to the crown, in concert with Braithwaite, who explains that Sidney "witness[ed] the Massacre of St. Bartholomew's" and that "[w]hen Queen Elizabeth sent English troops to help the Dutch in their struggle for freedom, Sidney, who was then the Governor of Flushing, participated, and owing to his reckless and chivalrous bravery, fell fighting at Zutphen in September, 1586," 798. H.D. echoes Braithwaite verbatim when she asserts, "He remains the most conspicuous figure of chivalry among English personalities."

Massacre of Saint Bartholomew. Thousands died in the violence between Catholics and Protestant Huguenots that erupted in Paris after the 1572 arranged wedding of Catherine de Medici's Catholic daughter to a Protestant prince who would become Henry IV of France.

Queen Elizabeth. Queen Elizabeth I, daughter of Henry VIII and Anne Boleyn, ruled England from 1558 to 1603. She was also, as H.D. remarks later, an occasional translator and writer, and the poem by Elizabeth I that Braithwaite reprints, "The Doubt of Future Foes," was probably written in 1568 after her cousin, Mary, Queen of Scots, went to England seeking her protection.

Fulke Greville. Fulke Greville, first Lord Brooke, was an aristocrat, a courtier, and a writer who lived from 1554 to 1628. As Braithwaite notes, Greville wrote *A Dedication to Sir Philip Sidney,* commonly known as *Life of Sidney*: "Attached very deeply to his friend, Sir Philip Sidney, he wrote The Life of the Renowned Sir Philip Sidney, 1652; and when he died styled himself on his tombstone: 'The Friend of Sir Philip Sidney,'" 788.

Edmund Spenser. An Elizabethan poet, Spenser is best known (as H.D. mentions below) for *The Faerie Queen.* He was born in London around 1552 and died there in 1599 on a trip from Ireland, where he served as an administrator during a turbulent period in Anglo-Irish history. Braithwaite writes, "he became, through the influence of Sir Philip Sidney, Secretary to Lord Grey of Wilton, Lord-Lieutenant of Ireland; and in 1586, received from the Crown a grant, including the castle and manor of Kilcolman, in the county of Cork, forfeited by the Earl of Desmond," 799. H.D. also reads in Braithwaite that "[i]n 1598 occurred what is called the 'rebellion of the Earl of Tyrone,' which forced Spenser with his wife and children to leave Ireland, for his estates were plundered and burned, to seek his native country where he died in 'extreme indigence and want of bread.'"

Sir Walter Raleigh. An Elizabethan writer, courtier, soldier, and North American explorer, Sir Walter Ralegh was born in Devon to a landed gentleman in 1554, and he was executed by order of James I in 1618 after thirteen years of imprisonment in the Tower of London and a failed expedition to Orinoco. It is now thought that few of the poems attributed to Raleigh were in fact written by him, and this may be true for the poems Braithwaite includes and H.D. mentions. Braithwaite writes of Raleigh that "[h]e served five years in France with the Huguenots, and subsequently in the Netherlands under the Prince of Orange. In 1579, accompanying his half-brother, Sir Humphrey Gilbert, he made his first expedition to America," 795. He also reports his beheading in 1618. Sir Walter Raleigh returns as a character in H.D.'s *Vale Ave* (composed in 1957).

New Place. The name of the large estate in Stratford Shakespeare purchased after attaining some wealth in the theater, a fact Braithwaite, 796, mentions in his biographical note.

Songs and Lyrics. H.D. here misnames her source, though she follows Braithwaite in referring to Elizabethan poetry generally as "songs and lyrics."

Queen Elizabeth. See also note on page 143. Braithwaite includes one poem by Elizabeth I, with which he opens his volume, but he does not offer a biography.

Blow, blow thou winter wind. . . . remembered not. These lines are from Shakespeare's *As You Like It*. Braithwaite anthologizes them as "Amiens' Song."

Notes to pages 76–80

Sidney. See note on page 143.

Spenser. See note on page 143.

Fletcher. John Fletcher was a Jacobean dramatist who lived from 1579 to 1625. He is known for *The Faithfull Shepheardesse*, as H.D. notes, but also as co-author, with Shakespeare, of *The Two Noble Kinsmen* and *Henry VIII*.

Sir Edward Dyer . . . Doctor John Dee. Born in 1543 in Somerset, Sir Edward Dyer was among the earliest Elizabethan poets and a member of the court of Queen Elizabeth I. The frequently anthologized poem from which H.D. quotes may not have been written by Dyer. Braithwaite, 785, reports that Dyer had been a Rosicrucian and was employed by Queen Elizabeth, but H.D. had conducted additional research on these two figures. In a letter dated August 10, [1945], Bryher recommends to H.D. Dee's diary as a good source on Elizabethan home life, comparing it to another book on Dyer. H.D. Papers, Yale Collection of American Literature, Beinecke Rare Book and Manuscript Library, New Haven, Connecticut. In response, H.D. writes that she has read nothing but Shakespeare and Dyer during her sojourn in Stratford (letter dated August 10, [1945]; Bryher Papers). Prague was a hub for alchemists during the Renaissance, and H.D. returns to this setting and theme in her novel, *The Mystery* (completed in 1951). Dyer himself appears again in her late poem *Vale Ave* (composed in 1957), which features Dyer's daughter, Elizabeth, in a secret romance with Sir Walter Raleigh.

My mind to me ... forbids to crave. The first stanza of a poem attributed to Sir Edward Dyer; Braithwaite entitles it "My Mind a Kingdom."

Marlowe. Christopher Marlowe. See note on page 142.

Raleigh. Sir Walter Raleigh. See note on page 143.

Tower. Castle on London's Thames River that, as H.D. notes, Elizabeth I and James I used as a prison. Sir Walter Raleigh was held there before his execution.

Fulke Greville. Braithwaite reports that Greville was "assassinated by one of his domestics," 788. See also note on page 143.

There was Elizabeth ... not forgotten. Shakespeare's granddaughter is Elizabeth; her mother was Shakespeare's daughter, Susanna Hall. Judith and Hamnet are Shakespeare's twins; Hamnet died at the age of 11.

Queen Elizabeth. See note on page 143.

Go, Soul, the Body's guest ... both the lie. See note on **Go, Soul ... the World the lie** on page 142. Here H.D. quotes more of the lengthy poem attributed to Raleigh.

Philomel, with melody ... with lullaby. These lines are taken from the fairies' song to Titania in act 2 of *A Midsummer Night's Dream*; Braithwaite entitles this song, "You Spotted Snakes." The lines H.D. extracts refer to another voiceless woman, Philomel, whose tongue was cut out after she was raped by King Tereus; she was later transformed into a bird.

Ladysmocks ... harebells soon. Ladysmocks are pale pink or lavender flowers mentioned in Shakespeare's *Love's Labour's Lost*, mary-buds are wild marigolds mentioned in Shakespeare's *Cymbeline*, and harebells are bluebells also mentioned in *Cymbeline*. Dating from the Elizabethan period, stylized knot gardens are designed in the form of a knot and contain aromatic and herbal plants.

Shakespeare's home in Stratford, New Place, has a knot garden. While in Stratford in the summer of 1945, H.D. studied the indigenous wildlife and the plants at the site of New Place. She writes to Bryher that she has spent so much time there that she has been "accepted as one of the inner circle" (letter dated July 24, [1945]; Bryher Papers). "I simply *live* in New Place Garden," she reports (letter dated August 4, [1945]; Bryher Papers). She writes her friend George Plank in a letter dated August 7, [1945?], that she fantasizes about being a tour guide and expert on botany in Shakespeare's work. George Plank Papers, Yale Collection of American Literature, Beinecke Rare Book and Manuscript Library, New Haven, Connecticut.

New Place. See note on page 144.

rosemary. See note on page 138.

Conqueror. William I of England, or William of Normandy, is also known as William the Conqueror. He was the first French king of England, ruling from 1066 to 1087.

Let Rome in Tiber melt—here is my—here is my—. Shakespeare struggles to re-member lines taken from Antony's speech to Cleopatra in the first act of Shake-speare's *Antony and Cleopatra*: "Let Rome in Tiber melt, and the wide arch / Of the ranged empire fall! Here is my space, / Kingdoms are clay." Antony reas-sures Cleopatra that he chooses her over his empire. As H.D. is checking over her manuscript, she writes to Bryher for the precise quote from the play: "Will you tell me if I have this quote right—'let Rome in Tiber sink—' I have a feeling it is 'melt.' It is that opening speech of Antony, as you know" (letter dated June 8, [1947]; Bryher Papers).

Judith . . . Hamnet. See note on **There was Elizabeth . . . not forgotten** on page 145.

To-morrow and to-morrow and to-morrow. Out, out brief candle. These famous lines are taken from the final act of Shakespeare's *Macbeth*, in which Macbeth reacts to the news of his wife's death.

When daisies pied . . . meadows with delight. These lines taken from Shakespeare's *Love's Labour's Lost* are included as "Cuckoo" in Braithwaite's anthology.

From you have I been absent in the spring, / When proud-pied April, dressed in all his trim—. These are the opening lines of Shakespeare's Sonnet 98, which is included in Braithwaite's anthology as "Absence." She has marked this poem in her copy of *Shakespeare's Sonnets* (London: Richards, 1945).

O master-mistress of my passion? This line is adapted from Shakespeare's Sonnet 20.

daisies smell-less but most quaint. This line is from *The Two Noble Kinsmen*. Braith-waite attributes the line to either Shakespeare or John Fletcher, and today the play is still thought to be a collaboration between them. See also note on **Roses, their sharp spines . . . But from it fly** on page 150.

Nor did I wonder . . . pattern of all those. These lines are also taken from Shake-speare's Sonnet 98. See also note on **lilies** on page 136.

Mary-buds begin / To ope their golden eyes. These lines are from Shakespeare's *Cymbeline*, which Braithwaite anthologizes as "Hark, Hark! the Lark."

Yes, marigolds . . . long-purples. Marigolds and king-cups are terms for a wild mari-gold, or mary-bud, mentioned in Act II of Shakespeare's *Cymbeline*. Deadmen's-fingers, or long-purples, are flowers mentioned in Act IV of Shakespeare's *Ham-let*. Telling Laertes of his sister's death, Gertrude explains that the long-purples in Ophelia's garland are called dead men's fingers by the "cold maids," who shy away from the "grosser name" given them by "liberal shepherds." See also note on **Ladysmocks . . . harebells soon** on page 145.

misereri. *Misereri* is the Latin word for pity. H.D. refers to Psalm 51, "Have mercy upon me, O God," which was set to music by countless composers and was tre-mendously popular in the Renaissance era.

I am sick, I must die. This is the penultimate line of all of the stanzas of a poem in

Thomas Nashe's play *Summer's Last Will and Testament*. See note on **Adieu, farewell . . . have mercy on us** on page 147.

Notes to pages 80–82

Thomas Nash. An Elizabethan playwright, satirist, and pamphleteer, Thomas Nashe lived from 1567 to around 1601. A controversial figure, he is best known for his prose writings and his play *Summers Last Will and Testament*. When H.D. writes of his "suspect" life, she doubtless refers to Braithwaite's note that he was expelled from school "for some youthful indiscretion" and that "he was put in prison," 794.

Marlowe. Christopher Marlowe. See note on page 142.

Raleigh. Sir Walter Raleigh. See note on page 143.

Adieu, farewell . . . have mercy on us. Lines from Nashe's *Summer's Last Will and Testament*, an excerpt from which Braithwaite entitles "In Time of Plague." H.D. quotes the entire excerpt. Braithwaite's note quotes another anthologist on the original production: "'when the play was produced it was sickly autumn, and the plague was stalking through the land[. . .] Very vividly does Nashe depict the feeling of forlorn hopelessness caused by the dolorous advent of the dreaded pestilence. . . . those pathetic stanzas, *Adieu! farewell, earth's bliss,* must have had strange significance at a time when on every side the death-bells were tolling,'" 765–66.

Helen. Nashe's poem references a figure central to the Trojan War, Helen, whose abduction by Paris sparked the war. H.D.'s mother's name was Helen, and the name recurs throughout her verse and prose writings.

Hector. Nashe's poem references Hector, the Trojan prince slain by Achilles during the Trojan War.

Thomas Nash . . . Marlowe. H.D. takes from Braithwaite that Nashe "became associated with Greene, Marlowe, and Peele," though he does not refer to them as associated with espionage, 794. With Nashe, Marlowe, Peele, Greene, Thomas Lodge and John Lyly are known today as "the University Wits."

Greene. Robert Greene (1558–1592) was an Elizabethan dramatist and prose writer who is seen today as England's first professional writer. H.D.'s reference to Greene's life as "suspect" and to the "mystery" of his death draws on Braithwaite, who writes that Greene "deserted a lovely wife, and lived a profligate live, dying, it is said, in absolute misery and poverty, from a surfeit of pickled herrings and Rhenish wine," the latter phrase a reference to Nashe's words on Greene's demise, 787.

George Peele. George Peele (1556–1596) was an Elizabethan playwright and poet best known for his plays *The Arraignment of Paris* and *The Battle of Alcazar*. Braithwaite, 794, makes reference to Peele's penchant for tavern life.

Queen Elizabeth. See note on page 143.

Tower. See note on page 145.

Give me my scallop-shell . . . thirst no more. These lines are attributed to Raleigh, and Braithwaite's note on the poem (which he entitles "His Pilgrimage") recounts that it was penned "in the Tower the night before his execution," 764.

Notes to pages 82–84

Ben Jonson. Ben Jonson was a poet and playwright who was born Ben Johnson in 1572 to a poor family and died in 1637. As H.D. notes, Jonson is known for his masques. Braithwaite's biographical note reports Jonson's "poor parentage," his Scottish ancestry, and his avocation as a means of "earning his livelihood," 791.

Michael Drayton. A poet and playwright, Michael Drayton was born in 1563 in Warwickshire, very near Shakespeare's birthplace. He is best known for his long poem *Poly-olbion*, and he died in 1631. Braithwaite's biographical note records his birthplace and the story of what H.D. refers to as "a spiteful entry" about Shakespeare's last night in a tavern with Jonson and Drayton, 784 (see note on **This is the entry . . .** on page 148).

Sir Walter Raleigh. See note on page 143.

Mary Arden. William Shakespeare's mother.

processions of Queens. Ben Jonson's *Masque of Queens*.

Queen and Huntress . . . preoccupation. This passage refers to Ben Jonson's *Cynthia's Revels*.

Tacitus . . . Terence. Tacitus and Livy were Roman historians. Plautus and Terence were Roman playwrights.

Lucy. See note on page 138.

New Place. See note on page 144.

Blow, blow . . . so unkind. See note on page 144.

This is the entry . . ." . . . there contracted." H.D. refers to the legendary story of Shakespeare's contraction of a fatal illness after a night at a tavern with Jonson and Drayton. She quotes Braithwaite's transcript of the diary of the Vicar of Stratford: "Shakespeare, Drayton, and Ben Jonson had a merry meeting and it seems drank too hard, for Shakespeare died of a feaver there contracted," 784.

Notes to page 84

Michael Drayton. See note on page 148.

Agincourt. H.D. refers to Drayton's poem about Henry V's victory at Agincourt, *The Ballad of Agincourt.*

Whether or not . . . beside the point. Here H.D. references characters from Shakespeare's *Henry IV* and *Richard II*.

Fair stood the wind for France . . . Such a King Harry. These lines are taken from Drayton's *The Ballad of Agincourt*. Braithwaite's note on the text remarks its importance as a national song; he also quotes another scholar on the relationship between Drayton's and Shakespeare's accounts: "It was not many years since the great theatrical success of *Henry V*; and the most famous of Drayton's odes may be taken as a lyrical epilogue, or rather intermezzo, by Shakespeare's countrymen," 745. Caux is the setting of Henry V's initial landing and battle at Harfleur. The Battle of Agincourt occurred on St. Crispin's Day, October 25. Shakespeare's *Henry V* features the St. Crispin's Day Speech that inspired Henry's outnumbered soldiers to fight.

Virginian Voyage. "The Virginian Voyage" is a poem by Michael Drayton.

Nymphidia . . . Queen Mab. *Nymphidia* is a poem by Michael Drayton. Here H.D. repeats the popular if controversial notion that Shakespeare's source for Oberon (in *A Midsummer Night's Dream*) and Queen Mab (in *Romeo and Juliet*) is Drayton's *Nymphidia*. Today it is unclear who influenced whom.

Notes to pages 84–85

John Webster. A Jacobean playwright, John Webster (1578/80?–1638) is best known for *The Duchess of Malfi*, from which H.D. quotes, and *The White Devil*. In the next section, H.D. will quote from Braithwaite that Webster was "a member of the Merchant Taylor's Company," 801. H.D. cites the name of a poem by Webster, "Vanitas Vanitatum", which is Latin for vanity of vanities, and she quotes two lines from the poem.

Great Plague. H.D. refers to an outbreak of the bubonic plague, in the 1660s, when St. Paul's was used to house the sick. In fact, Webster died before this outbreak. H.D. realized her error after the fact, writing to Richard Aldington in 1953, "What roughly is the date of the London plague? I am sure that I have juggled that date in my little Avon book, suggesting that Webster was deeply involved—he was certainly, but it may have been by hear-say, stories heard as a child. I did feel sorry that Pearson didn't pick on the few blunders, though there were some slight changes" (letter dated October 29, [1953]; H.D. Papers).

Strew your hair . . . and come away. Lines from Webster's *The Duchess of Malfi*, which Braithwaite entitles "The Shrouding of the Duchess of Malfi."

All the flowers of the spring / Meet to perfume our burying. Lines from Webster's "Vanitas Vanitatum," which Braithwaite extracts from *The Devil's Low Case.*

Notes to pages 85–90

Thomas Dekker. A playwright, poet, and satirist, Thomas Dekker lived from around 1572 to 1632. Braithwaite notes that he frequently collaborated with other writers and was (as H.D. quotes verbatim from Braithwaite) "one of the celebrated wits of the reign of James I," 783.

Thomas Middleton. A popular professional playwright, Thomas Middleton was born to a wealthy builder in 1580 and lived until 1627. He is best known for his revenge tragedies and for his political satire, *A Game of Chess*. H.D. quotes directly from Braithwaite when she notes that "little is known" about him and that he was "Chronologer to the City of London shortly before his death," 794. Braithwaite also writes of Middleton's collaborations with William Rowley, Philip Massinger, John Fletcher, and Ben Jonson.

John Webster. See note on page 149.

James I. King James I, England's first Scottish king and the son of Mary Stuart. He ruled England after the death of Elizabeth I, from 1603–1625.

Philip Massinger. A popular playwright in his time, Philip Massinger (1583–1640) is rarely studied today. Braithwaite stresses his collaborative ventures with other playwrights, and in this section, H.D. draws liberally from her source: that Massinger and Fletcher were "intimate friends[s]," that Massinger "was at one time page in the household of the Earl of Pembroke," that "[s]ome fifteen plays are to [Massinger's] credit," and that "Beaumont enticed [Fletcher] into authorship," 793–94, 786.

John Fletcher. See note on page 144.

Ben Jonson. See note on page 148.

Art thou poor . . . O sweet content. Lines from a collaboratively written play, *The Pleasant Comedy of Patient Grissill*, by Dekker and others. Braithwaite entitles the extract, "Sweet Content."

O, Sorrow . . . she finds a grave. Lines from Dekker's *The Noble Spanish Soldier*. Braithwaite entitles the extract, "O Sorrow, Sorrow."

The Blushing Rose and Purple Flower. The title Braithwaite attributes to lines he selected from Massinger's play *The Picture*.

Francis Beaumont. A poet and playwright, Francis Beaumont was born in Nottinghamshire in 1584 or 1585, and he lived until 1616. He is best known for his theatrical collaborations with John Fletcher.

Sir John Beaumont. Sir John Beaumont (ca. 1584–1627) was a baronet and court poet of mostly religious verse. His brother is Francis Beaumont. Braithwaite describes John Beaumont as "[a]n elder brother of the celebrated dramatist," 778. H.D. was concerned in 1952 that *By Avon River* contained an inaccurate description of the relationship between the Beaumonts, and Aldington sent her a clarification, reassuring her that the Beaumont lineage was complicated (letter dated May 12, 1952; H.D. Papers).

Roses, their sharp spines . . . But from it fly. These lines are from *The Two Noble Kinsmen*, and Braithwaite entitles this extract "A Bridal Song." Braithwaite attributes the lines to either Shakespeare or John Fletcher, and today the play is still thought to be a collaboration between them.

son of Richard Fletcher. H.D. reads in Braithwaite that John Fletcher "was son of

Dr. Richard Fletcher," 786. Richard Fletcher Jr. was chaplain to Queen Elizabeth I and later bishop of Bristol, Worcester, and then London.

Christopher Marlowe. See note on page 142.

grammar school boy from Stratford. William Shakespeare. Braithwaite's biographical note on Shakespeare mentions that Shakespeare had "a scanty Grammar school education," 796.

Luce's Dirge from *The Knight of the Burning Pestle.* "Luce's Dirge" is a song within the play *The Knight of the Burning Pestle*, which is attributed to Francis Beaumont.

Come, you whose loves are dead . . . men most true. These are the lines Braithwaite entitles "Luce's Dirge." Braithwaite extracts the song from *The Knight of the Burning Pestle*, attributed to Francis Beaumont. H.D. transcribes the entirety of his excerpt.

occult disasters . . . gold. This passage contains references to instruments used in occult practices. The crucible and philosopher's stone are used by alchemists to turn metal into gold, while the astrolabe is used by astrologers.

Doctor John Dee. See note on **Sir Edward Dyer . . . Doctor John Dee** on page 144.

The Queen. Elizabeth I of England. See note on page 143.

King James. James I of England. See note on page 150.

lulla, lulla, lullaby. See note on **Philomel, with melody** on page 145.

Then heigh ho, the holly: / This life is most jolly. Lines from Shakespeare's *As You Like It*. See also note on **Blow, blow thou winter wind . . .** on page 144.

Out, out brief candle. See note on **To-morrow. . .** on page 146.

white and purple, green and yellow. See note on **Come, you whose loves are dead . . .** on page 151.

daisies pied and violets blue. See note on **When daisies pied . . .** on page 146.

the marigold that goes to bed with the sun. Line from Shakespeare's *The Winter's Tale.*

Notes to pages 90–91

John Webster. See note on page 149.

Middleton. Thomas Middleton. See note on page 149.

Dekker. Thomas Dekker. See note on page 149.

John Donne. The preeminent metaphysical poet John Donne was born in London in 1572. Raised a Roman Catholic, he later became a Protestant minister and dean of St. Paul's. He died in 1631. His poetry was lauded by T. S. Eliot and by the New Critics. Though Braithwaite, 784, asserts that Donne became a Catholic as an adult, H.D. rightly suggests that his mother's Catholicism meant, rather, that he was Catholic as a child.

Thomas Nash. See note on page 147.

Come, come the bells do cry; / I am sick, I must die. See note on **Adieu, farewell . . .** on page 147.

Dirge of Francis Beaumont. See note on *Luce's Dirge . . .* on page 151.

Come away, come away, death . . . To weep there. Lines, as H.D. notes, from Shakespeare's *Twelfth Night*. Braithwaite anthologizes them as "A Lover's Dirge."

Notes to pages 91–93

Richard Crashaw. Like Donne, Richard Crashaw (1612?–1649) was a metaphysical poet, known chiefly for his wit and his religious verse. He was born around 1612 and lived until 1649, when he died in Loreto. In Braithwaite H.D. reads that "he was recommended to Rome by Queen Henrietta. He died soon after he became beneficiary of the Basilica Church of Our Lady of Loreto," 782. Though Crashaw's father was a Puritan, Crashaw himself apparently adhered to a Laudian belief in common ground between the Church of England and the Catholic Church until he adopted Catholicism in the 1640s when the English Civil War forced him into exile.

Supposed Mistress and *Shepherd's Hymn.* Abbreviated titles of two poems by Crashaw in Braithwaite's anthology.

Queen Henrietta Maria. The Catholic wife of King Charles I, who ruled England from 1625 to 1649.

Basilica Church of Our Lady of Loreto. The Basilica della Santa Casa is the reputed birthplace of the Virgin Mary, which according to legend was spirited away from Nazareth by angels.

Saint Teresa. St. Teresa of Ávila was a sixteenth-century Spanish mystic and saint. She belonged to the Carmelite order. H.D. refers to Teresa's purported vision of a seraph stabbing her in the heart.

Love, thou art absolute, sole Lord / Of life and death. H.D. quotes the first two lines of Crashaw's poem Braithwaite entitles "A Hymn to the Name and Honour of the Admirable Saint Teresa."

The Flaming Heart. Poem by Crashaw entitled "The Flaming Heart Upon the Book and Picture of Saint Teresa," a selection of which Braithwaite includes in his anthology. H.D. follows Braithwaite in dubbing it *The Flaming Heart*.

Haste therefore each degree / To welcome destiny. See note on **Adieu, farewell . . .** on page 147.

Thomas Nash. See note on page 147.

Live in these conquering leaves . . . self and sin. Lines from Crashaw's poem H.D. refers to as *The Flaming Heart*.

Notes to pages 93–94

George Herbert. A devotional poet and Anglican priest, George Herbert lived from 1593 to 1633. He was a close friend of John Donne's. Braithwaite reports that "[h]is life is said to have been pure and saint-like," 789.

John Donne. See note on page 151.

Edward, Lord Herbert of Cherbury. As H.D. notes, Edward Herbert (1582–1648) is George Herbert's older brother. He was a courtier, soldier, philosopher, and poet. Braithwaite includes two of his poems.

Roman convert at Loreto. Richard Crashaw. See note on page 152.

Romanized Dean of Saint Paul's. John Donne. See note on page 151.

I struck the board . . . replied *'My Lord.'* H.D. transcribes the entirety of George Herbert's "The Collar."

Notes to pages 94–95

John Ford. H.D., following Braithwaite's error, has confused the major poet and playwright John Ford with the musician Thomas Ford. John Ford (1586?– 1639/53?) was a playwright best known for *'Tis Pity She's a Whore.* Braithwaite attributes to Thomas Ford a song taken from John Ford's play *The Lover's Melancholy* and two songs taken from John Ford's play *The Broken Heart,* 787. In a note, he attributes the music of the hymn H.D. quotes to Thomas Ford.

Guests. As H.D. observes, Braithwaite, 765, does not assign authorship to the lyric, though he notes that Thomas Ford wrote the music.

George Herbert. See note on page 152.

Yet if His Majesty . . . in the manger. The entirety of the poem known as "Guests"; see note on *Guests* on page 153.

Notes to pages 95–99

Richard Rowland. Richard Rowlands (Verstegen) was a painter and printer who lived from about 1550 to 1640. H.D. draws on Braithwaite's biographical note when she writes that he was "educated at Oxford, and becoming a Roman Catholic took up his residence at Antwerp, where he prospered as a printer," 796. In a note, Braithwaite also explains further, "He removed soon after [attending Oxford], to Antwerp, and abandoning his English name, assumed the surname of his Dutch grandfather, Verstegen. In Antwerp he set up a press; wrote books, some of the cuts for which he engraved with his own hand," 763.

Our Blessed Lady's Lullaby. The only poem by Rowlands included in Braithwaite's anthology. H.D. does not quote from this poem.

Guests. See note on page 153.

Robert Southwell. Robert Southwell (1561–1595) was a Jesuit metaphysical poet. H.D. draws on Braithwaite's biographical note: "[I]n 1585 he was appointed Prefect of the English Jesuits' College in Rome; was subsequently returned to England as a missionary, where after three years imprisonment he suffered as a martyr at Tyburn, Febrary, 1595," 799. He was canonized as a saint in 1970. Braithwaite's note on "The Burning Babe" recounts Jonson's comment to Drummond of Hawthornden "that he would have been content to destroy his own writings if he could have written this poem," 763.

The Burning Babe. Poem by Robert Southwell.

As I in hoary . . . it was Christmas Day. H.D. extracts the first eight and last four lines of Southwell's poem, "The Burning Babe."

Francis Quarles. A poet and dramatist, Francis Quarles lived from 1592 to 1644. He is known for his poetry but also his volume of religious emblems. H.D. draws on Braithwaite's biographical note: "Was successively cupbearer to the Queen of Bohemia, Chronologer to the City of London, and secretary in Ireland to Archbishop Usher. On the breaking out of the Rebellion in 1641, he fled to England, where writings of a royalistic flavour and his attachment to Charles attracted the wrath of Parliament, who sequestrated his estate and plundered his books. The poet never recovered from the blow, which sent him to his grave," 795.

Elizabeth of Bohemia. See note on **Elizabeth . . . Frederick** on page 137.

My soul, sit thou . . . crowns the play. H.D. quotes the entirety of Quarles' Epigram 15.

William Strode. William Strode (1601?–1645) was a priest, a poet, and a playwright. Braithwaite lists Strode in the index but offers no biographical note.

Music. This is the title Braithwaite gives to a poem by William Strode.

O, lull me . . . soul for harmony. H.D. quotes the last stanza of Strode's "Music."

Sir John Beaumont. See note on page 150.

Francis Beaumont. See note on page 150.

John Fletcher. See note on page 144.

Of His Dear Son, Gervase. Poem by Sir John Beaumont.

Dear Lord, receive my son . . . every step I go. Lines from John Beaumont's poem, "Of His Dear Son, Gervase."

Phineas Fletcher. Phineas Fletcher was a poet who lived from 1582 to 1650, best known, as Braithwaite notes, 787, for his epic *The Purple Island*. Braithwaite notes as well that he was part of a literary family that included his brother Giles Fletcher and his cousin, the playwright John Fletcher (see note on page 144).

Drop, drop slow tears. Poem by Phineas Fletcher, anthologized by Braithwaite as "The Litany."

Drop, drop slow tears . . . through my tears. H.D. quotes the entirety of Phineas Fletcher's poem.

Giles Fletcher. Giles Fletcher (1586?–1623) was a minor religious poet, brother of the poet Phineas Fletcher, and cousin of the playwright John Fletcher. H.D. draws directly on Braithwaite's biographical note: "He took orders, but on account of the lack of appreciation on the part of his rural parishioners, 'grief,' as Fuller says, 'caused his early dissolution,'" 786.

It was to Drummond . . . Masques. See note on **Robert Southwell** on page 153.

William Drummond. William Drummond of Hawthornden (1585–1649) was a Scottish lyric poet. H.D. takes from Braithwaite's biographical note that "Drummond's sonnets, Hazlitt thought as perfect as any in the language," 785.

Flowers of Sion. Book-length sonnet-sequence by William Drummond.

John the Baptist. Figure in the Bible who baptized Jesus Christ.

'All ye whose hopes rely ... *Repent.*' H.D. records these lines in a sonnet from William Drummond's *Flowers of Sion*, which Braithwaite entitles "Saint John Baptist."

Henry King. English Jacobean poet. H.D. borrows from Braithwaite's biographical note, which relates that King was "Bishop of Chichester, and friend of Isaak Walton, Sandys, and Ben Jonson," 792. King's father immediately preceded John Donne as dean of St. Paul's, and both Donne and Jonson influenced King's poetry.

Exequy. Abbreviated title of Henry King's poem "Exequy on His Wife."

Sleep on, my Love, in thy cold bed / Never to be disquieted. Lines from Henry King's "Exequy on His Wife."

James Shirley. James Shirley was a Caroline playwright who lived from 1596 to 1666. He probably converted to Catholicism in his late twenties while serving as headmaster of St. Albans grammar school. He became a playwright when Charles I took the throne. H.D. draws on Braithwaite's biographical note: "[Shirley] was the last of the great group of dramatists who immediately followed Shakespeare. Intended for the Church, he became a Roman Catholic, and earned his living as a schoolmaster," 798.

Is the year only lost to me? See note on **I struck the board ...** on page 153.

George Herbert. See note on page 152.

Queen Henrietta Maria. See note on page 152.

Richard Crashaw. See note on page 152.

The glories of our blood ... in their dust. H.D. quotes the entirety of what Braithwaite entitles "Death the Leveller." It is an excerpt from James Shirley's mid-seventeenth-century play *The Contention of Ajax and Ulysses*. Braithwaite's note on the text identifies this poem as Shirley's finest, and not "imitative" like many of his other verses, 766.

Notes to pages 99–101

Robert Herrick. Robert Herrick (1591–1674) is a poet best known for his volume of secular and religious poetry entitled *Hesperides*. H.D. draws liberally on Braithwaite's biographical note, which relates that he "was son of a goldsmith in Cheapside. Educated at St. John's, Cambridge, he was presented in 1629 with the living of Dean Prior, in Devonshire. For being an ardent Royalist in 1647 he was ejected from the living, and returning to London he celebrated the event in verse. His poems for the most part were published anonymously, but in 1648 he issued a collection of them under the title of Hesperides. In 1662 he was restored to Dean

Prior, where he died and was buried," 789. (His expulsion from his position was actually in 1647, not 1648.)

George Herbert. See note on page 152.

Away: take heed, / I will abroad. See note on **I struck the board . . .** on page 153.

Fair daffodils . . . with you along. H.D. quotes the first stanza of Robert Herrick's "To Daffodils."

Welcome, maids of honour . . . girls neglected. H.D. quotes the entirety of Robert Herrick's "To Violets."

Pembroke's page. Philip Massinger. See note on page 150.

Sir John Beaumont's brother. Francis Beaumont. See note on page 150.

Julia . . . Anthea. Female figures to whom poems by Robert Herrick are addressed. H.D.'s late novel *Bid Me to Live,* ed. Caroline Zilboorg (Gainesville: University Press of Florida, 2011), takes the first line of Herrick's poem "To Anthea" as its title and Herrick's Julia as the name of its protagonist.

Royalists. Defenders of the Crown in the period surrounding the English Civil War.

Bid me to live . . . heart to thee. Opening lines of Robert Herrick's "To Anthea, Who May Command Him Anything."

James, Charles, the Commonwealth and Charles II. In order, rulers of England: King James I (who reigned 1567–1625), Charles I (1625–1649), the Interregnum Commonwealth government (1649–1660), and Charles II (1660–1685).

Sir Walter Raleigh. See note on page 143.

Say to the Court, it glows / And shines like rotten wood. See note on **Go, Soul, the Body's guest . . .** on page 142.

Prospero . . . *The Tempest*. Prospero is a character in Shakespeare's *The Tempest*; see also note on page 136.

Now my charms are all o'erthrown, / And what strength I have's mine own. Prospero's lines from the epilogue to *The Tempest*.

Hesperides. Title of a 1648 collection of poems by Robert Herrick.

Charles II. Charles II of England, who ruled from 1660–1685 following the Interregnum.

Notes to pages 101–104

Robert Herrick. See note on page 155.

Bid me to live. . . . See note on page 156.

Richard Lovelace. Known today as a "Cavalier poet" for poems (as H.D. notes) such as "To Althea, from Prison" and "To Lucasta, Going to the Wars," Richard Lovelace lived from 1618 to 1657. He was a soldier as well and endured two terms of imprisonment stemming from his Royalist views during the English Civil War. Braithwaite's biographical note, 793, stresses his military service and political difficulties.

Edmund Waller. A poet, translator, and member of Parliament, Edmund Waller lived from 1606 to 1687. During the English Civil War, Waller was tried for a Royalist plot but allowed to go into exile after giving testimony against his fellow conspirators. Braithwaite, 801, describes this episode in Waller's life in some detail, and H.D. notes his imprisonment.

Sir Philip Sidney. See note on page 143.

Althea from Prison . . . *Lucasta.* References to poems by Richard Lovelace.

Tell me not, Sweet . . . Honour more. H.D. quotes the entirety of Richard Lovelace's "To Lucasta, Going to the Wars."

Go, lovely Rose—. . . . sweet and fair. H.D. quotes the entirety of Edmund Waller's "Go, Lovely Rose."

Sir John Suckling. A "Cavalier poet" in the court of Charles I, Sir John Suckling lived from 1609 to about 1641. H.D. notes, following Braithwaite, Suckling's reputation as a libertine. H.D. quotes selectively from Braithwaite's biographical note: "In 1631, he joined the army of Gustavus Adolphus; and in 1639 raised an army of an hundred horse, leading them in battle between the Scotch and royal army. His life was one of wild and reckless dissipation. A loyalist, he was accused of scheming to save Strafford's life, and fleeing from England, he put an end to his disordered life in Paris," 800.

Gustavus Adolphus. Gustav II Adolf of Sweden, who reigned from 1611 to 1632. Gustavus Adolphus was king during the Thirty Years' War, a conflict in which Sir John Suckling participated.

I could not love thee, Dear, so much / Loved I not Honour more. See note on **Tell me not, Sweet . . .** on page 157.

Some bays, perchance. . . . the woman here. H.D. quotes the final stanza of Sir John Suckling's poem "Sonnet III." Braithwaite anthologizes the poem as "A Doubt of Martyrdom."

Thomas Carew. A "Cavalier poet" and courtier, Thomas Carew lived from 1594 or 1595 until 1640. As H.D. notes, following Braithwaite, he, like Suckling, had a reputation as a libertine. Braithwaite describes him as "fonder of 'roving after hounds and hawks' than diligently pursuing his studies," and H.D. draws as well on Braithwaite's description of his duties to Charles I: "cupbearer in ordinary and gentleman to the privy chamber," 780.

Charles I. Charles I of England, who ruled Britain from 1625 to 1649, when he was executed by the leaders of the Commonwealth during the English Civil Wars.

Song. "A Song" is a poem by Thomas Carew.

Ask me no more . . . bosom dies. H.D. reproduces the first and last stanzas of Thomas Carew's "A Song."

Henry Constable. Henry Constable (1562–1613) is best known as the author of one of the first Elizabethan sonnet sequences, *Diana*. Braithwaite's note, 708, on the text of the poem H.D. quotes informs his readers that Constable's lyrics appeared in the 1605 song book, *First Book of Songs and Airs*.

Diaphenia. Reference to Henry Constable's poem "Damelus' Song to his Diaphenia."

Diaphenia, like to all things blessèd . . . love me. H.D. transcribes the final stanza of Henry Constable's poem "Damelus' Song to his Diaphenia."

Sir William Davenant. A playwright and poet, William Davenant lived from 1606 until 1668. Though he claimed to be Shakespeare's illegitimate son, he was not, though he may have been his godson. Braithwaite's brief biographical note for Davenant reads that he "was godson of Shakespeare," 782, and his note for Carew relates that "[h]e was the intimate associate of Suckling and Davenant," 780.

Song. Braithwaite entitles Davenant's poem "Aubade" and places it first in the volume, but his note on the text, 687, records the title as "Song."

The lark now leaves his wat'ry nest. . . . at your eyes. H.D. quotes the first stanza of Davenant's poem that Braithwaite entitles "Aubade."

Notes to pages 104–110

Sir Henry Wotton. A diplomat and educator, Sir Henry Wotton (1568–1639) also wrote verse. He was a close friend of John Donne's. H.D. draws selectively from Braithwaite's biographical note, which relates that "[a]fter leaving Oxford he travelled for eight or nine years in France, Germany, and Italy, and on his return to England became secretary to the Earl of Essex. Wotton returned to Florence when Essex's political fortunes were broken, and was sent by the Grand Duke on a secret mission to James VI of Scotland. When James became King of England, he was taken into favour and thrice sent as ambassador to Venice, and also to some of the German States. Wotton's services in behalf of James' daughter, the unfortunate Queen of Bohemia, to whom he was affectionately attached, and whom he celebrated in the best of his poems, has become a noble episode in his career," 802.

Queen Elizabeth. Elizabeth I. See note on page 143.

Elizabeth of Bohemia. See note on **Elizabeth . . . Frederick** on page 137.

You meaner beauties . . . of her kind. H.D. includes the entirety of Wotton's poem, "On His Mistress, the Queen of Bohemia." Braithwaite's note on the text offers the following context: "The lady it praises was Elizabeth, daughter of James I. and wife of the Elector Palatine Frederick V., unhappily chosen King of Bohemia, September 19, 1619. Sir Henry . . . was employed on several embassies on behalf of this unhappy Queen, whose reign in Prague lasted but one winter," 706.

Philomel. See note on **Philomel, with melody . . .** on page 145.

another Elizabeth. Elizabeth I. See note on page 143.

Robert Devereux. A courtier, patron, and poet, Robert Devereux, second Earl of Essex, lived from 1565 until 1601. Braithwaite describes him as the "unfortunate favourite of Queen Elizabeth" in his brief biographical note, a dubious honor he attained as her interest in Sir Walter Raleigh began to diminish, 783. Devereux was eventually executed for treason.

A Passion of My Lord of Essex. Reference to a poem by Devereux. H.D. draws on Braithwaite's note on this poem: "This 'passion' is said to have been enclosed in a letter to Queen Elizabeth from Ireland in 1599," 753.

Tower. See note on page 145.

Raleigh's *Go, Soul, the Body's guest.* See note on page 142.

Her **thoughts and mine . . . know no cause.** H.D. quotes the final quatrain and couplet of a sonnet by Robert Devereux that Braithwaite entitles "The Ways on Earth."

Francis Davison. H.D. misreads Braithwaite's note on the minor poet Francis Davison (ca. 1575–ca. 1619), for it is his father, William Davison, who conveyed Mary Stuart's execution warrant. Braithwaite's note reads as follows: "Educated at Grey's Inn; eldest son of William Davison, privy councillor and secretary of State to Queen Elizabeth, who was disgraced for carrying her warrant of execution of Mary Stuart to the Council. Davison and his father were adherents of the Earl of Essex, and with him their political fortunes were broken," 783.

Mary Stuart. See note on page 138.

My only star. H.D. refers to the poem by Davison that Braithwaite entitles "Ode."

O cruel tiger! . . . will cure me. H.D. transcribes the final stanza of Francis Davison's "Ode."

Essex. Robert Devereux. See note on page 159.

the Queen. Elizabeth I. See note on page 143.

Sir Walter Raleigh. See note on page 143.

So when thou hast . . . can kill. The final stanza of the poem attributed to Sir Walter Raleigh entitled "The Lie." See note on **Go, Soul . . . the World the lie** on page 142.

Thomas Campion. A musician and poet, Thomas Campion lived from 1567 to 1620, and he is best known (as H.D. remarks) for his books of airs. H.D. takes from Braithwaite that "[w]ith Shakespeare and Herrick, he is . . . one of the finest lyrists of Elizabethan poetry," 780. He also notes that Campion published four Song Books and that he sought "to prove that English poetry was faulty in not following the classics." H.D.'s suggestion that Campion wrote airs for Shakespeare's plays is unfounded.

Herrick. Robert Herrick. See note on page 155.

Ben Jonson's familiar *Drink to me only with thine eyes.* H.D. refers to the opening line of Ben Jonson's "To Celia." Braithwaite's note to the poem points out that it is translated from Philostratus, 703.

Catullus' *Vivamus mea Lesbia, atque amemus*. Braithwaite's note, 709, to Thomas Campion's "Vivamus Mea Lesbia, Aique Amemus"—often anthologized as "My Sweetest Lesbia"—identifies its source in this poem by Catullus.

But, soon as once set is our little light, / Then must we sleep one ever-during night. H.D. quotes the last two lines of the first stanza of Thomas Campion's "Vivamus Mea Lesbia, Aique Amemus."

In imagine pertransit homo. A poem by Thomas Campion, frequently anthologized as "Follow thy Fair Sun, Unhappy Shadow."

Follow thy fair sun . . . still disdainèd. H.D. quotes four of the five stanzas Braithwaite includes of Campion's "In Imagine Pertransit Homo."

George Chapman. A poet and soldier, George Chapman lived from 1559 or 1560 to 1634. As H.D. indicates, following Braithwaite's note, he is best known for having produced the first English translation of Homer, 781.

Hero and Leander. Long poem by Christopher Marlowe. Braithwaite's biographical note on Marlowe reads that Marlowe penned "parts of a fine poem, Hero and Leander, which George Chapman finished," 793.

Muses that Sing. George Chapman's sonnet "A Coronet for his Mistress, Philosophy" is anthologized by Braithwaite as "Muses That Sing."

Abjure those joys . . . god is blind. H.D. prints the last quatrain and couplet of George Chapman's sonnet that Braithwaite entitles "Muses That Sing."

Follow still . . . still disdainèd. See note on Follow thy fair sun . . . on page 160.

Dante. Dante Alighieri (1265–1321) is the medieval Italian poet best known for his epic *Divine Comedy*, comprising *Inferno*, *Purgatorio*, and *Paradiso*. In the late 1940s, H.D. is reading and translating Dante's *Vita Nuova*. Handwritten marginalia in her copy of *The Tempest* indicates that she was identifying links between the two texts.

Come away, come away, Death. Line adapted from Shakespeare's *Twelfth Night*. See note on page 152.

Fair Daffodils, we weep to see. See note on Fair daffodils . . . with you along on page 156.

Yet stab at thee that will, / No stab the soul can kill. See note on Go, Soul . . . on page 142.

strown . . . on my black coffin. Line adapted from Shakespeare's *Twelfth Night*. See note on *Come away, come away, Death . . .* on page 152.

Come, come, the bells . . . I must die. See note on Adieu, farewell on page 147.

Christopher Marlowe. See note on page 142. Here H.D. draws on Braithwaite's biographical note that reads in part, "Tamburlaine the Great, his first great drama, was performed in 1588; this was followed rapidly in the next few years by three other plays, Doctor Faustus, The Jew of Malta, and Edward II, which made him the first great dramatist in English literature, and the master whose influence is shown in Shakespeare's early plays. Marlowe's life was wild and reckless, and in 1593 he was killed in a tavern brawl in Deptford, the particulars of which have never been quite understood," 793. H.D. also refers to Ben Jonson's assessment of Marlowe's "mighty line."

Tamburlaine the Great. Play by Christopher Marlowe.

Doctor Faustus. Play by Christopher Marlowe.

Is this the face . . . towers of Ilium. A reference to famous lines about Helen of Troy from Christopher Marlowe's *Doctor Faustus.*

Helen make me immortal with a kiss. Another line from Christopher Marlowe's *Doctor Faustus.*

Blackfriars Playhouse. H.D. refers to a theater in Elizabethan London where Shakespeare's company performed.

ghost in *Hamlet.* Reference to the ghost of Hamlet's father in Shakespeare's play. Shakespeare is reputed to have played this part.

Adam, Orlando's old retainer in *As You Like It.* Adam is Orlando's servant in Shakespeare's *As You Like It,* one of H.D.'s childhood favorites. Shakespeare is rumored to have played Adam.

The Jew of Malta and *Edward II.* Plays by Christopher Marlowe.

The Merchant of Venice . . . Henry V. Plays by Shakespeare.

This royal throne of kings . . . this England. Famous lines by John of Gaunt in act 2 of Shakespeare's *Richard II.*

"a merry meeting . . . contracted." See note on **This is the entry . . .** on page 148.

Elizabethan age . . . the Restoration. Eras in the history of English theater, which coincide with the reign of successive monarchs: the ages of Elizabeth I (1558–1603); James I (1603–1625); Charles I (1625–1649); the Interregnum (1649–1660), during which the monarchy was abolished and theaters were closed; and Charles II (1660–1685), when the monarchy was restored to the throne.

Lovelace. Richard Lovelace. See note on page 156.

Waller. Edmund Waller. See note on page 157.

Suckling. Sir John Suckling. See note on page 157.

Thomas Carew. See note on page 157.

John Milton. John Milton (1608–1674) was a major poet and prose writer who worked under Oliver Cromwell for the Commonwealth during the Interregnum. He is best known for his epic *Paradise Lost.* This passage of "The Guest" was added after H.D. wrote the holograph version. Braithwaite's preface offers the following explanation for the exclusion of Milton from his anthology: "Milton,

I have not included, for in my judgment his muse is not Elizabethan, though something more that was strong and independent enough in its genius to create a new dawn out of the Elizabethan nightfall," n.p.

Notes to pages 110–113

John Lyly. A playwright, prose writer, and poet, John Lyly lived from 1554 until 1606. He is best known, as H.D. notes, for his *Euphues*.

Euphues . . . Humour. This passage refers to the book for which John Lyly is best known. Euphuism is a prose style developed by Lyly that features affected and excessive rhetorical and poetic devices. H.D. learns from Braithwaite that Lyly was "ridiculed by his contemporaries, especially Shakespeare in Love's Labour's Lost, and Jonson in Every Man Out of His Humour," 793.

What bird so sings . . . in the spring. H.D. transcribes here an excerpt from John Lyly's play *Campaspe*, which Braithwaite anthologies as "Spring's Welcome."

Thomas Heywood. A playwright and actor, Thomas Heywood lived from around 1573 until 1641. Heywood not only wrote and acted in plays, but he also was a shareholder in a theatrical company, and his best known work is a prose defense of his profession, *An Apology for Actors*. It is from Braithwaite that H.D. learns that Heywood authored "part or whole of 220 plays, of which twenty-three have been preserved" and that "[h]is characteristic excellence was in homely scenes," 790.

Pack clouds, away . . . I'll borrow. H.D. includes the first stanza of an excerpt from Heywood's *The Rape of Lucrece* that Braithwaite entitles "Matin-Song."

Francis Bacon. A major statesman, prose writer, and thinker, Francis Bacon was born into a prominent family in 1561 and lived until 1626. Braithwaite's biographical note mentions the works that H.D. lists in her discussion and refers to Bacon as "[u]ndoubtedly the greatest of modern philosophers," 777.

The world's a bubble . . . born, to die? H.D. quotes the first and last stanzas of the only poem Braithwaite includes by Francis Bacon, which he entitles "The World." It is taken from Bacon's *Reliquia Wottonianae*.

Webster. John Webster. See note on page 149.

Middleton. Thomas Middleton. See note on page 149.

Mary. Mary Stuart, Queen of Scots. See note on page 138.

Dante. See note on page 160.

Inferno. Part of Dante's *Divine Comedy*. See note on **Dante** on page 160.

Purgatorio. Part of Dante's *Divine Comedy*. See note on **Dante** on page 160.

Duchess of Malfi. Play by John Webster.

Mad World my Masters. Play by Thomas Middleton.

Sophocles. Ancient Greek playwright of the fifth century B.C.E., best known for *Oedipus the King*.

Dekker. Thomas Dekker. See note on page 149.

Ford. John Ford. See note on page 153.

Massinger. Philip Massinger. See note on page 150.

Santa Maria Maggiore. The Basilica di Santa Maria Maggiore is a church in Rome, Italy. H.D. probably means to refer to Beatrice's church, Santa Margherita dei Cerchi in Florence, where Dante reputedly first saw Beatrice in 1274.

Trinita. Santa Trinita is another church in Florence, Italy.

Simonetta of Botticelli. Many Italian Renaissance artists, including Botticelli (1445–1510), painted portraits of this Italian noblewoman, Simonetta Vespuchi, celebrated for her beauty.

John Donne. See note on page 151.

poor corse. The line from Shakespeare's *Twelfth Night* reads "My poor corse, where my bones shall be thrown." See note on **Come away, come away, death . . .** on page 152.

Where I am clad in black / The token of my wrack. Lines from a poem by Thomas Lodge that Braithwaite anthologizes as "A Madrigal."

Thomas Lodge. A prolific Elizabethan playwright and physician, Thomas Lodge lived from 1558 until he died in 1625 tending plague victims. Braithwaite notes that Lodge was a physician, 792.

After death, when we are gone, / Joy and pleasure is there none. Final lines from a poem by Thomas Lodge that Braithwaite anthologizes as "Whilst Youthful Sports Are Lasting."

Accurst be Love . . . joys are pains. Final stanza of "Accurst Be Love!" by Thomas Lodge.

Notes to pages 113–114

Sir Edward Dyer. See note on **Sir Edward Dyer . . . Doctor John Dee** on page 144.

Sir Thomas Wyatt. Sir Thomas Wyatt (1503–1542) was a poet and diplomat in the court of Henry VIII. Braithwaite, 802, relates that Wyatt fell out of favor with Henry VIII because of his connection to Anne Boleyn but was restored to the court later in his life.

the Queen. Elizabeth I. See note on page 143.

Henry VIII. Henry VIII of England ruled England from 1509 to 1547. Elizabeth I was his daughter with Anne Boleyn.

Horace. Horace (65–68 B.C.E.) was a major Roman poet, best known today for his lyrical *Odes*. Braithwaite's note on the poem H.D. cites draws the connection between Horace and Wyatt: "It is one of the most elegant amatory Odes in our language. It is as beautifully arranged in all its parts as any of the odes of Horace," 725.

My lute awake! . . . I have done. H.D. transcribes here the first stanza of the poem by Sir Thomas Wyatt that Braithwaite entitles "To His Lute."

Eleanor of Aquitaine. Queen Consort of France while married to Louis VII of

France, then of England while married to Henry II of England. H.D. will discuss below her reputed "Court of Love," which promoted troubadours and courtly love. As Friedman notes, H.D.'s understanding of Eleanor of Aquitaine's "Court of Love" comes from her reading of Denis de Rougemont's *Love in the Western World*, trans. Montgomery Belgion (New York: Pantheon, 1940; repr. 1956).

Richard Lion-Heart. Richard I of England, son of Eleanor of Aquitaine and King Henry II of England, became king upon the death of his father and ruled England from 1189 to 1199.

O Richard, O mon roi, / L'univers t'abandonne. Lines from an eighteenth-century French opera by André Grétry and Michel-Jean Sedaine entitled *Richard Coeur de lion*, or *Richard the Lion-Hearted*. In a letter to Richard Aldington, H.D. confesses her embarrassment that she had thought the lines were Elizabethan (letter dated May 24, 1949; H.D. Papers).

Saracens. A term for Muslims during the medieval Crusades. H.D. fretted about this historical error. In a letter to George Plank, she regrets her "dreadful mistake" that "Richard Lion-heart was not captured by Saracens" (letter dated July 9, [1949]; George Plank Papers). Richard Aldington had corrected the error, explaining that it was in fact the Austrians who had held him for ransom (letter dated May 31, 1949; H.D. Papers).

Ben Jonson. See note on page 148.

Masque of Queens. A masque by Ben Jonson.

Samuel Daniel with his brother John. A playwright and poet, Samuel Daniel lived from around 1562 or 1563 until 1619. H.D. reads in Braithwaite's biographical note that Samuel Daniel "compos[ed] Court Masques which for a time rivalled those of Ben Jonson," 782. He also explains that his brother, John Daniel, was a musician in the court of Charles I.

William Browne. William Browne (1590/91–1645?) was a pastoral poet strongly influenced by Spenser. Braithwaite notes that he was "[e]ducated at Oxford and the Inner Temple," 779.

Edmund Spenser. See note on page 143.

Nicholas Breton. A prolific pastoral poet and prose writer, Nicholas Breton (1554/55–1626?) was, like William Browne, strongly influenced by Spenser.

Globe Theatre. The first Globe Theatre was built at the end of the sixteenth-century by Shakespeare's players. After it burned, a second Globe Theatre was built in 1614.

Greenwich Palace. Henry VII's favorite residence and the birthplace of Henry VIII, Greenwich Palace was also Elizabeth I's summer home.

Tower. See note on page 145.

Fear no more the heat ... come to dust. Lines from act 4 of Shakespeare's *Cymbeline*. Braithwaite includes them under the title, "Fidele."

Notes to pages 114–115

mulberry. H.D. refers first to a mulberry tree thought to have been planted by Shakespeare in the gardens of New Place. The 1756 legend that the tree was sold for firewood spurred a scramble for relics of the tree. She links this tree to one in the ancient Greek myth of Pyramus and Thisbe, which is performed in Shakespeare's *A Midsummer Night's Dream*.

Cynthia. See note on **Queen and Huntress** on page 148.

Cynthia now . . . no *Wall* between. These are references to Shakespeare's *A Midsummer Night's Dream*. Wall and Thisbe are characters in the play within the play performed by Bottom and his fellow players.

Fear no more the frown . . . come to dust. See note on **Fear no more . . .** on page 164.

Miracles of the Coventry Corpus Christi. H.D. refers to a cycle of medieval mystery plays known as Coventry Corpus Christi Pageants.

the king broke faith. H.D. refers to Henry VIII's break with the pope and Catholicism in the 1530s. His divorce from his first wife, Catherine of Aragon, resulted in his excommunication in 1533, and he placed himself at the head of the Church of England in 1534.

Notes to pages 115–117

Globe Theatre. See note on page 164.

Portia's caskets. The reference is to Portia in Shakespeare's *The Merchant of Venice*.

For the Capulet . . . violet. The reference is to Shakespeare's *Romeo and Juliet*.

the famous speech . . . Saviour. The reference is to Shakespeare's *Henry V*.

Malvolio in *Twelfth Night*. Malvolio is a character in Shakespeare's *Twelfth Night*.

Francis Bacon. See note on page 162.

Aeschylus. Ancient Greek playwright of the sixth century B.C.E., best known for his *Oresteia*.

Sophocles. See note on page 162.

Prince of Denmark. Reference to the title character of Shakespeare's *Hamlet*.

Aristotle. Aristotle is a major ancient Greek philosopher of the fourth century B.C.E., best known for his prolific writings on a wide range of topics and as a pupil of Plato.

katharsis. Aristotle discusses in his *Poetics* the cathartic effect of tragedy on the audience.

Fear no more the lightning-flash . . . come to dust. See note on **Fear no more . . .** on page 164.

Notes to pages 117–118

We know . . . Imogen. A reference to Shakespeare's *Cymbeline*.

Mary had sought . . . her sister, Mary. H.D. refers to Mary I of England (Mary Tudor, known as "Bloody Mary"), who ruled from 1553 to 1558; Elizabeth I was her half-sister and her successor. In her short reign, Mary I attempted to restore Catholicism to England and persecuted Protestants; when Elizabeth took the throne, she reversed Mary's acts and returned the country to her father's Protestantism.

Webster. John Webster. See note on page 149.

Middleton. Thomas Middleton. See note on page 149.

Dekker. Thomas Dekker. See note on page 149.

Ford. John Ford. See note on page 153.

Massinger. Philip Massinger. See note on page 150.

Let Rome in Tiber melt **. . . Cleopatras.** References to characters and a line from Shakespeare's *Antony and Cleopatra*. See note on page 146.

the great Queen. Elizabeth I. See note on page 143.

Chaucer. Geoffrey Chaucer (1343–1400) was an English medieval courtier and poet, best known for his *Canterbury Tales*.

Henry V. A play by Shakespeare.

Henry VI. A play by Shakespeare.

Richard III. A play by Shakespeare.

Henry VII. Henry VII of England ruled from 1485 to 1509. He was the father of Henry VIII, who succeeded him.

John Skelton. The poet John Skelton lived from around 1463 to 1529. He is best known for his invention of Skeltonic verse, consisting of a series of short lines of three to six words that retain the same end rhyme until a new set of rhyming lines begins. His time in Henry VII's court was spent as tutor to Henry VIII.

Henry VIII. See note on page 163.

There is Thomas, Lord Vaux . . . jester. These are sixteenth-century English poets associated with the court of Henry VII.

Provence troubadours. H.D. discusses the role of troubadours at some length in "The Guest." See note on **Mary . . . The trouvères . . .** on page 141.

England's fifth queen, the mother of Richard I. Eleanor of Aquitaine. See note on page 163.

School of Love. See note on **Eleanor of Aquitaine** on page 163.

Now cease, my lute . . . I have done. See note on **Fear no more . . .** on page 164.

Notes to pages 118–120

Edward VI. Edward VI of England, son of Henry VIII, ruled England from 1547 to 1553. Mary I was his successor.

Mary. Mary I of England. See note on **Mary had sought . . .** on page 166.

that other Edward who with his brother Richard. Edward V of England ruled for a few months in 1483 at the age of 13. H.D. refers to the belief that Edward V and his brother were executed by Richard III, who then became king.

Tower. See note on page 145.

Mary Tudor. Mary I. See note on **Mary had sought . . .** on page 166.

William of Normandy. See note on **Conqueror** on page 145.

Caedmon. Cædmon was an early English Anglo-Saxon poet who lived during the seventh century, known for his *Cædmon's Hymn*.

Cynewulf. Cynewulf was an early English Anglo-Saxon poet who lived around the ninth century, known for his religious poetry.

King Lear. A play by Shakespeare.

Cymbeline. A play by Shakespeare.

Holy Wars. A reference to the medieval Crusades.

Richard Lion-Heart. See note on page 164.

Drake . . . Magellan. These men were all European explorers in the fifteenth through seventeenth centuries.

Elizabeth. Elizabeth I. See note on page 143.

Augustine. Here H.D. conflates two Augustines. St. Augustine of Hippo is the most famous, the philosopher and Christian theologian from the Roman territory of what is now Algeria who lived from 354 to 430. Augustine of Hippo is a Church Father and is known for his writings, *City of God* and *Confessions*. Augustine of Canterbury is the sixth-century monk who was sent to Britain to convert the Anglo-Saxons to Christianity. He converted the English King Æthelberht to Christianity, founded the English Church, and in 597 became the first Archbishop of Canterbury.

Simon de Montford . . . Church of Provence. H.D. is particularly interested in this medieval French Crusader, Simon IV de Montfort, Fifth Earl of Leicester, because he led the Albigensian Crusade against the Cathars, a group of Provencal heretics who were virtually destroyed by this Crusade. H.D.'s notes on Ezra Pound's *The Spirit of Romance* record his characterization of the Crusade, with which she undoubtedly agreed: "a sordid robbery cloaking itself in religious pretense." H.D. Papers. But it is principally in the books of Denis de Rougemont that she would have learned about the topic. In her copy of *Passion and Society*, H.D. marked passages about the Catharist worship of the Virgin Mary as embodiment of their church and about the utter destruction of the Cathar society by de Montfort, including the "burning of their books" and "the slaughter and burning of the people," 95–99. She was also interested in his description of the troubadours: "For numbers of troubadours must have gone through a simulated marriage with the Church of Rome . . . while serving in their 'thoughts' another Lady—the Church of Love," 99. (The Church of Provence, in H.D.'s essay, is this Church of Love.)

Inquisition. H.D. refers to the earliest Inquisition, in the medieval period in France, which targeted Christian groups deemed heretical, prominent among them the Cathars of southern France.

troubadours. See notes on **Mary . . . The trouvères . . .** and **Eleanor of Aquitaine** on pages 141 and 163.

Thomas Wyatt. See note on page 163.

Henry VIII. See note on page 163.

Eleanor. Eleanor of Aquitaine. See note on page 163.

Henry II. Henry II of England ruled from 1154 to 1189. His wife was Eleanor of Aquitaine.

School of Love. See note on **Eleanor of Aquitaine** on page 163.

Round Table. King Arthur's legendary table at which he sat with his knights.

Plantagenets. The House of the Plantagenets ruled England from the twelfth to fourteenth centuries. The Plantagenets split into the houses of Lancaster and York, who battled in the Wars of the Roses. These wars ended when Henry VII defeated Richard III, the last Plantagenet king.

genista. A wildflower whose name is the source of Plantagenet (*planta genista*). The first Plantagenet, Geoffrey, reputedly wore a sprig of the plant in his helmet.

courtezia. Courtly love. This is the term Denis de Rougemont uses in his books that H.D. studied so carefully.

aubade. See note on **Mary . . . The trouvères . . .** on page 141.

John. A play by Shakespeare.

Richard II. A play by Shakespeare.

Richard II. Richard II of England ruled from 1377 to 1399.

Notes to pages 120–123

this fortress built by Nature for herself. See note on **This royal throne . . .** on page 161.

Edmund Spenser. See note on page 143.

Sir Philip Sidney. See note on page 143.

your need is greater than mine. H.D. references the popular story that Sidney refused a glass of water as he was dying at the Battle of Zutphen because he saw another soldier in greater need of it.

Sir Walter Raleigh. See note on page 143.

Kit Marlowe. Christopher Marlowe. See note on page 142.

if all the pens that ever poets held. This line is from a monologue in Christopher Marlowe's *Tamburlaine*. Braithwaite includes an excerpt of this monologue in his anthology.

Thomas Nash. See note on page 147.

the plague full swift goes by. See note on **Adieu, farewell . . .** on page 147.

Ben Jonson. See note on page 148.

Tower. See note on page 145.

Masque of Queens. See note on page 164.

John Donne. See note on page 151.

One short sleep ... thou shalt die. H.D. transcribes the last two lines of John Donne's well-known sonnet, "Death Be Not Proud," which Braithwaite includes in his anthology.

Sir Henry Wotton. See note on page 158.

Elizabeth of Bohemia. See note on **Elizabeth ... Frederick** on page 137.

Essex. Robert Devereux. See note on page 159.

Simon de Montford ... mendicants. See note on **Simon de Montford** on page 167.

troubadour. See note on **Mary ... The trouvères ...** on page 141.

Morte d'Arthur. *Le Morte d'Arthur* (1485) by Thomas Malory collects the legends of King Arthur. De Rougemont's *Passion and Society,* in a passage H.D. marked, links the Cathars and Malory's Arthurian romance, 185.

Assisi ... to Rome. See notes on **Poor Clare** and **Saint Francis** on pages 140 and 141.

Saint of Avila. See note on **Saint Teresa** on page 152.

Inquisition. See note on page 168.

Henry VIII. See note on page 163.

Wit with his wantonness / Tasteth death's bitterness. See note on **Adieu, farewell ...** on page 147.

For in that sleep of death ... give us pause. Lines from the well-known "To be or not to be" speech in Shakespeare's *Hamlet.*

Augustine's *City of God.* This book by St. Augustine stated his arguments against religions deemed heretical by the Catholic Church.

***Castle* of Teresa.** St. Teresa of Ávila wrote *El Castillo Interior* (or *The Interior Castle*) (1577) as a guide to spiritual growth and enlightenment.

Francis. St. Francis of Assisi. See note on page 141.

Robert Herrick. See note on page 155.

lilies of all kinds **of that *Winter's Tale.*** The phrase "lilies of all kinds" appears in Shakespeare's *The Winter's Tale.* See note on **lilies** on page 136.

Roman de la Rose. Medieval French poem about courtly love.

when Richmond proclaims ... the red. The line "We will unite the white rose and the red" is from Shakespeare's *Richard III,* spoken by the character Richmond. It refers to the War of the Roses. See note on the **Plantagenets** on page 168.

Tudors. The Tudor family assumed the monarchy from the Plantagenets; see note on the **Plantagenets** on page 168. The Tudors held the monarchy until the death of Elizabeth I.

Mary. Mary I. See note on **Mary had sought ... her sister, Mary** on page 166.

Elizabeth. Elizabeth I. See note on page 143.

Death thou shalt die. See note on **One short sleep . . .** on page 169.

Marlowe. Christopher Marlowe. See note on page 142.

Raleigh. Sir Walter Raleigh. See note on page 143.

Spenser. Edmund Spenser. See note on page 143.

Ben Jonson. See note on page 148.

Thomas Nash. See note on page 147.

The plague full swift goes by. See note on **Adieu, farewell . . .** on page 147.

Webster. John Webster. See note on page 149.

Thomas Lodge. See note on page 163.

John Donne. See note on page 151.

He may have . . . *forbeare.* Juliet is from Shakespeare's *Romeo and Juliet.* "Alas, poor Yorick," is spoken by Hamlet in Shakespeare's *Hamlet* to the skull of Yorick, exhumed by the gravedigger. See note on **Good Frend** on page 135.

Michael Drayton. See note on page 148.

Ben Jonson. See note on page 148.

Lucys. See note on page 138.

John Shakespeare. See note on page 138.

Mary Arden. See note on page 148.

Fletcher. John Fletcher. See note on page 144.

Long-purples . . . deadmen's-fingers. See note on **Yes, marigolds . . . long-purples** on page 146.

harebells. See note on **Ladysmocks . . . harebells soon** on page 145.

Marlowe. Christopher Marlowe. See note on page 142.

Cotswolds. Hilly area of England that includes Shakespeare's hometown of Stratford-on-Avon.

Lear. Titular character of Shakespeare's *King Lear.*

Birnam wood be come to Dunsinane. Lines from act 5 of Shakespeare's *Macbeth.*

Hail king! for so thou art. Lines from act 5 of Shakespeare's *Macbeth.*

Malcolm. Character in Shakespeare's *Macbeth.*

to-morrow and to-morrow and to-morrow. See note on page 146.

Prospero. See note on page 156.

Michael. Michael Drayton. See note on page 148.

Grecian . . . unities. The reference is to the Aristotelian rules of drama: that a play should have unity of action, unity of place, and unity of time. In H.D.'s copy of *The*

Tempest, she has marked the following in an introductory section on "Duration of Action": "In *The Winter's Tale* the represented time exceeds the stage time by sixteen years; in *The Tempest* the excess is perhaps half an hour," xiv.

Tamburlaine the Great. Play by Christopher Marlowe.

Touchstone. Jester in Shakespeare's *As You Like It*.

Twelfth Night fool. Feste in Shakespeare's *Twelfth Night*.

Come away, come away, Death. See note on page 152.

Ben. Ben Jonson. See note on page 148.

Aristotle. See note on page 165.

katharsis. See note on page 165.

And sighed his soul toward the Grecian tents / Where Cressid lay that night. Lines from Shakespeare's *The Merchant of Venice*.

Merchant. A reference to Shakespeare's *The Merchant of Venice*.

Marlowe's Jew. A reference to Christopher Marlowe's *The Jew of Malta*.

Jew of Venice. A reference to Shakespeare's Shylock in *The Merchant of Venice*.

Juliet . . . meat of me. Mercutio and Juliet appear in Shakespeare's *Romeo and Juliet*. As he is dying, Mercutio speaks the line "They have made worms' meat of me."

Oberon and *Midsummer Night's Dream*. Oberon is a character in Shakespeare's *A Midsummer Night's Dream*.

deadmen's-fingers or long-purples. See note on **Yes, marigolds . . . long-purples** on page 146.

courtezia. See note on page 168.

aubade. See note on **Mary . . . The trouvères . . .** on page 141.

Francis. St. Francis of Assisi. See note on **Saint Francis** on page 141.

Teresa. St. Teresa of Ávila. See note on page 152.

Aves and *Pater Nosters.* These are references to Catholic prayers, "Ave Maria" and the "Lord's Prayer."

Simon de Montford. See note on page 167.

Fioretti. The *Fioretti di San Francesco* is a popular book of legends about St. Francis of Assisi.

Diocletian. In the Greco-Roman Museum in Alexandra, Egypt, there is a well-known headless porphyry statue dating from the fourth century C.E. of this Roman Emperor who ruled from 244 to 311 C.E.

Capitoline Jupiter. The reference is to the Ancient Roman Temple of Jupiter, which is located on one of the seven hills of Rome, Capitoline Hill.

Juliet . . . too late. Juliet, Friar Lawrence, Romeo, Mercutio, Juliet's nurse, and Paris are characters in Shakespeare's *Romeo and Juliet*, which is set in Verona. Romeo is a Montague, Juliet a Capulet. Francis is St. Francis of Assisi; see note on **Saint Francis** on page 141.

Ben Jonson. See note on page 148.

Michael Drayton. See notes on page 148.

katharsis. See note on page 165.

Fletcher. John Fletcher. See note on page 144.

Marlowe's *Tamburlaine.* A reference to Christopher Marlowe's *Tamburlaine the Great.*

Mercutio . . . bridegroom. See note on **Juliet . . . too late** on page 171.

All lovers young, all lovers must / Consign to thee and come to dust. Lines from Shakespeare's *Cymbeline.*

Imogen is Fidele. Fidele and Imogen are characters in Shakespeare's *Cymbeline.*

Rosalind is Ganymede. When Rosalind disguises herself as a man in Shakespeare's *As You Like It,* she adopts the name Ganymede.

Juliet. Character in Shakespeare's *Romeo and Juliet.*

Kathars. See note on **Simon de Montford** on page 167.

Eleanor of Aquitaine. See note on page 163.

School of Love. See note on **Eleanor of Aquitaine** on page 163.

Mary. Mary I. See note on **Mary had sought . . . her sister, Mary** on page 166.

Elizabeth. Elizabeth I. See note on page 143.

Cynthia. See note on *Queen and Huntress* on page 148.

the Venetian story. A reference to Shakespeare's *The Merchant of Venice.*

In fair Verona, where we lay our scene. A line from Shakespeare's *Romeo and Juliet.*

Judith. See note on **There was Elizabeth . . . not forgotten** on page 145.

Capulet . . . too late. See note on **Juliet . . . too late** on page 171.

Michael. Michael Drayton. See note on page 148.

Nymphidia. See note on *Nymphidia . . .* **Queen Mab** on page 149.

Agincourt. See note on page 148.

Henry V. Play by William Shakespeare.

Hamnet. See note on **There was Elizabeth . . . not forgotten** on page 145.

But that the dread of something after death. Line from the well-known "To be or not to be" speech in Shakespeare's *Hamlet.*

plague. Great Plague. See note on page 149.

Queen Eleanor. Eleanor of Aquitaine. See note on page 163.

Michael said . . . Mary? H.D. shows Shakespeare struggling to distinguish Richard the Lion-Heart (see note on page 164), son of Eleanor of Aquitaine; Richmond's rival, Richard III of England, who ruled England from 1483 to 1485 (see note on **Plantagenets** on page 168); and Richard, the child probably killed with his brother, Edward V, by Richard III (see note on **that other Edward, who with his brother Richard** on page 166). He is also confusing Edward V with Edward VI, brother of Mary I of England. He then mistakes Mary I of England for the Virgin Mary (see note on **Mary had sought . . . her sister, Mary** on page 166).

deadmen's-fingers. See note on **Yes, marigolds . . . long-purples** on page 146.

Aristotle. See note on page 165.

katharsis. See note on page 165.

unities. See note on **Grecian . . . unities** on page 170.

Kathars. See note on **Simon de Montford** on page 167.

Henry. Henry II. See note on page 168.

Henry, the third. H.D. refers to Henry the Young King of England, who ruled from 1170 to 1172, between the ages of fifteen and seventeen. He was not Henry III because he predeceased his father, Henry II. His brother, Richard I, succeeded him and his father.

William. William I of England, or William the Conqueror. See note on **Conqueror** on page 145.

Cynthia. See note on *Queen and Huntress* on page 148.

Notes to page 130

Never harm. . . . lady nigh. See note on **Philomel, with melody . . .** on page 145.

She spoke of grapes . . . older. Cleopatra's line, "The juice of Egypt's grape shall moist this lip," appears in the final act of Shakespeare's *Antony and Cleopatra*. Her barge has purple sails. Antony and Caesar are also characters in that play. Imogen is a character in *Cymbeline*. The new "Triumvirs. Actium" concerns the shift in power in ancient Rome after the loss of Mark Antony to Octavius Caesar at the Battle of Actium, who had been (with Lepidus) the ruling political alliance. *"What's this? A cup, closed in my true love's hand?"* is a line spoken by Juliet in Shakespeare's *Romeo and Juliet*.

Michael. Michael Drayton. See note on page 148.

Essex. Robert Devereux. See note on page 159.

Raleigh. Sir Walter Raleigh. See note on page 143.

The Virginian Voyage. See note on page 149.

We are such stuff as dreams are made on. Line spoken by Prospero in act 4 of Shakespeare's *The Tempest*.

Notes to pages 130–131

Francis Bacon. See also note on page 162. Braithwaite's biographical note, 777, mentions that Bacon was educated at Trinity College, Cambridge University.

Let Rome in Tiber melt. See note on page 146.

Raleigh. Sir Walter Raleigh. See note on page 143.

Cynthia. See note on *Queen and Huntress* on page 148.

Mantua, Padua. Places in Italy that are also settings in Shakespeare's plays.

He had managed . . . Oberon. In Greek mythology, Hippolyta was an Amazon Queen, daughter of Ares, who was betrothed to Theseus but died before she married him. In Euripides' version, Hippolyta and Theseus had a child, Hippolytus, who is the subject of H.D.'s 1927 translation, *Hippolytus Temporizes* (New York: New Directions, 2003). In Shakespeare's *A Midsummer Night's Dream*, a character named Hippolyta is engaged to Theseus. In the opening scene, Hippolyta invokes Diana, the ancient Roman virgin huntress. For "Michael's Titania and Oberon," see note on *Nymphidia . . .* **Queen Mab** on page 149.

John Shakespeare. See note on page 138.

a Swan and an Arrow with suitable Latin. H.D. describes the coat of arms Shakespeare obtained for his father.

Lucy. See note on page 138.

things in heaven and earth. Phrase spoken by Hamlet in act 1 of Shakespeare's *Hamlet*: "There are more things in heaven and earth, Horatio, / Than are dreamt of in your philosophy."

Michael. Michael Drayton. See note on page 148.

Notes to page 132

day-lily. See note on **lilies** on page 136.

Judith. See note on **There was Elizabeth . . . not forgotten** on page 145.

Hamnet. See note on **There was Elizabeth . . . not forgotten** on page 145.

Or bid me go into a new-made grave / And hide me with a dead man in his shroud. Juliet speaks these lines in Shakespeare's *Romeo and Juliet*.

Juliet. Character in Shakespeare's *Romeo and Juliet*.

Francis Bacon. See note on page 173.

the Queen. Queen Elizabeth I. See note on page 143.

Michael. Michael Drayton. See note on page 148.

Queen Eleanor. Eleanor of Aquitaine. See note on page 163.

Campion. Thomas Campion. See note on page 159.

September 19 / November 1 / 1946. H.D. dates the composition of "Good Frend."

Index

blessèd," 104, 158; *First Book of Songs and Airs*, 158

Corcoran, Neil, 15–16, 24

Courtly love (*courtezia*), 4, 20, 22, 29, 126, 169; and Dante, 23, 29; and Eleanor of Aquitaine, 23, 120, 164; in the works of Denis de Rougemont, 141, 142, 168

Coventry Corpus Christi Pageants, 115, 165

Crashaw, Richard, 91–93, 98, 133, 152

—works by: "Live in these conquering leaves: live all the same," 92, 152; "Love, thou art absolute, sole Lord," 92, 152

Crown, Kathleen, 16, 23, 38n89

Crusades, 141, 142, 164, 167; in "Claribel's Way to God," 3, 17, 20, 23, 24, 68–70, 141; and courtly love, 3, 17, 23

Cynewulf, 119, 167

Cyprian, 66, 141

Daniel, John, 114, 133, 164

Daniel, Samuel, 114, 133, 164

Dante, 23, 29, 41n146, 108, 112, 160, 162, 163

Davenant, William, 104, 133, 158; "The lark now leaves his wat'ry nest," 104, 158

Davis, Bette, 6

Davison, Francis, 27, 106, 133, 159; "O cruel tiger," 106, 159

Dee, John, 77, 89, 144

Dekker, Thomas, 85–86, 90, 112, 117, 133, 149

—works by: "Art thou poor, yet hast thou golden slumbers," 86, 150; *The Noble Spanish Soldier*," 87, 150; "O, Sorrow, Sorrow say where thou dost dwell," 87, 150; "*The Pleasant Comedy of Patient Grissill*," 86, 150

Devereux, Robert (Essex), 6, 27, 29, 105–6, 121, 130, 133, 158, 159; "Her thoughts and mine such disproportion have," 105, 159

Diana, 174

Dido, 39n95

DiPietro, Cary, 24

Dobson, Silvia, 37n79

Donne, John, 90–91, 112, 124, 133, 151; "One

short sleep past, we wake eternally" ["Death Be Not Proud"], 121, 123, 169; and other poets, 90, 93, 112, 152, 155, 158; and religion 43, 90, 93, 151, 155

Drake, Francis, 55, 119, 138, 167

Drayton, Michael, 16, 17, 26–27, 41n129, 82–84, 133, 149; and William Shakespeare, 124–32, 148

—works by: *The Ballad of Agincourt*, 16, 17, 84, 129, 148–49; "Fair stood the wind for France," 16, 84, 148–49; *Nymphidia*, 26, 27, 40n129, 84, 129, 149, 174; *Poly-olbion*, 148; "The Virginian Voyage," 84, 130, 149

Drummond, William, 97, 98, 133, 153–54, 155

—works by: "All ye whose hopes rely," 98, 155; *Flowers of Sion*, 155

Dyer, Edward, 7, 27, 77, 113, 133, 144; "My mind to me a kingdom is," 77, 145

Edward III of England, 139

Edward V of England, 118, 129, 166–67, 172–73

Edward VI of England, 118, 119, 129, 166, 173

Edward VIII of England, 37n78

Eleanor of Aquitaine, 23, 113, 118, 120, 128, 129, 132, 163–64; as mother of Richard Lion-Heart, 172

Elizabeth (Queen Mother of Elizabeth II), 137

Elizabeth of Bohemia (Elizabeth Stuart, Winter Queen), 137, 138; and Francis Quarles, 22, 96; in "The Tempest," 2, 21, 22, 53; and *The Tempest*, 21, 39n105, 96, 104; and Henry Wotton, 104, 121, 158

Elizabeth I of England, 6, 20, 33n25, 54, 143, 145, 163, 164; and Francis Bacon, 132; birth of, 113; as character, 6, 33n26, 83, 128; court of, 81, 104, 143, 147, 151, 159; death of, 77, 90, 101, 106, 150, 169; and Essex, 6, 105, 159; and imperialism, 22, 27, 29; as poet, 76, 144; and Walter Raleigh, 82; reign of, 106, 119, 161; and Mary Stuart, 138; and Mary Tudor, 117, 123, 128, 166; and war, 27, 75, 143

Lucy, Thomas: and Michael Drayton, 26, 27, 124, 131; and William Shakespeare, 2, 25, 54, 83, 124, 131, 138

Lyly, John, 110, 111, 134, 147, 162

—works by: *Campaspe*, 162; *Euphues: The Anatomy of Wit*, 110, 162; "What bird so sings, yet so does wail," 110–11, 162

Magellan, Ferdinand, 119, 167

Mao, Douglas, 25

Mare, Walter de la, 35n40

Mark Antony (Marcus Antonius), 173

Marlowe, Christopher, 17, 28, 29, 80, 108, 109, 125, 134, 142–43, 160–61; as actor, 108–9, 123; birth of, 75, 76, 107; and Bry-her, 7, 34n32; death of, 76, 77, 81, 82, 108, 161; and espionage, 81, 123, 147; and John Fletcher, 89

—works by: *Doctor Faustus*, 108, 109, 143, 161; *Edward II*, 109, 143, 161; "Helen make me immortal with a kiss," 109, 161; *Hero and Leander*, 107, 160; "[I]f all the pens that ever poets held," 121, 168; "Is this the face that launched a thousand ships," 108; *The Jew of Malta*, 27, 109, 126, 143, 161; *Tamburlaine*, 108, 126, 128, 161

Mary, mother of Jesus (Virgin Mary), 70, 136, 140, 152; and the troubadours, 4, 23, 69, 129, 141–42, 167, 173

Mary I of England (Mary Tudor, Bloody Mary), 112, 117, 118–19, 123, 128, 129, 166, 173

Mary I of Scotland (Mary Stuart, Queen of Scots), 6, 138, 143, 166; death of, 106, 138, 159; as mother of James I, 150; in "The Tempest," 21, 53

Massinger, Philip, 86–89, 112, 117, 134, 150; "The Picture," 150

de Medici, Catherine, 22, 143

Melman, Billie, 33n26

Middleton, Thomas, 85–87, 90, 112, 117, 134, 149–50

—works by: *The Devil's Low Case*, 149; *The*

Duchess of Malfi, 86, 149; *A Game of Chess*, 150

Milton, John, 34n29, 44, 110, 161–62

Montfort, Simon de, 23, 120, 121, 127, 167

Moore, Marianne, 9, 13, 30n1, 36n42

Le Morte d'Arthur (Thomas Malory), 121, 169

Nashe, Thomas, 27, 80–81, 112, 134, 147; Great Plague of London, and, 17, 81, 90, 92, 121, 124, 147

—works by: "Adieu, farewell earth's bliss," 80–81, 90, 92, 108, 121, 122, 124, 147; *Summer's Last Will and Testament*, 80, 147

Nationalism, 16–17, 25, 26, 33n26, 37n79, 40n122

Octavius Caesar, 173

Olivier, Laurence, 16, 33n27

Orgel, Stephen, 20

Origen, 66, 141

Paris of Troy, 147

Pearson, Norman Holmes, 35n40; *By Avon River*, and, 2, 8, 35nn38,39, 36n41, 43, 149; prefatory note to "The Guest," and, 44, 74, 142

Peel, David, 137

Peele, George, 81, 134, 147, 145, 164

—works by: *The Arraignment of Paris*, 147; *The Battle of Alcazar*, 147

Philomel, 78, 105, 145,

Philostratus, 160

Plank, George, 6, 29, 30n1, 32n24, 33n27, 35n40, 41nn141,142, 145; *By Avon River*, and, 1, 31n2, 34n29, 164

Plantagenet, 120, 168, 169

Plato, 66, 141, 165

Plautus, 83, 148

Plotinus, 66, 141

Pound, Ezra, 136, 167

The Private Life of Henry VIII (film), 6

LARA VETTER is associate professor of English at the University of North Carolina at Charlotte. She is the author of *Modernist Writings and Religio-scientific Discourse: H.D., Loy, and Toomer*, and she is coeditor of *Approaches to Teaching H.D.'s Poetry and Prose* and *Emily Dickinson's Correspondences: A Born-Digital Textual Inquiry*. Additionally, she has published articles on H.D., Mina Loy, and Emily Dickinson in the *Journal of Modern Literature*, *Genre*, and *Literary and Linguistic Computing*. She is currently at work on a monograph about H.D.'s late-career writings.

www.ingramcontent.com/pod-product-compliance
Lightning Source LLC
Chambersburg PA
CBHW031955010726
47493CB00007B/2215